S0-CFS-083

Haunted on Bourbon Street

Books by Deanna Chase

The Jade Calhoun Novels
Haunted on Bourbon Street
Witches of Bourbon Street
Demons of Bourbon Street
Angels of Bourbon Street
Shadows of Bourbon Street (March 2014)

The Crescent City Fae Novels
Influential Magic
Irresistible Magic
Book Three in the Crescent City Fae series (June 2014)

The Destiny Novels
Defining Destiny (Dec 2013)

Haunted on Bourbon Street

A Jade Calhoun Novel

Deanna Chase

Bayou Moon Publishing

Copyright © 2011 by Deanna Chase

First Edition 2011

10 9 8 7 6 5 4 3 2 1

Library of Congress Control Number: 2011911981

ISBN: 978-1-940299-06-8   Trade Paperback
      978-0-9837978-1-4   eBook Version

Interior Design: The Printed Page, Phoenix, AZ
Cover Art: Janet Holmes

All rights reserved. No part of this publication may be repro-
duced, stored in, or introduced into a retrieval system, or
transmitted in any form, or by any means (electronic, mechanical, photocopying, recording, or otherwise) without the prior
written permission of both the copyright owner and the pub-
lisher of this book.

This book is a work of fiction. Names, characters, places, and
incidents are products of the author's imagination or are used
fictitiously. Any resemblance to actual events, locals, business establishments, or persons, living or dead, are entirely
coincidental.

Bayou Moon Publishing
dkchase12@gmail.com
www.deannachase.com

Printed in the United States of America

Acknowledgments

A huge thank you to my first readers: Susan, Angie, Kaye, Fay, and Suzanne. Without your encouragement and enthusiasm for more chapters this book may never have come to completion.

A special thanks to Jenn, my hard working critique partner; Angie, my diligent proofreader; Rhonda, my editor; and Lisa, my book designer. Your hard work and support has helped turn my dream into reality.

To Greg, my husband, thank you for being you.

Chapter 1

There was no way I was sharing my new two-hundred-square-foot apartment with a ghost. To be honest, I didn't know if the speculation was true, but I'd gotten the place at a steal because my landlord couldn't keep it rented. Considering the abundance of documented ghost lore in the French Quarter, I wasn't taking any chances.

On moving day I walked the two blocks to The Herbal Connection. The front window housed an elaborate book display of the title, *Vampires of New Orleans*. To the right were neat rows of Suck It wine with blood-tinged fangs on the labels. I grimaced. All signs led to the likelihood of just another tourist shop. Still, it was possible they had basic supplies I could work with.

As soon as I walked in I knew I'd found the perfect shop. The sandalwood scent dissipated and a gentle, salt-filled sea breeze tickled my senses. My favorite place on earth was the beach. Whoever ran the place was doing an excellent job. It took a highly skilled practitioner to cast an illusion tailored to each individual patron.

"Can I help you?" A southern drawl floated from the back of the shop. As she stepped from behind a display, my eyes settled on a more expensive, classier version of my Aunt Gwen. The two could almost be twins, except the shop lady had salon-dyed auburn hair and wore white linen slacks, topped off with a coral blouse, while Gwen had natural gray curls and always wore her standard red T-shirt and coveralls. Of course, Gwen rode her tractor daily, and I had no trouble picturing this woman sipping mint juleps on a veranda.

I smiled. "Hello. Yes, I need a sage and cedar smudge stick if you have it."

"Of course we do, dear." She crossed the room and held out her hand. "I'm Bea, owner of the shop."

My clammy hand met her cool grip. "Jade. Nice to meet you."

"Cleansing negative energy?"

I nodded.

She grinned. "You must be new in town."

Looking down at my faded jeans and simple cotton T-shirt, I wondered if I had a fresh-from-Idaho vibe radiating off me. It was possible. I'd only been in New Orleans for a month. "Is it that obvious?"

She laughed. "No. I would have remembered if you'd been here before."

Why? Did she have a photographic memory? While I'd been told my willowy frame and long strawberry-blond hair combined with my pale Irish skin was striking, I hardly stood out in the sea of characters who wound their way through the French Quarter on a daily basis.

She rushed to explain. "Most people who come in here don't know what they're looking at. I know almost everyone in New Orleans who has knowledge of the craft."

Oh. Doing a simple cleanse was miles from using craft. I didn't particularly like being mistaken for one who manipulated spells.

She hummed softly as she packaged my items, and when I handed her my credit card she peered at me. The beach breeze vanished, replaced by the sandalwood scent. A warm sensation wrapped around me in a slow circle. It took me a moment to realize it was coming from Bea. She was reading me with a witch's spell. Instantly I dropped my barriers and sent out my senses. If she could read me, I could do the same to her. Only, I wasn't a witch. Empaths don't need spells to read other people.

Excitement mixed with a heavy dose of curiosity radiated from her in light, feathery waves. I realized her energy was a lot like mine. Most people's emotions are a little thick and sometimes hard to wade through. Hers felt light, inviting and familiar. What exactly could this woman do, and what had she learned about me? I'd assumed she was just a witch practitioner; now I knew she was also some sort of intuitive.

I stepped back, blinked, and the sea-salted air returned.

"There's something special about you," she said.

More like a curse. I pasted on a smile and pretended nothing had happened. "That's what my mother always used to say."

Her eyes sparkled, and she leaned in closer. "Very interesting, indeed." She placed her hand over mine, and a spark sent a jolt to my shoulder.

Jumping back, I pulled my hand out of her grasp.

Her smile turned to a grin, and she clapped her hands together in delight. "Oh, my dear! You simply must come by my house for tea some afternoon. We have much to talk about. Here's my card." She slipped it in the bag.

I grabbed the handle and turned to go. "Um, okay. Thanks."

"You're welcome, Jade. I look forward to hearing from you soon."

I waved as I pushed the door open to the street, knowing I wouldn't call her. My last memory of my mother blowing me a kiss as she headed off to her coven meeting flashed in my mind. Tears burned the back of my eyes. I blinked them back. Bad things always seemed to happen when witches and intuitives got together. No. It didn't matter how curious I was about Bea, I knew it was best to keep to myself.

Buildings, especially old buildings, often retain an imprint of emotions from previous residents. When I'd first visited my new place I'd sensed a profound sadness. It was easy to understand why new tenants hadn't felt comfortable there. People didn't need to be empaths for negativity to unknowingly work its way into their being.

Fortunately, after a thorough smudging, when I opened myself up the place felt brand new. No sadness, and no evidence of a ghost. If there was one, it was gone now. Satisfied, I spent the next few hours hauling my stuff up the three very steep flights of stairs, and by the time the delivery men arrived with my new mattress, I'd sweated enough to soak right through my shirt. I'd sent them off with their tip and was headed toward the shower when a knock sounded at my door.

I cast a longing glance at my bathroom before I answered. Mortification rooted me to my wide pinewood floors, and my face burned as I stared at the man who never failed to make my stomach quiver.

"Hey," Kane said.

"Uh, hey."

He held up a box wrapped in elegant gold paper. "I come bearing gifts."

Did my landlord bring presents to all his new tenants?

"Pyper asked me to bring it up."

Of course. Pyper was my boss and Kane's business partner. Kane owned the building and, with Pyper's help, managed the attached strip club. Pyper also ran the coffee shop next door, where I worked part time. I wasn't certain, but I thought maybe they had something going on the side. "Thanks. That was sweet of her." I opened the door wider. "Come on in. It's moving day, so the place is a little messy."

"No, it's okay. I don't want to bother you." His gaze traveled the length of my body. I couldn't help myself. I knew I shouldn't do it. Reading someone's emotions was such an invasion of privacy, and I knew at that moment I resembled a character from a Tim Burton movie, but I let down my barriers and probed anyway.

To my surprise, mild appreciation mixed with humor filled my senses, until his gaze landed on my face. His energy changed to something close to pity. I flinched and raised my shields. Pity? The man felt pity for the way I looked. What else could I expect from a guy who owned a strip bar? Stupid, shallow, piece of... Whatever. It wasn't like I would actually ever date him anyway. The strip club thing aside, he was taken. I think.

I tried to hide my scowl and reached for the gift. "Okay, then. Thanks for stopping by."

"No problem." He turned to go, then looked back. "Hey, do you want to come down to the club later? It's ladies' night."

The invitation caught me off guard. I blinked. "Ladies' night?"

"Yeah, free admission and free drinks all night."

Right, because my idea of the perfect evening included watching naughty librarians and pussycats strip down to their dental floss, while drinking myself into oblivion. "No, thanks. It's been a long day."

He glanced past me into the apartment and nodded. "Right. Just thought I'd ask."

I waited until he'd disappeared down the stairs then slammed the door. Son of a bitch. The closest thing to a date invitation I'd had in months had been to a strip club. What was wrong with me?

I flopped on my new mattress because I didn't have any other furniture yet and plucked the envelope off the present. I let it slide through my fingers for a few moments before turning it over. It read: *Jade, Welcome home.* My foul mood vanished. A smiled tugged at my lips. I didn't have many friends. Okay, I had one friend and right then, things were...awkward. It happens when your best friend starts dating your ex.

Being an empath has made it difficult to maintain personal relationships. When I'd been younger and hadn't understood I was different, I'd alienated a lot of people with my ability. Let's just say my perceptions weren't appreciated. So Pyper's attempt to reach out to me meant more than she could possibly know. Especially since I'd learned to keep my gift to myself. In the last ten years I'd only told one other person—my ex—about my ability.

Giddy with anticipation, I grabbed the box and carefully peeled away the tape, preserving the paper. For what, I didn't know. I never save wrapping paper. In fact, people who did usually annoyed me. Not that I don't want to save trees, I'm just usually too impatient to see what's inside. Red tissue paper lined the inside of the white gift box. I fished through, finding a personal coffee maker, a mug with *The Grind* scrawled across it and a round jar of something called Honey Dust.

I read the label: *An edible body powder.*

Laughing, I put the jar down and ripped the card open. Heat radiated through my body as I read the words. *Welcome to the building. Sincerely, Pyper and Kane.*

Had the Honey Dust been Pyper's idea or Kane's? If it was Kane's, somehow I thought I should be offended, but the image of him running his lips over my dusted skin sent ripples of anticipation through my body. I waved a hand in front of my face, fanning myself. *Calm down, girl. Kane is Pyper's man.* Surely she had included it as a joke.

I set the mug and the coffee maker on the counter and carried the Honey Dust to the bathroom. The lure of my claw-foot tub was too much. As I waited for it to fill, I ran back to the kitchen to grab a bottle of merlot. My bags sat opened with stuff bulging out of them. Without any furniture, I had nowhere to store any of it, but I couldn't have cared less. I had my own place, all to myself, and nothing else mattered. Except the bath waiting for me.

Content after slipping into the tub, I lifted the wine bottle to my lips. So what if I didn't have any glasses yet? I wasn't above drinking straight from the bottle.

An ominous rumble boomed outside, indicating an afternoon storm. Sighing, I set the wine on the floor, leaned back and closed my eyes, reveling in the rhythmic rain as it drummed on the roof.

When my toes started to prune I reluctantly pulled the plug and ran the shower to soap up and wash my hair. While drying off, I saw the round jar sitting on a shelf just to the left of the tub. The Honey Dust. My lips quirked into a small smile.

Feeling a little naughty, I opened the container. A sweet honeysuckle fragrance filled the bathroom. Before I could do anything else, the dust rose from the jar all on its own and swirled in a circle around me, caressing me with tiny invisible kisses.

I froze and then called out, "Hey, stop it right now!"

The whirlwind stopped at my command, and I almost choked on the thick dust of powder lingering in the air. Feeling utterly violated, I catapulted out of the tub, crying out when my ankle smashed against the side of the tub. With limbs flailing, I somehow managed to grasp the edge of the sink and save myself from cracking my skull on the toilet. How embarrassing would that be to be found dead, naked in your bathroom, in a pile of Honey Dust?

Breathing hard, I ran to the other room and pulled on the first clothes I found, grabbed my purse and slammed the door behind me. My bare feet moved faster than I thought possible down the stairs. As I jumped the last three steps into the hallway I angled right toward the exit, colliding with something—or someone—solid enough to knock me on my ass.

"Holy shit, Jade. Where's the fire?" Pyper grunted, trying to get her feet back under her.

"Oh God! I'm so sorry." I covered my face in horror.

"It's all right. I'll live." Her voice floated down from above me. "Here, let me help you up." When I didn't respond, her tone went soft. "Are you okay?"

I peeked out from behind my fingers and squeaked, "I have a ghost."

Her posture relaxed as she leaned against the wall. "Oh, okay," she said, dismissing me.

"No really, I think the apartment has a ghost."

"Why? 'Cause Kane said so, and now every little thing is freaking you out?" She rolled her deep blue eyes.

"No. Because just now, as I was putting on a sampling of the Honey Dust you gave me, it kicked it up and made it whirl around me like a mini tornado. I didn't even have the window

open. You can't tell me there isn't something weird about that."
I pleaded, staring into her widening eyes.

Great. I'd known her less than two weeks, and already I'd
become the resident freak.

"Really? That's interesting," she said more to herself than to
me. Standing up, she angled toward the stairwell. "Come on."
She put her foot on the first step.

"Where?" I didn't move. She wasn't seriously going up there,
was she?

"Upstairs. I have to see this," she said, her eyes now gleeful.

"No! I am not going back up there."

"Come on, Jade, who will believe you if you don't have a
witness? Kane doesn't count, since no one believes him either."

"You go if you want. I'm going to stay right here." I pressed
against the wall.

"Oh no, you aren't." She grabbed my hands and tugged me
up.

Planting my feet, I set my shoulders and didn't budge as she
tried to pull me along. "No."

Looking me full in the face, she burst out laughing. The
laughing continued until tears streamed down her face.

"What in the world makes you think this is so hilarious?" I
demanded.

Gasping to catch her breath, she wheezed out, "The Honey
Dust. You have a perv ghost." Laughter overtook her again, causing her face to turn beet-red. It clashed with the blue highlights
in her thick black hair.

I sighed, resigning myself. Her hysteria somehow calmed me
enough to reconsider. "You are going to pee yourself laughing
at my situation. Let's go." Moving past her, I headed back to
my apartment.

My bravado quickly waned as we hit the second floor landing.
Had it not been for Pyper's firm hand on my wrist, I'm certain
I would have turned and fled. When we reached my door I
raised my eyebrow as Pyper took a key out and unlocked it. It
was natural for her to have a key. I just wouldn't have thought

she kept one on her person. However, I said nothing and let her tug me into the room.

She walked to the bathroom and held the door wide open.

I crept up behind her and peeked over her shoulder. The harmless-looking Honey Dust jar sat capped in the middle of my bathroom.

I gasped.

"What?" Pyper turned to look at me.

"I, ah, well, I didn't stop to put the cap on the jar. I just dropped it…" My voice trailed off as I backed away from the room. Legs turning to jelly, I sank down onto my mattress. Pyper disappeared into the bathroom. Visions of me in a straitjacket, surrounded by white rubber walls, filled my mind.

A few minutes went by before she popped up beside the door-jamb. "Come in here," she called as her head jerked back inside.

I sat motionless, my mind fixated on the rubber walls.

"Get in here," she demanded.

My mind blank, I followed her voice and stopped in the door frame. Pyper was squatting, pressed up against the wall, studying the jar in the middle of the floor.

"What?" I asked.

"This is so interesting," she replied, not looking up.

I waited for her to continue.

"The jar is in the middle of a layer of the Honey Dust. Do you see it?" She used her finger to make a circle in the air above the jar.

I glanced down. "Yeah. So?"

"There's something missing." Her eyes twinkled.

Looking back at the jar and the floor caked in dust, I saw nothing else out of place—or missing, for that matter. Puzzled, I stared at her.

"Footprints!" she exclaimed. "Where are your footprints? It looks like the whole jar was dumped in here. No way could you have dumped the whole jar out, replaced the top, and set it here without leaving footprints."

I inspected the scene. The jar sat in the middle of my bathroom with a thick layer of Honey Dust covering the floor from the tub to the door. She was right. I couldn't have placed the jar where it was without disturbing the smooth layer.

Pyper turned and walked into the main room. "Whoever you are, reveal yourself!"

My eyes flew open in shock. "What the hell?" I hissed. "You're not supposed to invite ghosts to reveal themselves."

"How else do you think I'm going to see it?"

"Shhhh." I was terrified of what her invitation might bring.

An unfamiliar energy, mixed with bitterness and satisfaction, invaded my senses. I turned to Pyper, my voice barely a whisper. "Someone is here."

"Huh?" She took a step toward me and then jumped, wrapping her arms around her chest. "What the hell was that?" She twisted her head, searching the room.

Ice numbed my hands and moved up my arms, making me shiver. I pointed to a shadow, black as coal, moving across the far wall. We stood, paralyzed, while the image grew larger and moved toward us. Pyper's sudden fear inched its way into my awareness. Instinct took over, and I forced as much calm as I could in her direction.

Her panic started to ease, but just barely. I renewed my efforts, forcing my will toward her. Pain pierced my heart and shot through my veins. Gasping, I clutched my chest, staring in horror at the black shadow as something grabbed my essence and yanked.

"No!" I shouted in defiance and snatched my energy back.

The shadow hovered in front of us for a moment, unmoving, then shattered into a million pieces like confetti. I stood staring, transfixed by the cascade as it faded into nothing until Pyper tugged on my hand. I glanced at her, and we both ran for the stairs.

Chapter 2

"What was *that*?" Pyper huffed as we burst through the back door of The Grind, the coffee shop where we both worked. Luckily it was next door to my apartment building, because I had forgotten shoes again.

"No idea."

She motioned for me to follow, leading me to her office.

I collapsed in the closest chair, grateful to have my shaking legs out from underneath me. What the hell had just happened? I'd sent calming energy to Pyper and ended up feeling like my essence had been sucked out. Only, it hadn't had Pyper's emotional signature. Something much more powerful had taken it.

"One thing's clear. Your ghost is definitely a pervert," Pyper said.

"Huh?"

"He felt me up. Didn't you see me jump? He grabbed my boob." She crossed her arms over her chest. "We need to call Kane. He's the only person I know who will believe us."

"No!" Walking around barefoot on Bourbon Street through sticky, alcohol-soaked garbage and drinking-induced bodily fluids during Mardi Gras held more appeal than telling him about my Honey Dust experience.

"Why not?"

"I don't—" My phone buzzed. My hands trembled as I fished it out of my pocket. This was bad. The trembling only started when my energy was compromised. The screen flashed Kat's name. I took a deep breath and hoped I sounded normal. "Hey, what's up?"

"I'm outside the café. I was going to get you a chai latte, but it's closed. Come get me so I can see your new digs," she said.

I grimaced. "My apartment isn't really available right now."

Pyper sent me a questioning glance. "Are you okay? You don't look too hot."

Covering the phone, I whispered, "I'm fine."

Kat raised her voice. "Hello…who are you talking to, and if your apartment isn't available, where are you and where's all your stuff? I've been home. Your room is cleared out. What's going on?"

"I'm all moved in, it's just…let me come get you, and I'll tell you about it." After Kat's affirming response, I snapped the phone closed. "I need to go," I told Pyper.

"Go where?" She stood up. "You can't leave now. You look like you're going to pass out." She gently pushed me back into the chair.

"My friend is here. I can't just leave her standing outside." The motion of standing and sitting back down turned my stomach. *Please don't let me ralph right here.*

"I'll go get her." She left before I could protest. How would Pyper find her? They hadn't met, and Pyper didn't even know Kat's name.

A familiar energy drew my attention to the door as Kane walked in. He rummaged through the desk and pulled out a bag of mint chocolate cookies. "Pyper said you needed sugar and to make sure you stay put."

I took a cookie, bit into it and shrugged in agreement. Where else would I go? Surely not to my new apartment. Panic bubbled in my chest. I couldn't stay there. I'd never get any rest. Would Kane let me out of my lease? The queasiness returned as I thought of staying in Kat's spare room for another night. Maybe I'd get lucky, and Dan would be out with the guys.

Kane offered me a soda from a small refrigerator.

"Thanks." Clutching the can with one hand, I tried to open it with the other. Unfortunately my fingers shook too badly. I couldn't even grab the tab to pop it.

"I got it." Kane took the can. When he set it back on the desk it had a straw poking out the top. "Drink."

"Thanks." I took a long sip.

Kane grabbed a chair and sat next to me. His gaze shifted to my still-trembling hand. Balling it up in defiance, I pressed it into my thigh. I wasn't this weak, damn it.

He reached over and covered my hand with his, sending a thick layer of protection through my weakened defenses. At first it felt like a cloak, shrouding me, but then it turned into more of an energy meld.

Whoa. That never happens. I could consciously take in others' emotions if I wanted to, but it takes effort. Was he aware of the effect he had? Could he control it, or was it just happening? Warmth spread from his touch through my limbs, steadying my twitching muscles.

Heat prickled my neck under his watchful gaze. I tried to pull from his grasp, but his fingers tightened on mine. "Thanks, but I'm okay now," I murmured.

He raised one eyebrow. "You look like you're going to fall over any minute. I'm hanging on just in case."

"I'm not going to pass out," I said in a steady voice, drawing my hand from his. As our hands parted, the shivers started. Wrapping my arms around my middle, I glided my hands up and down my bare arms, trying to generate heat.

"Here." Kane stood, grabbed a sweatshirt from behind the desk and handed it to me. "Use this."

"Thanks." I pulled it over my head and was rewarded with a trace of his fresh, rain-scented cologne.

"We're here," Pyper called from the doorway.

"Jade!" Kat ran to my side. "Are you okay? Pyper told me what happened." She took my hand in both of hers. "Use me," she whispered.

"Only if you calm down."

Her panic swirled around me like a windstorm before she managed to rein her emotions back in. I squeezed her hand to let her know I appreciated the offer, but didn't tap her energy. Irrationally, I didn't want to taint what I'd just experienced with Kane.

Kat had been around the last time I'd been stupid enough to compromise my energy. When we were roommates, our neighbor had witnessed a shooting and had been so distraught she'd stopped talking. I'd thought if I could ease her burden by siphoning her distress, she might be able to help the police investigation. It had worked. Too well.

While she helped the police nail down a suspect I spent a week in bed, recovering. For the first few days the only way I could get up was if Kat was touching me, lending me her strength. It had been her idea for me to try and take it. She'd said, "If you can take the bad stuff, why can't you take the good?" Since I didn't think I could get worse, I'd tried it and used her emotional strength to heal. Still, I'd had to take it from her. It didn't just happen like it did with Kane.

"You need to lie down," Kat said.

"I'm all right." I looked her in the eye. "Besides, I'm not too keen on going up to my apartment right now."

"Then you'll come home with me." Kat stood, tugging on my arm.

I pulled back and shook my head. "No. Thank you, but in my condition I don't think I can stomach Dan." Her boyfriend—my ex—and the reason I'd found my own apartment.

It was quite the shock to move to New Orleans and find that not only had Dan moved here as well, but he was also dating my best friend. I'd been more hurt by the fact that Kat had been afraid to tell me than I was that the two were dating. Dan and I had made such a mess of our relationship; there really was no hope of reconciliation on either of our parts. As for the two of them dating? I understood. The three of us had been inseparable in high school. It wasn't unreasonable to think they might make a connection. Of course, since Kat had left Boise right after our college graduation, I hadn't expected it to happen from two thousand miles away.

Kat sighed. "Jade—"

I cut her off. "No, Kat. I told you before I get sick to my stomach when he's around."

She studied me for a long moment. I knew she was thinking it was all in my head. I'd thought so too, at first, but lately it was getting worse. Either way, I didn't want to be in the same room with him. She pulled out her phone. "Okay, let me see what I can do." After walking to the far side of the office, she dialed.

My heart swelled. Finally, she'd heard me about Dan.

Kat snapped her phone shut. "Okay, he's on his way."

"What? Dan's coming here?" I stood up, ready to bolt from the room.

"No. Why would I call him? You know this is so not his thing. I called my friend, Ian. He hunts ghosts."

I hadn't known what I was expecting, but the person who showed up definitely wasn't it. A man in his early thirties, looking as if he'd stepped out of a skateboarding magazine, strode up to me.

"Hi, Jade." He waved.

"Ian? I didn't realize it was *you* who was coming."

His lips quirked into a lopsided, sexy little smile and pale blue eyes searched my face as he reached for my hand. I'd met Ian once before, shortly after I'd gotten to New Orleans. He'd been at one of Kat's dinner gatherings. Grimacing in embarrassment, I realized I'd monopolized most of our hour-long chat. I hadn't even remembered his name.

"Nice to see you again." He paused and tilted his head toward a marquee on my building. It read, *Hundreds of beautiful women and three ugly ones.* "You live above a strip bar?"

I glanced at Kane's club, Wicked, and shrugged. "The price was right."

"Interesting marketing tactic." He laughed.

Kat appeared beside me and handed over a pair of flip-flops she'd purchased from the corner store. "I'm off to get some food. Want anything?"

After Ian and I placed our orders, I gestured for him to follow me. My plastic shoes clattered on the brick pathway as we entered my wisteria-perfumed courtyard. Humidity hung in the air, finally warding off my chills. I shed the sweatshirt as I sat at a wrought-iron table. "Thank you for coming so quickly. I hope I didn't interrupt anything important."

He shook his head. "Nope, perfect timing. You saved me from some rather dull reports, actually."

"Reports? Ghost hunting reports?" Visions of a school lab, with Willow and Buffy fighting demons, filled my head.

"Oh, no. Research reports. I'm an assistant to a meteorologist at the University. I type up his reports and help out when needed."

Nothing about his appearance—tousled sandy blond hair, wire-rimmed glasses and torn-up Converse—said professional. But his easy smile and the warm inner glow radiating from him put me at ease. "So, ghost hunting is a hobby of yours?"

"Sort of. More like an obsession. Tell me, what can I do for you?"

What did I want him to do for me? Validation? Expulsion of my ghost? "Well, I don't know. What do you normally do?"

"There isn't a lot of 'normal' about it." His smile widened. "However, why don't you tell me what prompted Kat to call me, and we can go from there?"

I took a calming breath and told him about the Honey Dust and the black shadow.

"Honey Dust?" His eyebrows rose with the question.

"It's an edible skin powder." I averted my eyes. When I dared a glance he was writing in a note pad, his lips turned up in a sly smile. I bent my head, hoping my face wasn't as flushed as it felt.

He put down his pen and took a long swig from a can of Coke. "Ah, that is exactly what I needed," he said with a sigh. "Long night last night, you know."

"Oh?"

He started writing again. "Yeah, the video tape jammed, and we had to stop in the middle to fix it. Then, of course, we had to start all over. But the mood was shot, so we didn't really get much action."

I stared at him, my brow pinched in confusion.

He chuckled, then sobered as I frowned. "I'm sorry," he said. "It's just I get that look a lot. I meant I was out late on an investigation. The best time for measuring paranormal activity is at night between nine p.m. and six a.m. We had some equipment issues."

"Obviously, I know nothing about what you do."

"No problem. I always forget not everyone lives, eats and sleeps ghosts twenty-four-seven. Let's get to it, shall we?"

I nodded, urging him on.

"I'll need to inspect your apartment, but I'd like to bring my team, John and Riley. We each use different equipment to measure activity, so it's better if I can get both of them here."

I nodded again, and he took out his phone and dialed. Five minutes later, the other two men were on their way.

"Okay, where will you be while we do our thing?" Ian asked.

"Why?"

"After we take some baseline measurements, I'd like to get you back up there to see if there's any activity related to you. Sometimes spirits are attracted by certain energies."

Of course they were. I wondered how I'd gone this long without one attaching itself to me. "I guess I'll be here."

"Perfect. As soon as my guys get here I'll get right to work. Are you staying at Kat's tonight?"

Was I? "I guess so. Staying at my place doesn't seem like a great idea." I bit my lip to keep from scowling.

Ian shrugged. "I haven't ever seen a ghost do more than just spook someone, so you could probably stay at your place. We'll be here late, though. Collecting data can take a while to get conclusive results."

"Only spooking, huh? That's good to hear." Too bad I wasn't like most people. With my energy I'd end up possessed.

After Kat returned, the three of us ate our po'boy sandwiches and chatted about nothing ghost-related. I'd almost forgotten why Ian was there until his phone buzzed and he had to go meet his fellow ghost hunters.

I handed him my apartment key. "Just come get me when you're ready."

"Will do." Ian took a few strides before I stopped him.

"Wait, don't you have a fee or something for this?"

"Um, yeah. I do, but let's see where this goes first. Consider this a free consultation. If we need to proceed, then we can discuss it."

"That's awfully nice of you." I smiled.

"Ah-ha! There it is. I wondered if I'd get a genuine smile out of you. Looks good." He winked. "Consider it the friend rate. Later, Kat."

She waved. We watched as he left the courtyard, his phone pressed to his ear. The side door to the building banged shut.

"He's hot! Is that the ghost hunter?" Pyper asked as she joined us.

I nodded. "He is pretty yummy, isn't he? In a schoolboy kind of way."

"Schoolboy." She snorted. "Thinking of sneaking off behind the bleachers?"

I laughed. "That's a thought." Then I finally noticed her electric-blue hot pants and deep-cut halter top. "What *are* you wearing?"

Her features transformed into a sexy pout. "What? You don't like my stripper outfit?"

Kat started coughing mid-sip, and Pyper laughed.

"You strip at the club, too?" I asked.

"Actually, I used to, and now only when necessary. We're short-handed tonight. "

After the initial shock of Pyper's announcement wore off, the three of us stayed in the courtyard chatting for the next few hours until Ian called me for my part in the investigation. Kat had convinced me to stay at her place. I wasn't happy about it, but my choices were limited. And if I didn't get to sleep soon I really would pass out.

Dragging my feet up the third flight of stairs, I tried to be reasonable. Three other people were in my tiny, almost empty apartment. What's the worst that could happen?

I knocked on the closed door, unsure if I should just walk in. In seconds, Ian appeared.

"Ready, Jade? All we're going to do is take some measurements. But first I need you to say a protection spell."

"A spell?" I frowned. I didn't practice, and for good reason.

"More like a prayer. It's just standard procedure."

"All right." A prayer spell wasn't going to kill me. They were harmless.

Ian smiled reassuringly. "Don't worry. Just repeat after me."

I nodded.

"Gods of the afterlife, we are here as mere observers. We ask for your guidance to walk with you in our quest for knowledge. We seek to do no harm and ask for protection from those whom would seek to harm us."

I repeated Ian's words and then asked, "Ready?"

"Yep. Okay, so I want you to walk slowly around the room while we take measurements. Don't speak unless I ask you to."

I circled my apartment, while Ian followed holding some kind of electronic meter. The two other guys were busy manning their own equipment. One held a palm-sized video recorder and the other juggled three different cameras.

I had no idea how accurate any of their readings would be. Ghost hunting wasn't in my knowledge base. But I did have a weapon they didn't know about. Deciding it was best to be in the know, I let my guards down and took in the lingering emotions. Ian's excitement tingled up my spine.

"You really enjoy this, don't you?" I asked.

"Everyone has a passion. Now, don't talk. We're taking measurements."

I mouthed 'sorry' and zeroed in on the camera guy's boredom and the videographer's impatience. Seems Ian's helpers didn't share his passion. Blocking the three of them, I concentrated on any other emotional imprint. Nothing. I kept my senses open. When we neared the bathroom, trepidation slowed my steps. Ian nudged me. I had no choice but to suck it up.

The Honey Dust still covered the floor, and the sweet honeysuckle scent brought the afternoon's events right back. I almost felt the mini tornado swirling around me. But as I stood there taking it in, nothing penetrated my emotional energy. It just felt peaceful.

Ian steered me to the center of the living area and asked me to say something.

"Hello?" I called.

Silence.

"Are you here?"

After a moment, Ian nodded. I tried again. "If you're here, give us a sign."

We tried a few more rounds of calling the ghost out, but nothing happened. With my part finished, I asked Ian to leave the key with Pyper, and left to find Kat.

I found a note on the empty table in the courtyard. Kat was waiting for me in the club. What? That's the last place I'd expect her to be.

As I rounded the corner I spotted a bride-to-be dressed in a short, black sequined dress and a white veil, surrounded by a group of women decked out with condoms and penis pops. The group moved as one to the front of the entrance. Is it normal for a woman to have her bachelorette party in a strip club? Huh.

I moved to join the back of the line, trying to avoid a crowd of men moving toward the party girls.

Someone grabbed my arm, startling me.

"Hey!" I cried out.

"You don't need to wait in line," Kane said. Was it weird my insides turned gooey every time I heard him talk? "Your friend's inside at the bar."

"Thanks." I smiled up at him. As I walked through the door I turned back to wave and caught him watching me. My insides were warm and mushy...until emotional energy slammed into my gut, knocking the wind out of me.

I would have fallen if the wall hadn't been directly behind me.

Gasping for air, I envisioned a glass silo then mentally put myself in it. The pain in my gut lessened enough for me to breathe, but didn't fully vanish.

The biggest problem with being an empath is I couldn't effectively block out others' emotions in a highly charged atmosphere. And this placed was *charged*. Usually an individual person's energy has a distinct imprint. I could feel his or her energy and knew the specific owner, much in the same way I could pinpoint the sound of a voice to a particular person. But in situations like this, it was a shouting match of emotional energy. Only, I felt the pain in my stomach, not my ears.

With so much energy surrounding me I couldn't focus. If I didn't merge my senses with someone else, I'd collapse...soon. With emotional chaos making my head spin, I reached out blindly. Unfortunately, I chose the wrong person.

My stomach rolled as rage crawled up my spine, wrapping around my neck as if to strangle me. Gagging, I pulled my energy back and placed my mental image safely back into my glass silo. Jesus! Nothing short of evil resided in that body. On the outside he looked completely normal: an average, balding, thin man sitting in the corner, rolling an unlit cigarette between his fingers. I made a mental note to somehow warn Pyper and the staff to stay away from that one. Sometimes my gift comes in handy, and other times it's downright unnerving. In this case, it was definitely both.

My eyes watered. I didn't notice Kat until her hand touched mine. "It's okay, zone in on me," she said.

The pain subsided, and I gave her a weak smile. "Thank you, again." Having someone to focus on usually worked better than my cylinder, but it had to be a person with nontoxic energy or else it was useless.

"No, it's my fault you're in here. I got a hankering for a margarita."

No wonder she seemed relaxed. "How many have you had?"

"Two or three…or maybe this is the fourth one. I can't remember. Pyper wouldn't let me pay for them." She giggled.

I laughed. "Okay. Let's go sit."

When we got to the bar, Kat handed me her drink and left to use the restroom. Sitting, I tapped my mental cylinder again. This time, it held. Thank God.

"What can I get you?" The bartender's radiant heart-shaped face turned toward me, breaking into a smile that extended to her eyes. Her spiky red hair glowed under the bar lights.

"Bottled water, if you have it."

"Three dollars." She set a bottle, dripping with melted ice, on the counter.

Yikes. "Thanks. Can you tell me where I can find Pyper?" I wanted to tell her to look out for Ian so she could get my key.

She nodded to the stage. "Right up there, but she goes by Candy when she's working. Don't tell the masses though." She winked. "You're not here for an audition, are you? Those are usually during the day when the club isn't open."

I choked, spitting the water out. "Oh, no. I just needed to talk to her for a moment." A vision of myself on stage made me shudder.

"Too bad. I'd have liked to see that." She grinned and turned her attention to a waiting customer.

I watched in fascination as Pyper rode the pole to the beat of "Cowboy" by Kid Rock. Multi-talented didn't begin to describe her as she climbed the two-story-high pole, using just her arm strength. Once she was two-thirds to the top she wrapped her legs tightly around the pole, released her hands while arching her back and spun around for a good thirty seconds. Damn. That was impressive.

The men hooting in the front row were clearly not put off by the implications of a woman who could hold herself up with her thighs. A fact demonstrated when they whipped their dollar bills out and waited for her to give them a moment of personalized attention.

Mesmerized by Pyper's performance, I didn't notice the man sit down next to me until he spoke.

A whiskey stench assaulted my senses as a male voice whispered low and hot into my ear. "What the hell do you think you're doing, bringing Kat here?"

It's a good thing my protection cylinder held, because I knew if it hadn't, my po'boy dinner would have ended up on the club floor.

"Dan," I replied. "Who invited you?"

Chapter 3

I quickly scanned the club for Kat, but she still hadn't come back from the restroom.

"Kat called me, drunk off her ass." Dan moved to stand in front of me. His hostility filtered through my defenses, making my skin crawl. Where had that come from? We certainly weren't friends anymore, but we had formed sort of an unspoken understanding to ignore each other. He leaned in. "Stay away from her."

My temper flared. I planted my palm on his chest, pushing him back as I stood. "Or what, Dan? Are you going to keep her under lock and key?"

"Don't *ever* touch me again," he seethed.

Like I wanted to? My hand ached with a slow burn from the contact we'd just had. My physical reactions to him were getting worse. "Then leave me alone. Kat doesn't need to be rescued. She's a big girl."

His eyes narrowed as he pushed me, knocking me down onto the stool. "You expect me to believe she came into a place like this on her own? Have you decided to become a stripper now? I'm not surprised. Or maybe you just switched teams since you can't seem to hold onto a man."

Stunned, I stared up at him from the stool. In a million years I'd never guess he would assault someone, and especially not me. No matter how angry we were with each other. Not after what the three of us had been through the summer before our sophomore year in high school. It was clear he'd been drinking, but I'd never known him to be an angry drunk. Worry for him eroded some of my anger. What the hell was going on?

"Excuse me." The bartender leaned across the bar, tapping Dan on the shoulder. "Maybe you should take a step back."

Dan cut his eyes to her. "Mind your own business."

"This *is* my business. Now step back, or I'll have you thrown out." She signaled to someone across the room, but I couldn't see who with Dan blocking me.

"You can't throw me out. I haven't done anything." Dan dismissed her and turned to a man sitting to my left. "Stupid dykes."

All my concern for Dan's mental state fled as I registered his vile words. It was like he'd been possessed.

"I heard that." A vicious scowl spread over the bartender's face. "This is your last warning. Leave the lady alone, or you won't like what happens next."

Dan laughed and placed a possessive hand on my arm. "Me and the *lady* go way back," he slurred. "I'm not bothering you, am I, Jade? I mean, it's not like you don't know how I *feel* about you."

His touch sent a ripple of disgust through me. Twisting my arm, I did my best to dislodge it from his grasp. "Let go, Dan. I mean it."

"I think you better do as she says." Kane appeared at Dan's side.

"Who the hell are you?" Dan turned, his body poised for a fight.

"The manager. I suggest you remove yourself from my club." Kane appeared relaxed, but his voice was laced with a dangerous edge.

"Oh. Good." Dan let out a menacing laugh. "Just the one I was lookin' for. If you're thinking of hiring this bitch," Dan pointed at me, "you should know she's a mind-reading freak."

In a blink of an eye, Kane twisted Dan's arm behind his back and shoved him toward the exit.

"Let go, you bastard," Dan howled, kicking out as he struggled. "I'm doing you a favor."

The music drowned out Kane's reply, but icy fury radiated off him. Dan appeared livid, but his energy betrayed intense satisfaction. What had he thought he'd accomplished? Had he shown up specifically to hurt me? I watched as Kane literally threw Dan out the door and then followed him.

"Jade?" Kat put her hand on my arm. "What's going on?"

"How long have you been standing there?"

"I just got back. Was that Kane throwing Dan out of the club?"

"Yeah."

"Wait. What was Dan doing here? Did you two fight? I thought you were ignoring each other." Her eyes stayed glued to the door, and disappointment rippled from her.

I heaved a heavy sigh. "Look Kat, Dan physically attacked me and when the bartender asked him to step back, he lost it. This is on him, not me." Delayed adrenaline coursed through my veins, making me shake.

She twisted so fast she stumbled, but caught herself on the neighboring stool. Her bloodshot, slightly glazed eyes struggled to focus on mine, making me wonder just how much she'd had to drink. "Dan would never do that. Have you forgotten what happened in that foster home years ago? He saved us. Both of us."

A frustrated growl slipped from my lips. "No. Of course not. How could I?"

That was the summer I'd lost my mom, and I'd been put into the system before Aunt Gwen had come to take care of me. On the Fourth of July the pair of them had come to pick me up from the foster home on the way to the fair. Only we'd never made it out of the house. A cold shiver snaked down my body as I remembered.

Dan had risked his life to save the two of us from unspeakable things, enduring far more than a fifteen-year-old boy ever should have. By some miracle Kat and I had made it out with minor injuries. Dan hadn't been as lucky. He'd put himself between our attacker and us over and over again and would have surely died protecting us if the police hadn't shown up when they had.

From that day on, the three of us had formed an unbreakable bond of friendship. Until Dan and I had screwed it up with our relationship.

"I better go make sure he's okay. See you back at my place," Kat said.

"Don't count on it," I said to her back as she wobbled through the crowd, but I doubted she heard me over the music. Gritting my teeth, I turned back to the bartender. "I'm so sorry."

"Why?" Her brow dimpled as she frowned.

"Because it's my fault Dan was here." My hands started trembling. I balled them into fists, furious at my reaction.

"Did you invite him here or something?"

"What? No."

"Then how is it your fault? It's obvious you don't harbor any love for the dude." She shrugged. "Don't worry about it. It's not the first time some random drunk started trouble."

"He's not so random," I said quietly.

"Really, don't worry about it. Kane will take care of it. I'm Charlie, by the way."

I shook her hand. "Jade, and thanks for the help."

She cocked her head in interest. "So, is it true?"

"What?"

"What he said. Can you really read minds?"

"No." Technically I couldn't read minds, so it wasn't a lie.

"That's too bad. I'd love to have a gift like that." Charlie turned to wipe down the bar and then asked, "Wouldn't you?"

"No. I wouldn't," I answered truthfully. My shoulders relaxed as I smiled at her.

It wasn't long before Kane strolled back in, his expression cool as if nothing had happened. He walked straight toward me. Just as he reached the bar I said, "I am so sorry. I don't know what his problem is."

"You don't? I do."

"You do?" My hands started to shake again.

"Being an asshole is his problem. Don't worry, the other bouncers have been instructed that he's not allowed in here again. Ever."

"Ever?"

"Is that a problem?"

The tension in my jaw eased as I let out a long, slow breath. "No. Thank you, Kane. I'm sorry he caused such a scene."

He nodded, staring at me with intense curiosity radiating off him. I willed myself to keep eye contact and waited. He clearly had questions, but as time ticked by it became equally as clear he wasn't going to ask. And I wasn't offering.

"Well…thanks again, I appreciate the help. If you need anything from me, let me know."

His gaze traveled the length of my body, then back up. "Maybe later." With that, he turned and walked off.

"Uh-oh! Looks like the boss has his sights set on a new girl," Charlie sang as she did a little dance next to me.

"What?"

"I saw that look. I may not be into guys, but I know how one looks when he's interested."

"But what about Pyper?"

"What about her?" she asked.

"Uh…aren't they together?"

Charlie laughed, long and hard to the point of almost crying. "Honey, if Pyper had a thing with Kane, you'd know it. Subtlety's not her strong suit when it comes to men." A wicked smile played at the corner of her mouth. "No. They're just business partners. And the boss man has his eye on you."

After the adrenaline rush wore off, pressure built behind my left eye, threatening a migraine. If I didn't leave the club soon, someone would be carrying me out. I thanked Charlie once more and made a quick getaway. The pressure didn't start to ease until I entered the narrow walkway to my building's courtyard. By the time I reached the inner sanctuary, the brick walls had succeeded in blocking out the commotion of Bourbon Street. Sighing in relief, I flopped into a chair.

"Jade?" Pyper called. I followed the sound of her voice and found her leaning against the side entrance. "I thought you were going to your friend's house."

"Change of plans. What brings you out here?"

She walked over and sat next to me. "Just taking a break. What about you?"

"Waiting for Ian to finish so I can get to sleep."

Pyper sat up, her eyebrows raised. "Really? You're not afraid?"

I lifted one shoulder. "I was up there with Ian, and nothing happened—even when I tried to speak to it. I figure I better get it over with." My halfhearted smile faltered at her skeptical look. "It'll be fine."

She pulled a business card out of her bag. "My cell's on there. If anything else happens or if you just get spooked, call me, and you can come to my place. I live next door above the café."

I furrowed my brows. "Thanks. That's kind of you, especially since we hardly know each other." I liked her and thought we were on our way to being friends, but trust wasn't something that came easy for me. I'd suffered too many past betrayals. Depending on anyone was just asking for trouble. Look at Kat, for example.

I realized she hadn't seen the exchange between Dan and I, and the whole thing was so out of character for him, but when I'd told her what happened she'd dismissed my claims without even considering them. Being drunk wasn't a good enough excuse. She seemed to comprehend Dan being thrown out of the club just fine. That alone should have given her a clue something wasn't right. The whole exchange left me feeling empty and alone.

"What can I say? I feel guilty we rented you a haunted apartment. I really thought Kane was full of shit. If you want out of your lease, I'll make it happen."

Ah. Guilt made people do a lot of things they normally wouldn't do. Still, I appreciated both offers. "Thanks, but I think I'll stick it out for now. Hopefully Ian can come up with a solution for a ghost-free apartment." At this point I didn't have many options. So unless the ghost sent knives through the air at me, I'd already decided I was staying. "But if things get worse I might take you up on it."

"You've got guts. I like that in a woman."

"Me too," Ian said as he strolled up behind us. "Jade, here's your key. We've got everything we need, but it'll take a few days to compile the data. I'll call you, and maybe we can get together for dinner and go over it?"

"Sure, sounds good. Thanks, Ian." I stood and gave him a hug goodbye.

"Hmm, sounds like you've got yourself a date," Pyper said after Ian left.

"What? No, it's not a date. Is it?"

"Sure looks like it from here." Pyper stood. "I've got to get back inside. Don't hesitate to call if you need anything."

The moment of truth. Was I ready to go back up to my apartment? No, but sleeping in the courtyard wasn't an option. I could always take Pyper up on her offer, but how weird would that be? I barely knew her. Maybe I'd break down and use my almost-maxed-out credit card for a hotel room.

Music from The Charlie Daniels Band started playing from my cell phone, interrupting my inner monologue. I smiled as I flipped it open. "Hey, Gwen. How's my favorite aunt tonight?"

"Better than you, sweetie. You've pushed yourself too far."

"I know it. I'm sorry. Am I keeping you up?" Gwen has psychic tendencies, and there isn't anyone she's more in tune with than me.

"Yes, but it's not the first time, and it won't be the last. I called to tell you, you've made the right decision, so stop stressing over it and get to it." She paused then added, "I need to rest at some point tonight."

"Wait, my decision? You mean the one to stay in my apartment tonight?"

"Is that what you were mulling over when I called? If so, then yes." She chuckled. "The message came through loud and clear."

The tension eased from my limbs. If Gwen said it was okay, then it was okay. I brought her up to speed on the day's events, minus the run-in with Dan. I'd be willing to bet she already knew, but no need to rehash it. Gwen was even less of a fan of his than I was—if that was even possible.

"Wow," she said. "You do have a lot going on. I'm getting a strong vibe your apartment is okay, but still be careful. If it bothers you again, tell it to leave. Be firm, but respectful. You don't want to piss him or her off."

"I will, and thanks. I needed to hear your voice tonight."

"I know. Get some rest and restore that energy. Do as I say, now. I'll know if you don't."

Grinning, I said my goodbyes, with promises to take care of myself. As I let myself into the building, I felt better than I had all day.

With more than a little trepidation I pushed my door open, praying Gwen was right. I trusted her completely, but even that couldn't put all my fears to rest. After a mental sweep around the room I mustered up the strength to visit my bathroom. I couldn't go to bed without brushing my teeth.

Honeysuckle scent still clung to the air, but the bathroom had been cleaned and the jar of Honey Dust sat innocently on my bathroom shelf. *Thank you, Ian!* Maybe a date with him wouldn't be so bad. After completing my bedtime ritual I made a beeline for my new bed. Grateful the day had finally come to an end, I set my cell phone alarm to wake me for work the next day and passed out.

A cool breeze caressed my shoulder, prompting me to pull back the thin sheet. I welcomed the reprieve from the warm, humid night. I didn't need to feel the mattress shift to know I wasn't alone. His playful energy engulfed me, and a slow smile spread on my lips when his warm breath tickled my ear. Purring as he caressed my neck, I tried to roll toward him but his arm clasped around my middle, trapping me.

Wiggling, I tried to escape from his firm grasp but stilled when he trailed his fingers from my belly upward between my breasts.

How had I ever gone so long without this?

I held myself still, reveling in the building tension as he explored. But when he brushed his thumb over my nipple, I trembled, and a small moan escaped from my lips. His desire shot through my veins, overriding any self-control. I reached out, aching with need, desperate to feel his body pressed tight against mine. My arms circled, pulling him close. As I pressed my lips to his, he vanished. An agonizing pain shot through my heart.

My eyes snapped open. I clutched my chest and sat up, my body still trembling from the invisible touch. I focused on the eerie yellow moon shining through the window. Who exactly had I been dreaming about? No face or build came to mind. My only recollection was the imprint of his touch and lingering, wicked desire. With a sigh I lay back down on the pillows.

What was that about? Okay, hanging out in the strip club had side effects. Or was that a benefit? My thoughts drifted to Kane, and the desire returned full force. Damn it! That man was just too sexy for his own good.

Chapter 4

The rest of the week fell into a comfortable routine. I worked the café in the mornings and spent the afternoons at the glass studio—the real reason I'd moved to New Orleans. The hot glass school had offered me a job teaching beadmaking. I'd been making and selling glass beads online ever since college and had built a pretty solid business over the last seven years. But the income wasn't really enough to afford to live here, hence the part-time café gig.

Kat, who already lived here, had referred me and did more than a fair amount of coaxing to get me to move. Too bad she'd neglected to mention Dan had relocated from Idaho or that they'd started dating. Otherwise I'd still be living in Boise.

By Friday I'd decided I'd earned an afternoon off. I'd just poured a large glass of wine when a knock sounded at my door.

I opened it to find Pyper, with new streaks of neon pink running through her black hair. "Wow! Where'd you find time to do that? Your hair looks awesome!"

She raised her hand to a freshly dyed lock. "Right after I left the café. It came out great, right?"

I nodded as she made a beeline for my counter. "Thank God," she said dramatically. "You have wine."

I laughed. "Rough day?"

"You have no idea." She filled her glass to the rim and drank half of it before taking a breath. "Better already."

"I'd offer you a seat, but…" I waved a hand around the empty room. "I haven't had time to look for furniture yet. I'm planning a date with Craigslist tomorrow."

"Don't worry, I can't stay. One of the girls just called and quit. Something about taking a job in Miami. Now we're really in a bind. We have three VIP parties tonight." Desperation seeped from her. "Please, Jade? Would you help us out tonight?"

"At the club?" I asked, surprised.

She nodded.

"I don't—"

"Please?" Pyper pleaded.

"I'm sorry, but I'm not interested in stripping."

"What? Oh, no. Charlie needs help tending bar, and I'm filling in for one of the waitresses. You do such an excellent job at the coffee shop. I know you'd be perfect."

I frowned, biting my lip. "I'm really not interested in working at the strip club." Even though I could use the extra cash, it would be rough trying to block all the energy flying around that place. And on a Friday night. I cringed.

"Oh. Well, I guess…" Pyper drank the rest of her wine and studied the room. Her lips turned up in a slow grin. "I'll tell you what. You help me out tonight, just tending bar, and I'll hook you up with some furniture and movers."

"Huh? How?"

"We have a whole storage room full of old furniture downstairs. I'm sure there's plenty there to fill this place. You said you were looking for used stuff anyway." She shrugged. "Plus, I can get a couple of the guys to haul it up here."

Free furniture and movers? Maybe I could suffer the energy land mine for one night. "How long do you need me?"

"Yes!" Triumph streamed off her. She knew she had me. "Three, maybe four hours."

"All right, but I've never tended bar before. Don't expect what you get at the café."

"Don't worry. Charlie will have plenty for you to do. Thank you very much! Come down around nine so she can catch you up to speed before it gets busy." Pyper twirled and danced to the door. "You're a lifesaver."

After Pyper disappeared I searched for my phone, intending to call Ian. We'd been playing phone tag for the last two days. I still didn't have the results from his ghost hunt. It didn't seem to matter much, since I hadn't seen or felt anyone since the day he'd taken the readings. I was just curious at that point. If the ghost left me alone, I was more than happy to let it be.

I dialed and waited.

He picked up on the third ring. "Jade! Finally, we connect."

"About time. You're busier than me, it seems."

He laughed. "I don't know about that. Our schedules just seem to be clashing. However, I managed to free my calendar for tomorrow night. Are you up for dinner and maybe a little jazz music?"

"Sure, sounds great. I'm working until two, so any time after that I'm free."

We settled on six p.m., meeting at my apartment. I looked around, wondering where Ian would sit. The bed was the only surface in the room, leaving the other option the floor. Wonderful. Instead of indulging in the nap I'd been hoping for, I grabbed my keys and went in search of Pyper.

Pyper wasn't at the café so I rapped on the club door, hoping to be heard over the faint music pulsing inside. I waited and then knocked harder. On my third try the club door swung open mid-knock.

"Oh, hello," I stammered, staring into Kane's chiseled face.

"Jade." He smiled, and his curiosity pushed at my consciousness. "You're not here for the auditions, are you?"

I frowned, eyeing my dusty threadbare jeans. What was with these people? Did I look like a stripper? I smoothed my hair. More than a few locks had fallen out of my ponytail. I opened my mouth to protest then noticed Kane's cocky smile and a fair amount of amusement clinging to him. "Funny. Is Pyper here?"

He chuckled and waved me in. I glanced around, taking in the blue, crushed velvet walls, chairs and love seats I hadn't noticed before. Things looked different in the daytime. Even the ceiling was done in velvet.

He stepped beside me and guided me with his hand on the small of my back. Electric heat ran up my spine, causing me to shiver. I could almost feel his ego swell as pleasure ran through him. Damn it. He'd felt that. It was all I could do to keep walking and not run for the door. "Have a seat. I'll grab you something to drink. Pyper might be a while," he said.

I sat at the bar, watching Kane glide behind the counter.

"What's your poison?" he asked.

"You don't have Guinness, do you?"

"Guinness?" He raised one eyebrow.

"Yeah, you know—the Irish pub beer?" I tapped my fingers on the bar. "What? It's been a long week." And my wine sat untouched back at my apartment.

"Nothing. I just don't know many women who drink Guinness." He reached into a small refrigerator and pulled out the dark bottle. "In a glass?"

"Doesn't matter."

He popped the cap and handed it over. I grabbed it and turned around, checking out the scene on the stage in front of me. A group of five women stood listening intently to Pyper.

Kane came out from behind the bar and sat next to me, his own beer in hand.

"Drinking on the job?" I asked.

"One of the perks to being the owner." He raised his bottle in a mock salute.

I couldn't argue with that. Nodding, I touched his beer with my own and drank.

We sat in silence, our attention on the stage. Pyper seemed to be giving some sort of instruction. Intrigued, I leaned to the right, trying to see past one of the girls blocking my view. Kane's musky scent filled my senses. My world tilted. Reaching out, I grabbed onto the closest thing. Kane's thigh. His muscles tensed, and I wanted nothing more than to run my hand higher along the firm surface. My eyes met his. The deep pools of melted chocolate made me bite down on my lower lip. His eyes shifted at the movement and just when I thought he would lean in...

"What's goin' on?" Piqued interest invaded my senses.

The spell broken, I jumped, snatched my hand back and turned my attention to Pyper as she came to a stop in front of us.

"Love the pink," Kane said in his normal tone, apparently unaffected by whatever had just happened.

She smiled. "I thought you might."

"Jade was waiting for you." He got up and left without saying another word.

"What's that goofy look about?" Pyper asked.

"Huh?" I tried to put my face into a neutral expression. "I don't know. Just out of my element, I guess. Sorry to bother you while you're working, but I was hoping I could get a look at the furniture."

"No problem, you're not bothering me. My assistant has this under control."

I grabbed my beer and followed Pyper to a door at the end of the hall. After unlocking it, she flipped the light and ushered me into a room reminiscent of Aunt Gwen's attic. A tiny walkway had been forged through the clutter of cardboard boxes and old furniture. Dust covered every possible surface, making my nose twitch.

"All of this has been left by past residents?" I asked in disbelief.

"As far as we know. Most of it was here when Kane bought the building."

Kane. Just his name sent my stomach into flip-flops.

Stop that. You are not interested in a strip club owner. Too bad he was so damn yummy.

"Jade?" Pyper waved her hand in front of my face.

"Hmmm?"

"Did you hear me? I said, feel free to take anything you want. We're planning to donate it anyway."

"Oh! Thanks." I moved around the room, inspecting the old furniture. The place was packed with everything from antique settees to metal folding chairs. Moving slowly, I selected a small writer's desk, an old couch destined for a slipcover, and a lamp base in desperate need of some paint. I needed a chair for the desk, but decided to hold out for something a little more comfortable.

"Jade, check this out!" Pyper called from the back of the room.

I picked my way through the mess and followed the direction of her pointed finger. In front of me stood the most beautiful, thick, honey oak headboard I'd ever seen. Intricately carved wooded vines trellised from the center out to the edges. I ran my hand over the tiny blossoms nestled in the clusters of leaves and let my guards down. Love and joy radiated from it. "What flower is this?"

"Bougainvillea. You see a lot of them around here."

"It's perfect."

"I think you'll want those, too." Pyper pointed to two matching nightstands.

Grinning, I nodded.

She pulled out her iPhone and dialed. "Kane, I need you to come to the storage room." She huffed in exasperation. "No, we're not trapped under anything heavy. Just get your butt in here."

My smiled faded. This stuff belonged to him. I was no expert, but even I could tell the bedroom furniture was worth a pretty penny. "How much do you think he'll want for it?"

"Who? Want for what?" Pyper asked in confusion.

"Kane. The furniture." I waved to the headboard. "That other stuff, the desk and couch, well it's seen better days. I can see giving them away. But the bedroom set, just look at it."

Pyper shook her head. "You can ask him, but I doubt he'll take anything for it. He really wants to turn this room into an office, so the more stuff gone, the better."

"I'm here. What do you want?" Kane said from right behind us, sounding irritated.

Pyper smiled, unleashing all of her charm on him. "Kane, darling, we need you to flex those bulging muscles and help us move some stuff up to Jade's place."

He rolled his eyes. "Your charms don't work on me." However, he smiled, and I sensed amusement entering his energy.

"Wanna bet?"

His smile turned into a grin. "Don't start something you can't finish." He glanced at me and nodded.

I waved, feeling like an intruder.

Pyper showed him the bed and night stands. "We'll get the rest."

"We will?" I asked as I stared at the couch.

"Of course we will. Come on."

Forty minutes later Pyper handed me an ice pack as I sat on my couch.

"You poor thing. Don't feel bad, I trip all the time. Let me see it." She gently pulled my hand away from my head. "It doesn't look too bad, considering you face-planted the corner of your desk." She ran a finger along the skin above my eyebrow.

"Ouch!"

"Sorry." She rummaged in her purse and pulled out a small bottle. "Here, take a few of these."

As soon as I downed the pills and a glass of water, a shirtless Kane walked in, carrying my desk. I'd left it on the second floor landing after tripping and almost knocking myself out. I cleared my throat. "Thank you," I croaked out.

"No problem."

Shifting the ice for a better view, I watched Kane. I just could not tear my eyes away from that chest. The view was more than enough to make me forget about my throbbing head. My hand twitched, aching to touch him, and I yelped in pain. "Oh, shit! That hurt."

A shadow blocked the sun shining in through the window. I gazed up into Kane's worried expression. He placed a pillow at the end of the couch. "Here, lie back."

I did as he said, speechless once more from the heart-aching view.

He took the ice bag from me and gently laid it on my head. "Just relax. We'll take care of the rest."

I gave him a weak smile, not trusting my voice.

For the next hour I entertained myself by watching Kane, still shirtless, and Jeff, a club bouncer, move in my furniture and put together my bed. All kinds of Kane fantasies were entertained as his rippling muscles flexed under the weight of the headboard. That bed had some serious potential, and I had plenty of material to work with. I'd been having vivid sex dreams every night for the last four nights. My libido was definitely in overdrive. My mind had formed a particularly fascinating scenario involving caramel when Kane stood up and announced they were finished.

"Already?" I sat up.

Kane glanced at his watch. "Already? We've been at this for two hours."

"Right. What do I owe you?" I reached for my purse.

"For what?"

"The furniture and your time. Jeff's too."

"Didn't Pyper already tell you that stuff was free?" To my disappointment, he pulled his shirt back on.

"Yeah. But it's such nice stuff. I should pay you something for it."

Kane stood with his arms folded and shook his head.

"Well, for your time then." I pulled my wallet out, intent on not letting this go.

"I'll collect later." Kane said with a wry grin. "As for Jeff, you can just give him a tip. He's already on the clock for the club."

"That isn't right! He's been doing my work, not yours. Let me pay his hourly wage."

Kane shook his head again. "No. I was going to get him to clean out the storage room anyway. It doesn't matter if it goes up here, or if it goes to the restoration place."

I stared at him. Was he for real? "At least let me take you to dinner sometime as a thank you."

"I'm counting on it." Kane walked away, signaling to Jeff it was time to go.

"Wait!" I pulled out forty dollars and pressed it into Jeff's hand. "Thank you both so much."

Jeff looked at the cash, then at me, then to Kane.

"Take it," Kane said as he opened the door.

Jeff smiled and nodded, following Kane.

"Thanks again," I called as they left.

Immediately, I pulled out fresh sheets and went to work on making up my new bed. When I'd finished I topped it with my favorite down comforter and added poppy red and coral pillows for color. Standing back, I felt the lure of crawling into my new sanctuary. But my stomach growled. Loudly. I hadn't eaten since my break at the coffee shop and couldn't put it off any longer. I pulled my phone out and ordered a small veggie pizza.

With twenty minutes to wait, I showered and was draped in a robe when I heard the knock.

Grabbing my wallet, I raced to the door. When I opened it, my jaw dropped, and instinctively I cinched my robe tighter.

"Dinner's ready," Kane said, sweeping past me with the pizza box and a paper bag.

"Uh…"

He handed me the box and pulled me to the couch. "Sit."

"How—"

"Do you have a bottle opener?"

"On my keychain." I pointed to my keys on the counter.

He chuckled and pulled out two beers. Popping the caps, he asked, "Always prepared, huh?"

"Swiss army knife."

He handed me a Guinness. I smiled. I could get used to a man who remembered my beer of choice. "I found the delivery guy outside looking lost," Kane said as he sat next to me.

"Thank you."

"No problem. Dig in."

I wasted no time and sighed with pleasure at the first bite. "Yum." I held out the box, offering him a piece.

He peered in. "Where's the meat?"

"I don't like pork."

"I hear they have other meat options."

I swallowed my next bite. "So I like veggies on my pizza. Get over it. It's not like I knew I'd have company"

His eyes roamed over me. "So I see."

"Aren't you supposed to be working?" Didn't he have naked employees needing his attention?

"Supposed to?" He pursed his lips. "In a matter of speaking, maybe. But Pyper has it under control. Besides, it isn't busy right now."

"Damn. She works all the time. When does she sleep?"

"I don't think she does." Kane grabbed the last piece, and we ate in silence.

When I finished I asked, "How much was the pizza?"

He shook his head.

"I can't *not* pay you for my dinner. I can just call and get the total from the pizza place."

"Sure you can 'not pay' me. I ate most of it." He wadded up his napkin and tossed it into the empty box.

"You only ate half, and you brought the beer." I opened my wallet and thrust a twenty at him.

"It wasn't that much."

"I don't care. Just take it," I said, frustrated. I wasn't used to being taken care of, and I wasn't a freeloader either. "Look. Thanks for all your help, but I can take care of myself."

"I can see that." His eyes twinkling, he got up and moved toward the door.

I followed and thrust the twenty at him again. "Take it, or I'll put it in your pocket myself."

"Really?" A mischievous grin spread over his face. His anticipation prickled my skin.

I groaned inwardly. Not the smartest comment I'd ever made. To save face, I took a deep breath and moved in. His arm came around me as I slipped the twenty into his back pocket. My breasts pressed up against his chest, and the thin material of my silk robe did nothing to hide my now aroused and pointed nipples.

Kane lowered his head. My breath caught just before he pressed a light kiss on the bruise above my eye.

He smiled down at me. "You can let go of my ass now."

As if burned, I jumped back, folding my arms over my chest.

Chuckling, he opened the door. "Bye, Jade. Thanks for dinner."

I closed the door and stood there wondering what in the hell just happened. The room suddenly became very cold, snapping me out of my trance. I turned toward the window and saw the outline of a medium-built, fair-haired man. The apparition grew into an almost solid image, took two steps, and vanished.

Shock rooted me to the floor.

Chapter 5

What the hell was that?

My heart hammered against my chest, and I stopped breathing at the same time. The combination made my head spin. I forced myself to take deep breaths. My right arm wasn't shooting with pain, so I knew I hadn't suffered cardiac arrest. Though for a minute there, I wasn't so sure. When my heart slowed to a relatively normal rate, I moved cautiously through the apartment, scanning the emotional energy.

When I'd completed my circle without incident, my shoulders relaxed. Had I imagined the apparition? I didn't think so. Maybe it wasn't just my apartment that was haunted. Maybe the ghost haunted the whole building, and he'd left for the night. I could only hope. Grateful I had somewhere to be, I wasted no time getting ready for work.

After searching my closet, I dressed in a long pencil skirt and a wrap-around top, cut low in the front. Slipping on my only pair of heels—cute, strappy, black ones—I checked myself out in the bathroom mirror. Perfect if I was headed out for a date. Maybe a little overdressed for working a bar at a strip club, but I didn't have anything else suitable. It would have to do.

Grabbing my keys, I took one last look at my apartment. Satisfied my ghost was still absent, I locked the door behind me and headed for the club.

A few minutes later I paused, letting my eyes adjust as I entered Wicked. The lights were dim as usual, but the place hadn't started to fill up yet. Eight-thirty was still on the early side for a strip club. A cute, tiny blonde dancing on stage caught my eye. I frowned, wondering why anyone would want to strip down and get felt up by random guys every night. It made my skin crawl thinking about it.

I closed my eyes and focused on constructing my emotional barrier. Once my cylinder was in place I made my way over to the bar toward Pyper and Charlie. "Hey, I'm a bit early."

"Good, that'll give Charlie more time to get you up to speed." Pyper stepped closer. "That's one hell of a shiner you have above your eye."

"Thanks." I reached up, trying to cover it with a piece of my hair.

Pyper laughed. "You're fighting a losing battle."

"Ah, give my girl a break. It takes talent to look that hot with half your forehead black and blue," Charlie said, waving toward a stool. "Sit down. I'll get you a drink."

Seeing Pyper nod, I happily obliged.

Charlie set a tall, slender glass of ice and a diet Coke on the counter and held up a bottle of rum in question.

"No thanks. I took some pain pills. I don't think that's a good combination." Apparently drinking on the job was optional. Why not? It *was* a strip club.

"You're such a good girl," Charlie said, winking at me.

I snorted. "I need lessons on misbehaving." I'd forgotten what it felt like to let loose every once in a while. Ever since I landed in New Orleans I'd been the height of Miss Responsibility. Something was seriously wrong with me. I had done nothing but work since I got here. Eyeing Pyper, I mentally penciled in a night on the town. No doubt she'd coax me into something not suitable for the PG-13 crowd.

"No time like the present," Charlie said, spiking my drink with some Captain Morgan's.

"Oh crap. I'm gonna need a keeper by the time the night is over." I scowled, but picked up my glass and took a long swig. "Ahhh."

Both of them laughed.

"I need two hurricanes," someone said behind me.

I swiveled, finding Holly, the assistant manager from the café, in a bar maid outfit.

"Hey, I didn't know you were working here, too," I said.

She shrugged. "Pyper needed help."

"That's a common theme."

"You're working here?" She looked me up and down and then focused on the stool.

"Yes, when Charlie's ready for me." I frowned as hostility crept into my awareness.

She gave a curt nod, grabbed the drink tray and left.

That was odd. What did I do to annoy her? I watched her serve the drinks to an oblivious couple, now sharing one chair. The intense desire and excitement whirling around them made me blush. It was then I realized the alcohol was chipping away at my emotional barrier. I pushed the glass aside.

"Quite the show they're putting on." Pyper sat next to me.

"You might want to offer a room for them to rent."

Pyper grinned. "Rooms by the hour. That'll really class the place up." She leaned closer, passing a glass to Charlie. "Fill me up, will you?" Her tired eyes drooped with fatigue.

"Do you ever sleep?" I asked.

Her smile vanished, and anxiety flowed over me in waves. "Not these days. Insomnia, I guess." She shook her head and pasted a smile back on her face. "Thanks again for helping out. I really appreciate it."

"No problem."

Pyper put her hand on my arm. "I just don't want you to feel taken advantage of. You're starting to grow on us, and we'd like to keep you around." She winked in Charlie's direction.

"Damn straight," Charlie piped in. "Best thing that's happened around here since Roy was ousted."

"Roy?" I asked.

"Previous owner before Kane bought the place. Serious jackass," Pyper explained. "Anyway, I've got some work to do. See you later." She waved and headed toward the offices.

An hour later, I wiped down the bar, wishing I had a sandwich. The rum, combined with the pain pills, hadn't been the best idea. My barriers had vanished altogether, and I hadn't been able to block out the rapidly intensifying energy in the club.

As I worked my way through the line of customers, Mr. Evil, the man I'd noticed the first time I'd come in the club, appeared at the table closest to the bar. As before, he held an unlit cigarette, but his anger was subdued this time. Maybe he'd invested in therapy. He stared intently at Pyper, never taking his eyes off her. I didn't blame him. She'd changed into a silver push-up bra and a tiny black leather skirt, no more than eight inches long. Just enough to give the illusion it covered her bum.

"I thought you had the night off from stripping?" I asked when she joined us.

"So did I, but one of the girls hasn't shown up. Strippers." She rolled her eyes and laughed. "No one else was reachable, so I'm it." She searched the crowd until she spotted Kane. My heart did a little jig in my chest, until I saw him put his hand on Holly's back as he walked with her. He gave Pyper a wave. "That's my cue," she said and stepped toward the stage.

Right at that moment, the lights flickered off and on, and the music volume shot up to deafening levels. I cringed, my eardrums responding with sharp stabs of complaint, and squinted in confusion at the DJ booth. What the holy hell?

A faint prickle of glee entered my system, causing the hair on the back of my neck to rise. I turned toward the mental intrusion just as the tequila bottle I'd been holding ripped from my hand. Pain exploded through my skull.

Everything went black.

Groaning from the sunlight piercing my eyelids, I rolled over and shoved my face deep into the pillow. A flash of searing pain bolted me upright.

"Son of a bitch!" I gasped as my hands flew to inspect the damage. The goose-egg-sized lump made my stomach turn. With my eyes closed I took a few cleansing breaths before I felt the mattress shift beside me. Peeking through my fingers, I peered down at a sleepy-eyed Kane. His tousled dark hair and the glimpse of his bare chest momentarily made me forget my aching head. I searched my muddled brain for some recollection of how I ended up in this predicament, but it was blank.

"Morning," mumbled my bed partner as he sat up. "Let me see." He moved my hands and gently touched my forehead.

I closed my eyes to block out his sheer maleness, hoping my hormones would downshift from overdrive. With his touch, concern, tenderness and protectiveness illuminated from him, wrapping around me like a blanket. I lay my head back down on the pillow, too exhausted to analyze this turn of events.

"How did I end up here?" I asked as I admired the rich walnut armoire and four-poster bed I was snuggled into.

"Do you remember anything from last night?" he asked.

I took a moment to think. "Not much. The last thing I remember is Pyper leaving the bar to go on stage, and suddenly everything went haywire." I glanced up at him. "I'm guessing I was knocked out."

He nodded.

"What got me?" I asked.

"Tequila bottle."

"Jesus! Taken out by Cabo Wabo. It was a full bottle too. Is it toast?"

A strong mix of humor and exasperation overrode his concern. Kane snorted. "Considering what happened next, I'd hardly say it matters much at this point."

I pushed myself up with my elbows and raised my eyebrows in question.

"Do you remember the lights flickering on and off and the music, that awful music?"

I nodded. The music had sped up, effectively giving us a Chipmunks' version of a Prince song. "That's the last thing I remember."

"That's because as Pyper left the bar and headed to the stage, all the loose bottles on the shelves shot up and circled her like a tornado. The one you'd been holding jerked out of your hand and bounced off your forehead on its way to join the others."

"Right. Flying liquor bottles." I laughed. "Come on, tell me what really happened. I ran into something again, right?"

Kane stared at me, shaking his head. His exasperation quickly stamped out any traces of humor.

I stared back finally remembering the tequila bottle flying from my grip.

Shit. A tornado. Just like the Honey Dust. A full minute went by as I digested the information. I found myself focusing on his shirtless chest and tan six-pack. My eyes glazed over as I imagined pulling the rest of the covers off him to explore further. Blinking, I caught his eye and flushed. He picked up a tee shirt and put in on.

"Sorry," I mumbled, my ears growing fiercely hot.

He just sat there, wearing that sexy, cocky smile of his.

Clearing my throat, I said, "Okay, so that really happened. Fill me in on the details."

Kane sat back against the headboard and handed me his pillow. I snuggled into it, catching a faint trace of his crisp, earthy cologne.

"I was headed to the bar when Holly hijacked me. We'd just turned toward my office when Prince turned into Alvin."

A private moment with Holly in his office? A vile image of the two of them kissing flashed through my mind. Irrational? Yes, but there it was.

He continued. "Then the music stopped, and all the bottles from the bar started flying, including the one you held. I saw you go down and ran to help."

"My hero," I said with a small smile.

He grimaced, looking pained. "It took me a moment to realize the bottles were circling Pyper. Thank God whatever it was stopped, because I don't think I could have broken through to get to her."

"They just stopped?"

"Yeah and shattered all over the floor. We're lucky everyone moved out of the way. Someone could have gotten seriously hurt."

Through my mounting horror I couldn't help wondering what the patrons had thought of bottles flying through the air. Suddenly I was intensely glad I'd been passed out and missed the whole thing.

Kane reached out and gently caressed my forehead, again. "You had us worried."

The tenderness in his voice warmed me and scared me at the same time. Imagining sexy times excited me, but getting intimate was another thing entirely. "Pyper wasn't hurt?"

He shook his head. "Just shook up."

I breathed a sigh of relief and sat up. For the first time I noticed I was wearing my own Nick and Nora owl pajama bottoms and camisole. Who'd changed my clothes? I pulled the covers up, feeling exposed.

"Pyper helped you into your pajamas," Kane said, reading my mind. "She also brought your toiletries. They're in my bathroom."

My stuff was mingling with his in the bathroom. *Yikes.* "Okay, thanks. But how did I get here?"

"I carried you."

Too bad I'd missed *that.*

"Then, I went back for Pyper. I'd left her in Charlie's care and by the time I got back, she'd settled down enough to insist we get your stuff so you'd be comfortable when you woke up. She stayed in her room—" he pointed to the wall on our right, "—and I stayed here with you, just to be sure you were okay."

Wait what? "You and Pyper live together?" Hadn't Charlie told me they weren't a couple? Maybe she was misinformed.

"No. This is her place, but I keep stuff here for when I stay over. I guess you could say this is sort of my room."

"Oh." I didn't know what to make of that. Friends with benefits?

His eyes crinkled as his lips quirked up. "We aren't a couple, just business partners and best friends. Sometimes I work so late I crash here."

"I didn't ask." His ego swelled, pushing on my mental barriers. *Crap.*

"Yes you did. You just didn't voice it."

I rolled my eyes and looked away, catching a glimpse at the clock. "Shit, I have to get to work." I jumped up, causing a dizzy spell and almost fell back onto the bed. I put one hand on my throbbing head and the other on the bedpost to steady myself.

Kane scooted over and eased me back down. "No you don't. Pyper said to tell you not to come in today. She's got it covered."

"But—"

"No, the last thing we need is you passing out in the café. She'll call me if she needs help." He got up. "I'll go make you some breakfast. Stay here and rest, or grab a shower if you want. All your stuff is in the bathroom."

I nodded, watching him head out the door. Kane wasn't at all what I expected him to be. I'd judged him on the fact that he owned a strip club, and while I'd never met a strip club owner, I'd pegged him as a cross between Hugh Hefner and Larry Flint. In other words, a ladies' man who thought about sex, women and more sex. Why else would a person go into the strip club business? I suspected he had some of those qualities, as most men did, but clearly he was made of a lot more. He'd been genuinely concerned about me, took care of me, and he was still doing it this morning. Smiling to myself, a warm feeling of pleasure grew in my chest.

Not wanting to have breakfast in my pajamas I got up and headed for a bath. The oversized tub took up half the bathroom. Feeling deliciously pampered, I couldn't resist turning on the jets.

I would have stayed there until my entire body shriveled into a raisin, but the smell of coffee and Kane's call that breakfast was ready lured me out.

My backpack sat on the counter filled with my makeup bag, toothbrush, deodorant and, to my surprise, the Honey Dust. Why Pyper thought I'd need it for an overnight when I was knocked out, I didn't know. But considering what happened the night before, I couldn't believe she'd included it. Was she possessed? I hadn't even touched it since the day I'd moved in. Maybe it was an act of defiance against the spirit. I set my shoulders and decided if she was brave enough, then so was I. What's a little Honey Dust compared to flying bottles?

"If you're here, Ghost, please stay away. You're not invited into my space." Hopefully that would keep him out. Looking around to be sure I was alone, I lightly dusted myself with the sweet scent. The air didn't stir, and nothing suddenly appeared. Feeling victorious, I put the jar away, and dressed in the clean jeans and tank top Pyper had picked out for me. After pulling my hair into a bun and slapping some makeup on, I ventured into the rest of the apartment to join Kane.

I shuffled over the rich pecan hardwood floors, awestruck. I'd never been in a more soothing living room. The overstuffed mocha couch and loveseat were covered in peach pillows, complementing the vanilla cream walls. The aroma of fresh coffee filtered from the kitchen. Did the apartment always smell like freshly ground beans? It *was* directly above the café. I stopped in the adjoining dining room at the ten-foot-tall windows, letting the sun warm my face.

Kane appeared from the kitchen and stepped up behind me, handing me a steaming mug.

"Thanks," I said, glancing back over my shoulder.

He hesitated then brushed his warm lips along the nape of my neck, gently kissing me. The flick of his soft tongue melted any resistance I might have mustered.

My breath caught soundlessly.

"Humm," he murmured. "Honey Dust tastes better on you than I thought it would."

Chapter 6

Kane moved away and retreated to the kitchen. I grabbed the window frame, steadying myself. Kane just kissed me. On my neck. *Thank you, Pyper, and your silly Honey Dust fetish.* I absently raised my mug and then sputtered as the scalding coffee seared my tongue. "Ow!"

"You okay?" Kane rounded the corner with two plates.

"Uh, yeah. Hotter than I expected." I held the mug up and opened my mouth to ask if he'd kiss it and make it better, but clamped it shut when my brain took over. If he wanted to kiss me—real on-the-lips-with-tongue-and-everything kissing—then he would, but I wouldn't beg for it.

He gave a sympathetic smile and put the plates on the table. "Breakfast. Hope you like waffles." He passed me a silver carafe of syrup as I sat.

The waffle was cooked to perfection, golden brown on each side and smothered in fresh blueberries. I drizzled the syrup and sighed in pleasure with the first bite. "Yum."

Satisfaction seeped from him as he watched me.

"What?" I asked.

"I'm glad to see you have an appetite. If you'd had a concussion you probably wouldn't be very hungry right now."

My insides turned to Jell-O. Suddenly I wished I'd had the nerve to ask for the kiss. No one but Kat and Gwen had gotten remotely close to caring for me in years, and here I had this gorgeous piece of eye candy doing just that. Of course he could be trying to make sure I didn't sue his ass, but considering my inside information source, I really didn't think so.

"Thank you for…everything," I said, meaning it.

He nodded. "My pleasure."

After breakfast, Kane left and I cleaned the kitchen then went back into his room to gather my things. I found my outfit from the night before folded on the dresser and packed it in my backpack on top of my toiletries. The bed remained unmade. I stopped, running my hand over the side Kane had slept in. His lingering concern touched my heart. Overwhelmed, I sat on the bed. It felt good to have a decent man care about what happened to me. Not wanting to let the feeling go, I curled up on his pillow, closed my eyes and breathed.

A man, cloaked by shadows, inched toward me. A soothing calm reached my awareness. The moonlight should have illuminated him, but his features remained unclear in his shadowy form. It didn't matter. My body recognized him. For the last week he'd visited me almost every night.

He stopped next to the bed and waited.

"What's your name," I asked.

He stood still and silent. No matter what I asked, he never spoke. It was his body that did all the talking.

"I wish I knew your name."

A stream of tenderness, longing and a hint of desperation caressed my soul. The sensations tingled in my belly. I shifted and patted the bed, extending an invitation.

He sat, and my arm brushed his solid thigh, sending heat to my center. Wanting to be touched, I lifted my face to his open hand. He cupped my cheek and traced his fingertips down the length of my neck. Moments went by as I delighted in the familiar sensation.

I reached out, exploring the solid, yet still mysterious figure. My fingers danced across his hot skin, feeling what my eyes couldn't see. His fingers tensed and curled in my hair. Longing worked its way into my consciousness. Without thought I pulled him to lie beside me. Desperate to see my lover, I used my fingers to trace his cheeks, eyes and, finally, his mouth.

I struggled to make out his features, succeeding in just a rough outline. Focusing on his lips, I titled my head, giving him the answer he waited for. Our lips met, and all inhibitions were lost.

It took a while for my brain to process the annoying chirping in my ear. One eye popped open, and I sat up with my body pulsing from the reoccurring dream. Once again I found myself in Kane's bedroom. Except he wasn't there, and the chirping was my ringtone.

I groaned and snatched my cell from the bedside table. "Yeah?"

"Jade? It's Pyper. Ian's here to do more readings. Can you come down?"

"Sure," I croaked. "Give me a few minutes."

In serious need of a cold shower, I headed for the bathroom.

Ten minutes later, refreshed and smelling like a rain forest, I headed to the first floor of the building and found the club's back door propped open. That was unusual. But if Ian was interviewing multiple people, he might have gotten tired of answering it. A few wall lights were on, giving me just enough light to see where I was headed. Trying not to disturb anything Ian might want to inspect, I stayed close to the walls, but it quickly became clear the place was spotless, completely cleaned up. And empty. Where was everybody?

I sat, staring at the stage trying to make sense of the ghost activity. Other than the energy suck after Pyper called out the ghost, my experiences with it had been mild. Honey Dust and an apparition were hardly threatening. But bottles flying around a crowded club? A chill ran down my back thinking about it. At least my suspicions were confirmed. It was haunting the whole building, not just my apartment.

Unless it was just haunting *me*.

No, it had attacked Pyper the night before. Had she pissed it off that day in my apartment?

I took a deep breath and walked to the stage. Maybe it had left some sort of emotional imprint. The events of the night before played in my mind like a movie reel. I saw Charlie and myself behind the bar, both hopping around, busily mixing drinks. I was watching Kane, surprised to notice he was keeping an eye on me. Pyper took her first few steps to the stage. Then the bottles flew. Dark emotions—anger, jealousy, disgust, and intense longing—wrapped around me. I could barely see Pyper through the whirlwind of bottles, but a faint trace of her terror reached me. The emotions intensified as if feeding on her fear. My body spasmed, unable to filter it all. I couldn't breathe. Lightning bolts of synapses crisscrossed through my brain before my vision turned to snowy static.

I woke, lying on the stage, with Pyper holding my hand. "What happened?" I asked, disoriented.

"You tell me," she said. "I was headed into the office to make a phone call when I saw you standing there. You looked like you were in some kind of trance. Then your face went white, your eyes got wide and you collapsed. Something frightened you."

"No, not frightened, exactly." The truth was, I wasn't sure what just happened. I hadn't been scared. My own emotions had been buried under the onslaught of the darkness I'd just experienced while the scene had replayed for me. Even the parts I hadn't been conscious to witness. Did I imagine what I thought happened? My empathy gift said otherwise.

"Then what?" Pyper looked at me expectantly.

What indeed? "Startled?"

"That look was not a startled one," she said.

How could I tell her what had happened without revealing my ability? Panic formed in a little ball at the pit of my stomach. "Maybe I just overdid it after last night." I stood, shaking slightly.

She stared at me for minute. "Yeah, maybe. I think you should sit down."

She had a point, but I didn't want to stay that long. "Where is everyone?"

"Next door, waiting for you."

"Oh. I thought we were meeting here. Let's go." I took off, not caring if she followed. I needed to get out of club. It just felt...wrong.

I entered the back room of the café from the adjoining hallway and found Kane.

"I was starting to think you fell back asleep," he said.

"No, I thought we were meeting next door. Is Ian out front?" I peeked through the tiny window from the back room of the café. Ian was sitting at one of the tables with a woman sporting bright red curls.

I bit my lip. Why was Kat here? She'd called a few days after the incident in the club. I hadn't picked up, and she'd left a message asking if we were okay. I hadn't called her back. It still stung that she hadn't even considered I'd been telling the truth. Before all the drama happened, I wouldn't have believed it either. But if Kat had been the one saying it, I would have at least listened.

As I lingered, trying to find the nerve to face my friend, Dan entered the café and strolled up to their table, holding a bouquet of sunflowers.

My breath hitched, and buried memories flooded back. Dan and I standing in his parent's sunflower field on a hot summer day as he gazed down at me with a powerful wave of tenderness bursting from his essence. I'd reached up, caressing his jaw with my thumb and he'd kissed me for the first time. A romantic, emotional kiss that had ended with his arms wrapped tight around me as if he'd never let go. That was the summer we'd fallen in love, before I'd lost his trust and he'd lost mine.

Dan bent down and kissed Kat's cheek. Her smile turned sweet as he handed her the bouquet. He always gave sunflowers. As homage to his parent's livelihood, I'd supposed. But it still hurt seeing the familiar gesture.

Sadness settled in my chest. Dan had only recently turned into a massive jerk. Once he'd been a kind, attentive partner I'd been ready to spend my life with. And here he was, displaying a small piece of the man I'd once known. No wonder Kat didn't see what I did.

Had I been just as blind? No. I'd had the added benefit of knowing what he was feeling. He'd loved me. I had never doubted it. Now he carried an emotional poison—at least when he was around me. Somewhere deep inside I wondered if I was to blame.

Kat stood, wrapped Dan in a tight hug and sat as he strolled off again and disappeared onto Bourbon Street.

"That's your friend, right?" Kane asked, following my gaze.

I tilted my head, stealing a peek at his thoughtful expression. He'd remembered. "Yes."

"What are you waiting for?" Kane nudged me, and I had no choice but to walk through the door.

I stopped behind Kat and cleared my throat. "Let's sit outside." I didn't know where this conversation would lead, but we didn't need an audience.

"Where the heck have you been?" Kat turned and frowned, her eyebrows pinched.

"Here," I gestured vaguely around the shop and glanced at Ian. "Hi."

"Hey. I'll be right back." He got up and headed toward the counter.

"I've been calling you since last night. Didn't you get any of my messages?"

Shaking my head, I searched for my phone in my purse. I hadn't checked to see if anyone had called. No doubt Gwen had been trying to reach me as well. "Oops, I must have left it in Kane's room."

"You slept with Kane?" she whispered, looking over my shoulder.

I glanced back to see the man in question watching us. I waved and he nodded. "No, well, yes…" Her eyes bulged with shock. I tried not to laugh. "I slept in his bed, but nothing happened."

"Why the hell not?"

"Stop staring. Let's talk about this outside."

She grabbed her flowers and followed me. I glanced at them but said nothing. Conversations about Dan never went anywhere good.

Once we were seated she blinked a few times then reluctantly gave me her full attention. "Kane is sex on a stick."

"Watch it, girl, you're drooling." I handed her a napkin, and my shoulders relaxed. I should have known girl chat about a hot guy would diffuse any awkwardness.

Ignoring my napkin, Kat switched gears. "Ian left me a message you'd been attacked last night. I've been calling ever since. Geez, Jade, you've had me in a panic all day."

I tensed. Now she was worried about me? "I wasn't attacked. My head just got in the way."

"I wish you'd have called," she said quietly. "Who else do you have to look after you?"

"I'm sorry. I was in no shape to call anyone. Besides, I have friends here. Pyper and Kane took care of me. See?" I held my hands out. "I'm fine. No need to worry."

"Except for the giant bruise on your forehead. And I'd hardly call these people your friends. I mean they work at a strip club, for God's sake."

"So what?" My fists clenched in aggravation. "A minute ago you were wondering why I hadn't thrown myself at Kane, and now you're judging him and Pyper? You don't even know them. Pyper isn't some doped-up stripper. She owns the café and helps manage the club. And as for Kane, he was a perfect gentleman. Get off your high horse and drop the preconceived notions. At least they were there for me when I needed them." I stared at my hands, trying to forget I'd been making the same sort of assumptions about Kane since I'd met him.

Kat's pain, mixed with frustrated anger, assaulted me. I closed my eyes, quickly building my silo barrier. Damn it. I would not feel guilty. Pyper and Kane had proven to be better friends in the short time I'd known them than Kat had in the last three months. I wouldn't stand for her insulting them.

"What do you mean, 'At least they were there for you when you needed them'? When have I ever not been there for you?"

"Never mind." I shook my head. "It's not important."

Her eyes narrowed. "It's about Dan again, isn't it? God, Jade, I wish you two would just let it go already."

"And I wish you'd wake up!"

"I don't want to be in the middle of this." She closed her eyes for a moment then looked at me pleadingly. "Can we just agree to not talk about him?"

"Fine."

"Thank you."

"Excuse me." Ian cleared his throat. "Sorry to interrupt, but I sort of need to talk to Jade."

"You're not interrupting," I said. "We're done here."

Kat stood. "I have to get home anyway. I just needed to be sure Jade was okay. Thanks for letting me know, Ian." She gave him a quick hug and left without saying another word.

I slumped and waved for Ian to sit. "Sorry about that. We're having…issues."

"It'll blow over soon enough. You know how Kat is. She's protective." Ian set a paper cup in front of me. "Pyper thought a chai might perk you up."

"She's protecting the wrong person." Closing my eyes, I took a long swig of the chai and sighed. Yep, I'd needed that. "Thanks."

Ian took notes while I gave him a detailed account of the night before and the vision I'd just had in the club, minus the crazy emotional turmoil.

"Excellent." He grinned.

"I'm glad you think so," I said dryly. "I'd just like it to stop."

"I've got a plan for that. After Kane called I left a message for my aunt, who has some tricks for us to ward off your ghost. I should hear back from her later today."

Kane had called Ian? Did they know each other? Weird. "Okay, when can we get that done?"

"As soon as possible, but I need to take readings from inside the club first." He stood up. "Ready?"

I nodded and followed him into the café. We found Pyper and Kane sitting with their heads together at a table in the corner.

"We're back." Ian waved.

Pyper straightened and smiled at him. "Oh, good. We were just talking about you. Have a seat." She patted the chair next to her.

He gave her his sexy half-smile and squeezed in beside her.

Kane was staring at me, and suddenly my head swam. I grabbed the edge of the table and took cleansing breaths to center myself. His hand rested on the small of my back as he leaned in and whispered, "Maybe you should go up to Pyper's and lie back down."

"Probably." But I made no move to leave. I wanted to know what we were going to do about the ghost. "Okay, Ian, what's the plan?"

"Kane's going to let us take some measurements down here, so I'll get started with that shortly. I've got a lot to do in an hour."

"An hour? But you stayed half the night in my apartment."

Kane stiffened beside me. I looked at him, bewildered.

"Kane said he'd open the club a little late, but he has an event scheduled. Since we can't measure activity with other people around, I'll take what I can get. Though I would like to log some data with you and Pyper in there to see if either of you sets anything off."

"Just me and Pyper?" I asked.

"Yes. It seems the two of you have some kind of connection with whatever may be lurking here. I'll take some basic measurements and have each of you come in for a reading. After I record the data I can compare the results and see if we have any similarities or anomalies," Ian explained.

"No." Kane said.

"No?" I asked before anyone else could respond. "What do you mean, no?"

Kane turned serious eyes on me. "I mean, I don't want you and Pyper involved anymore. You went into some sort of trance today in there, and Pyper could have been seriously hurt last night. I will not allow that to happen again."

The blood rushed to my head. Combined with my fight with Kat and feeling like I had no control over what was happening,

I snapped. "Who are you to tell me what you will and will not allow to happen?"

"Your boss."

I huffed. "Right. *Boss*. I had no idea taking orders from you on my personal time was in the job description. Besides, you may be the owner of the club, but technically I work for Pyper, remember? I only filled in tending bar as a favor to her. Why in the hell else do you think I would *work* at a strip club?"

"For the money," he said calmly. "Like all the other girls."

"You son of a bitch." I glowered at him, pissed off, mostly because he was right. I did need the money, but he didn't have to know that. "You know damn well I only filled in as a favor to Pyper."

He opened his mouth to say something, but Pyper cut him off. "That's true."

Kane turned to her. "Which part, the favor part or the son-of-a-bitch part?"

"Both," she said lightly. She turned her attention to Ian. "Of course, we'll both help." She waved her arm toward me.

I smiled at Kane's incredulous expression.

"Oh, stop being a bully," Pyper continued. "We're both big girls. If we want to help Ian figure out what's going on, we will."

Kane stared at her until she raised an eyebrow. Then he studied me. I resisted the urge to stick out my tongue. *Real mature*, I told myself. Finally, he asked Ian, "Is there something you do to keep people safe in these situations?"

Ian nodded. "Yes. So far we haven't had any mishaps…though this situation seems a bit more volatile than most we've been involved with."

"Really?" I asked. "How so?"

"Well," Ian paused, rubbing his chin. "Most of our clients come to us because they see images, like a vision, or they get a sixth sense something is there. Rarely do we come across cases where the spirits are interacting on as personal a level, as they seem to be doing in this case."

Kane stayed silent but continued to glare at all of us.

Ian glanced at him, shifting uncomfortably. "But don't worry, there are things we can do to discourage interaction. As soon as I hear back from my aunt we'll set up wards to keep the ghost inactive."

"Sounds great." Pyper handed him a card. "My cell is on there. Give us a ring when you're ready. Come on, Jade, let's get some takeout and head to my apartment."

Without glancing back, I fell into step behind Pyper.

Once back at Pyper's I found my phone and grimaced at the multitude of calls from Kat and Gwen. I should have remembered to call my aunt. Chances are, she'd felt the void when I'd been knocked out and most certainly would have felt my energy shift while I'd been in the club that afternoon. I dialed, and spent a full twenty minutes assuring her I was fine, and promised to check in more often.

"It's good to have someone to worry about you." Pyper handed me a mug of chai.

I nodded. "Thanks." Emotionally exhausted, I leaned back and closed my eyes.

Promptly at nine o'clock, Pyper's cell phone rang. She answered and a moment later tucked her feet under her. "Ian wants just you for now. Then we'll switch."

"Here goes nothing." I got to my feet, waved and took off down the two flights of stairs. My heart pounded. I wanted nothing else but to go back up to Pyper's apartment and just hang with her.

Ian waited for me at the back door of Wicked. We wasted no time saying our protection spell and repeating the procedure we'd followed the week before in my apartment.

For the last hour I'd been having an internal debate, trying to decide if I wanted to open myself up and use my gift this time. On one hand it would give me insight, but on the other I might pass out again. And I was really tired of being treated like an invalid.

As Ian followed me around the room, making appreciative noises at whatever results he received, I couldn't stop my curiosity. I had to know. Letting my guards down, I took in the lingering emotions. They were stale, and I was reminded of the smell of warm beer left out overnight after a party. Dingy lust, mixed with tired anticipation, swarmed in my head then suddenly was chased away by disgust and hatred.

I froze and scanned the room.

"Did you see something?" Ian's voice and energy lit with excitement.

I shook my head, still trying to hone in on the direction of the intrusion. There wasn't a clear path, just a whirlwind of toxic emotions.

"Say something," Ian whispered.

"Why are you here?" I asked in a clear voice. The disgust gripped my senses until all I could see was a red haze. I gasped as I fought it. "Let go! You do not have permission to invade my aura." The red cleared, and the toxic waste gripping me vanished. A pure white energy, something close to joy, filled my being. "Thank you."

"Who are you thanking?" Ian asked, stepping up next to me.

"I don't know. The goddess, maybe. Did you get what you needed?"

"More than enough. I can't wait to analyze this." Ian bounced like a little boy on a sugar high. He steadied himself and examined me. "What just happened there?"

I shrugged. I didn't want to share my ability with Ian. Unfortunately I was too tired to come up with a great explanation. "Can we talk about it later, after you do your analysis?"

His face fell, but he recovered quickly. "Sure. It's probably better to talk about it after the scientific stuff is laid out anyway."

I turned to go. "I'll send Pyper down when I get back upstairs."

"I guess we'll have to reschedule our date?" Ian said with a question.

Oops. I'd forgotten all about it. "Sure." I smiled. "I'm also still waiting to hear what you found out during the first investigation."

"Oh, right! I have a bunch of charts and stuff for you, but basically it boils down to some spiked EMF readings, indicating there was something there, but nothing definitive. I think we can safely say something is causing havoc. We just don't have solid proof. Yet."

I pursed my lips. "All right, but you know I don't care about proof. I just want it to leave us alone."

Ian's smile soured. "Of course. I'm working on it."

"I know." I grabbed his hand and squeezed. "Thanks. I really do appreciate everything."

He pulled me toward him and kissed my cheek. "You're welcome. Any time. I'll call you about dinner."

I nodded and, trying not to read too much into his kiss, went to get Pyper. Halfway up the stairs, I spotted her coming toward me.

"Ian called already," she said.

"Okay. Is the door open? I need to get my stuff."

"Yeah, Kane's up there." She winked. "Go easy on him. He isn't used to anyone but me putting him in his place."

I laughed.

"See ya." She squeezed past me and disappeared at the bottom of the stairwell.

A moment later I let myself into her apartment. "Kane?"

"In here." His voiced carried from his room.

I stopped in the doorway, watching him make the bed. Now that my irritation had worn off, I felt bad I'd snapped at him. Even though he'd kind of deserved it. I really didn't like to be told what to do. Still, he'd only been being protective. "Sorry I lost it on you earlier. It's been a rough few days."

He turned, eyeing me. "It's all right. I admire women with spunk."

"I can see that."

His lips quirked. "Oh? Who have you noticed me admiring?"

"Just Pyper. You two are obviously close, and she has more spunk than anyone I've ever met."

"I don't know. Charlie might give her a run for her money. That girl can run a bar, keep the dancers in check and throw trouble-making losers out on their asses. Between the two of them I don't know why they need me."

For the eye candy. I hid a smile. "If Pyper is the club manager and Charlie runs the bar and helps her out, what exactly do you do?"

"I'm supposed to be taking over for Pyper so she can devote her full attention to the café, but my other work keeps me too busy. I should just promote Charlie and leave it all in her capable hands." He sat down on the bed and kicked off his shoes.

I leaned against the doorframe, enjoying talking with him. "Your other job?"

"Yeah, I'm a financial advisor. Independent contractor, so I set my own hours."

"That's interesting. I didn't know that." Well, well, well. Mr. Strip Club Owner had a respectable job. Not that it mattered. Hadn't I already decided I didn't care what he did for a living while defending him to Kat? Or had I? I still couldn't see myself dating someone who worked in the sex trade.

Fantasizing about? Appreciating? Drooling over? Yes. But not dating.

The thought brought me back to reality, and I grabbed my bag off the dresser. "I should go. Thanks again for looking after me."

His eyes met mine. "Any time, Jade. Any time."

Chapter 7

I scowled at the line snaking its way out the front door of The Grind. What the hell? Usually the place was empty at eight o'clock on a Sunday morning. Since I wasn't scheduled to work and craved a chai, I dragged my feet to the back of the line and waited.

Five minutes later the line had barely moved. I craned my neck to see what was going on inside. A mass of bodies blocked my view. I started to move past the crowd when a petite blonde grabbed my arm. "Hey, what do you think you're doing?"

Her irritation did nothing to help my already grumpy mood. I stared pointedly at her hand. "Let go."

"I'm not going to let you cut in line. We were here first."

A slightly darker blonde clone stood next to her, nodding in agreement.

"You have about two seconds to let go before I make you do it."

At that moment someone else grabbed my opposite shoulder. I whirled, ripping my arm out of the blonde chick's grip, and came face to face with Kane.

"Everything all right?" he asked.

The blonde started babbling about line jumping while my irritation rose to startling levels. How dare he interfere? Through my angry haze I didn't hear what Kane said, but the blonde backed off and reclaimed her place in line.

"Let go," I said.

He released his grip. "Sorry, I just meant to guide you away from the crazy."

"I can take care of myself," I snapped.

The confusion in his eyes made me instantly regret my tone. "Sorry."

Damn, why did I have to be so cranky? The sex dreams had to stop. Every morning I woke frustrated, and hanging out with Kane didn't help. I was pretty sure he was the reason I was having them in the first place.

"Rough morning?" he asked.

"Something like that."

"A chai might help."

I stared, impressed he remembered my drink of choice. He didn't miss anything. "I can't—out of time to wait any longer. I have to get to the glass studio. I have a class starting today."

"Don't worry. I'll have it done before you know it." He guided me into the café, ignoring my protests.

"Thank God," Pyper said when she spotted us. "We've had one tour group after another this morning. Jade, I thought you had class this morning."

"She does," Kane said as he joined her behind the counter. "She needs a chai before she goes."

Pyper immediately started fixing my drink.

I protested, but neither of them paid any attention and wouldn't let me pay. "Thanks. You didn't have to do that."

Pyper smiled. "There have to be some perks to this thankless job."

As I left I sent the blonde clones a sickly sweet smile and toasted them with my cup. It was a petty thing to do, but for some reason I couldn't shake my mood, even after Pyper and Kane had been so kind. I quickened my step, hoping to walk off some tension. Otherwise, teaching would be a disaster.

I cleared my mind and imagined holding a glass rod in my hands. Melting glass was my passion. The first time I'd lit a torch and introduced the glass into the flame, everything else in my life ceased to exist. I focused on that feeling, letting everything else go. My shoulders relaxed as the tension eased.

For years, making beads had been my sanctuary. I didn't know if it was the concentration required when working with molten glass or the mesmerizing flame, but when focused on a piece, I didn't feel anyone's emotions. No one's but mine. It was a gift I cherished.

I arrived a half hour early and went to work prepping torch stations. The eight-week beginner's course was designed to teach students how to set up a studio, understand the properties of working with glass and master the art of round beads. How advanced we got in technique all depended on how fast the class progressed.

At eight-forty the bell indicating a visitor rang. Pulling the door open, I said, "You're a little bit early, but…"

The older woman from The Herbal Connection stood in front of me, casually dressed in jeans and a long-sleeved cotton shirt. If it hadn't been for her light energy invading my senses, I wouldn't have recognized her.

"I'm sorry, dear. I hope I'm not an imposition." She wore a pleasant smile.

"Oh no! I'm sorry. Come in. I was just surprised. It's Bea, right?"

She nodded, peering thoughtfully at me like she had the first time we'd met. "I was hoping I'd run into you again."

I wasn't. Had she known I was the teacher here? I bit back the frown threatening my lips and smiled. "Would you like some coffee while you wait?" I gestured toward the snack counter. "I only have decaf. I stopped serving the caffeinated kind after students got too jittery. Shaking hands and hot glass are never a good mix."

Her arm brushed mine as she moved toward the coffee carafe. She paused. "No need to be nervous. I don't bite."

Had she read me, or was my mental state just that obvious? I busied myself, arranging work stations until the bell rang again. I practically ran to let the other students in.

The first hour of the class I spent lecturing on proper safety procedures involving the torches, propane lines and eyewear. After answering all their questions on setting up a home studio, we got started. The group took to the techniques faster than any of my other classes. By the third hour I found myself relaxed and thoroughly enjoying myself. Bea turned out to be the star of the class, mastering the lessons first.

"Done!" she exclaimed, proudly holding up her bead.

I carefully took the cool end of the metal mandrel she'd wound her bead on and admired it. "Wow, you did an excellent job. Perfectly round, with even dots spiraling around it. Okay, someone open the kiln so we can get this beauty in there."

A young woman, just barely eighteen, jumped up and held the metal door open for me. I slid the mandrel in, beaming at Bea. "Okay, make another one. Then you'll have a pair."

Bea settled back into her chair, intent on her task. I scanned the rest of the class and found they too were almost finished and doing quite well. I wondered if Bea's energy had anything to do with it. Pure white essence mixed with a calmness and joy radiated from her, circling everyone in the room, including myself. It's typical for people's moods to affect each other, both good and bad. I'm in a unique position to witness it firsthand. Despite my impulse to stay away from Bea, I found myself undeniably drawn to her.

"Bea! Look, I did it!" Sandy, the eighteen-year-old, exclaimed. She held her mandrel up. "It's not as nice as yours, but at least it's round."

"It's beautiful, Sandy," Bea said from the station next to her. She rolled her chair back and held the kiln door open. "Put it in next to mine, and then get another one made. Next week, Jade will show us how to make earrings."

Sandy grinned and did as instructed.

I nodded an acknowledgement at Bea, thankful for her help, as I instructed another student on adding molten glass to her bead.

Before long I stood in front of the work stations, calling the class to order. "Excellent first day!" Pride radiated off them. "Next week when you come in, I'll have the very first beads you ever made. Don't worry about how they look." Though I already knew they were much better than any of my other students. "Whatever they look like, we're going to turn them into a piece of jewelry just for you. Think about how cool it will be to tell anyone who asks where you got that fantastic jewelry—you can say, 'I made them, even the beads.'"

A cheer went up, and the class dispersed.

"Thanks for your help," I said to Bea.

"Me? I didn't do anything." Her smile gave her away.

"Right. Okay, but thanks all the same."

"You're welcome. Since you seem to think I did you a favor, I'm wondering if you can do something for me in return?"

I waited.

"Come have tea with me sometime after class when you're free. There's something I'd like to show you." Her face gave off nothing, and suddenly her energy vanished.

"Mysterious." I gazed at her. Very unusual. Bea hid her emotions from me as if by will, but all day I noticed her energy putting the students at ease. It could be a dangerous combination if she really did have control over what she was doing, and I was certain she did. However, I hadn't felt anything but pure white light from her, a sign of goodness. I had to admit, I was intrigued. So what if she was a practicing witch? It wasn't as if she had asked me to join a coven. And if she did, I'd walk away.

Besides, she seemed too pure to be a witch. I didn't have a clue what she was. "All right."

Her white light brightened with my agreement. "Wonderful! I can't wait." She waved goodbye as she headed toward the door.

I sat down, exhausted and contemplated heading home to take a nap. The idea sent my heart racing. Ian hadn't shown up with the protection wards yet, and I really didn't want to face the possibility of more ghost sightings. I hadn't seen or felt anything the night before, but I'd slept like the dead (if the dead dreamed of hot guys, that is). A whole room of ghosts could have been loitering and I wouldn't have noticed.

Sliding my protective glasses on, I picked up a flint striker and lit my torch. The familiar orange flame calmed my pulse as I picked up a rod of glass and introduced it to the heat. My attention focused as the glass formed a soft, molten ball. Soon all other thoughts left my head as I pulled thin strands of glass to use later as decoration. With my work station full of prep, I grabbed a steel mandrel and started creating a complicated focal bead.

Hours later, after packing my kiln full of beads, I organized my work station and cleaned up glass scraps until the work surface shined. A true testament to how much I didn't want to go home. Organization was not my middle name. With a sigh, I turned out the lights and headed home.

Walking past the line formed in front of Wicked, I waved to one of the dancers standing out front and entered the side door. With nervous energy making me nauseous, I forced myself up the three flights of stairs. *Please let the ghost be taking the night off.*

As I slid my key into the lock, a note taped to the door caught my attention.

Jade, if you need to, for any reason, come on down to Pyper's apartment. I'll be there. Kane.

A silly grin broke out on my face. For any reason? I'd keep that in mind. Feeling a weight lifted, I entered my apartment and flipped the lights on. I peered around the room. Everything *looked* calm. Still hesitant, I stepped inside, let my guard down and tapped into the emotional energy. Nothing unusual. To be sure, I circled my apartment three times. Faint waves of familiar comfort washed over me, and I knew nothing lingered except traces of my own essence. I sighed in relief and got ready for bed.

Not long after I pulled the covers back and snuggled in, the dreaming started.

My eyes flickered at a movement and I sat up, startled. Across the room a man leaned against the window frame, unbuttoning his shirt as his pale blue eyes searched mine.

Automatically I covered my bare chest, feeling exposed and aroused at the same time. His familiar energy engulfed me, and my breath caught. Finally, I could put a face to my dream lover.

A soft chuckle escaped his lips as he ran a hand through his tousled, sandy brown hair and moved toward me. He reached out, soothing the side of my face.

Tingling with the caress, I clasped my hand over his and leaned back.

"Join me," I urged.

Watching as he stepped out of his jeans, I inhaled sharply at the sight of his well-defined thighs. His thumbs reached the elastic of his boxers, slowly sliding them over the concave of his hips. My eyes fixated on his silhouette as he stood there completely exposed, adoration streaming off him.

His obvious love filled me with a heartbreaking tenderness as his eyes roamed slowly down my body and back up again. The action reminded me of someone carefully memorizing every detail. With a slow, seductive smile, he lowered himself and caressed my hair, fanning it out behind me on the pillow. I reveled in the silky smooth sensation, losing myself. When his hand finally stopped he leaned in close, his warm mouth hovering over my own. Too impatient to wait longer, my hand shot out, pulling his head down the last few inches and tasted the sweet warmth beneath his lips.

A small sigh turned into a gasp as he jerked back, his surprise and anger filling my senses. Intense jealousy blocked his emotions, startling me. My senses followed the stream, and I found Kane, his fists raised, standing just behind my lover. Realization dawned. Kane had pulled the man off me.

With my heart pounding, my eyes flew open. Moonlight spilled through the darkness of my empty apartment.

The next day, Ian arrived with dried herbs. He mounted them near my front door and balcony window then took off to do the same for the club. He'd said his aunt had put them together and invoked them to ward off evil. I hoped Auntie knew what she was doing. Not just anyone could invoke a charm.

After two ghost-free days I decided the ghost repellent was working and took an afternoon off from the glass studio to work on my Etsy website. It had been too long since I'd updated it. I set my laptop up on the balcony and settled in for some serious photo editing. After a few dozen or so pictures my mind started to wander.

A small smile played at my lips as I recalled the X-rated dreams I'd continued to have. They started out exactly the same, with the sandy-haired, blue eyed man I now referred to as Mr. Sexy appearing at my bedside. His light-as-a-feather touch sent my senses into overload, simultaneously relaxing me and sending electric shock waves through my veins. But each time as Mr. Sexy leaned in, intent on replacing his fingers with his lips, Kane appeared.

In that instant, Mr. Sexy evaporated and Kane replaced him. His roving hands and eager lips set off my already primed body with a passion so fierce and memorable, all of my past real-life experiences paled in comparison. Though, to be honest, I didn't have a lot to compare it to. Dan happened to be one of only two people who had actual carnal knowledge of my body.

Heat rose to my face as I recalled the intimate details of my dream. Who knew my subconscious could be so imaginative? And with two men. Too distracted to work, I hauled my laptop inside and went to the kitchen, searching for a bottle of wine. I knew I'd brought a few bottles with me from Kat's house. I'd emptied one, but where had I put the other? Ah, yes, in the suitcase I hadn't yet emptied. Leaving it close to the closet was good enough, right?

Inside, I found an unopened cream envelope. I picked it up, reached for the wine bottle sitting in the middle of the bag and headed back to my kitchen.

After uncorking the bottle, I poured a glass and sat on my couch, fingering the neat scrawl of my name in Kat's handwriting. I took a sip of the rich cabernet and pulled the card out. Two women huddled close on the front, with a single word at the top. *Girlfriends.*

A gift-card-sized envelope fell out as I opened it. Kat's handwritten note read:

> *Jade, I know things have been difficult with the "situation," but I want you to know you're my best friend, and no man will ever change that. I love you, Kat.*
> *P.S. Put the label on your bathroom door. Every girl needs privacy.*

Searching the envelope, I found the black and white label. *No Ghosts Allowed.*

I laughed, remembering our ghost speculation the night before I'd moved out. Kane had said it was haunted, but none of us had taken him seriously.

The thought wiped the grin from my face. I ripped the gift card open and found a generous gift certificate to a local home furnishing store. Tears sprang to my eyes. I'd let my feelings about Dan get in the way of our friendship. I hadn't heard from or spoken to her since we'd argued that day in the cafe. While I wasn't mad anymore, I was disappointed. In her quest to remain Switzerland between me and Dan, she'd all but shut me out.

I reread her card, letting the words sink in and then grabbed the phone. Her voicemail picked up on the third ring.

"Kat, I just found your card and am calling to say thank you. I'm sorry about our fight. It's not fair to put you in the middle of me and Dan's B.S. Call me so we can make plans to spend this ASAP. I love you, too." Setting the phone down, I wiped the fresh tears from my eyes and headed back for my wine. On the way I picked up the No Ghosts Allowed label. Snickering, I placed it in the middle of my bathroom door.

"Do you see that, ghost? You are not allowed in the bathroom. Some things are private." I retreated back to the couch, and an image near the window made me spin. I gasped. A vague, shadowy, outline grew stronger until a man, a man I recognized stood near my window. Mr. Sexy.

Oh. My. God. My dreams were haunted by a ghost. I stood paralyzed, transfixed, waiting. Our eyes met and Mr. Sexy's lips quirked up. Then he dissipated.

I ran to the phone and dialed, still staring at the place he'd vanished from.

"He's back," I said into the receiver.

"The ghost?" Ian's voice climbed an octave higher.

"Yes. I just saw him." Draining my glass, I wondered what I should say. I'd been having dream-sex with my ghost? I reached for the wine bottle.

"What did he do?"

"Nothing. He just appeared, then left."

"Are you okay?"

"Yeah. I think so. Just a little freaked out." I sat down, afraid I might fall.

"Understandable, but he sounds harmless enough. That kind of apparition is pretty tame. What happened right before he appeared?"

"Uh, I spoke to him. Told him to stay out of the bathroom. You know, privacy."

Ian chuckled. "That's what you get for talking to him. If I were a ghost, I'd follow you in there too."

"Perv." I cleared my throat. "You really think there isn't anything to worry about?"

"Probably not. He likely appeared because you spoke to him. As long as nothing sinister is happening and you don't feel threatened, it should be fine."

Threatened? Not exactly. More like invaded. "Okay, but will you be around later if I need you?"

"Sure. Do you want me to come over?"

I mulled it over for a minute. I really did want to relax and work on my online store, but at the same time I knew any hope of concentrating was shot now. "Do you want to come watch a movie?"

"Sure. Give me about forty-five minutes, and I'll be over. Want me to bring a DVD?"

"Yes, surprise me." I didn't really care what we watched. I just didn't want to be alone. "And if you have any more ghost repellent, bring it too."

"Will do."

I sat rigid on the couch. A ghost invaded my dreams. How was that possible? I'd seen an outline of him before in my apartment, but not a detailed one. It couldn't just be my subconscious. I'd never seen him before.

Shaking my head, I recalled the very real emotions of Mr. Sexy. Every day I let my guard down in the apartment and didn't feel his intense emotions while awake. Only while dreaming. I shivered. If he did visit me in my dreams, did he stick around to witness my intense and very private scenes with Kane? I didn't think so. In those scenes the only emotions I remembered were Kane's, which felt just as real.

Lowering my head to my hands, I rubbed my temples. Kane certainly wasn't a ghost, and I dreamt of his emotions too. Dreaming while reading emotions was something I'd never experienced before. I'd just thought it was a new dimension in my dream world. Now I didn't know what to think. I guessed it was possible Mr. Sexy visited me in my dreams, and then my subconscious took over, pushing him out and replacing him with Kane—the one I actually wanted to be with.

Should I tell Ian about the dream visits? What would I say— that I spent my nights getting intimate with my ghost until Kane showed up and things got even more imaginative? God, no! I could barely even think about my dreams without heat burning my cheeks. They were like nothing I'd ever experienced before and way more intimate than anything I'd ever shared with anyone, including my two ex-boyfriends.

Maybe I could just tell him Mr. Sexy appeared in my dreams and leave Kane out of it altogether. I sighed heavily. I didn't want to talk about any of it, but if I wanted help, I'd have to.

The alarm buzzed at four-thirty a.m., and the springs creaked as Ian rolled over. I slid out of bed, eyeing the coffee maker. I bypassed it and tiptoed my way to the bathroom. I could get coffee at the café, but I just didn't function well until I'd had my first cup. After showering, I spent ten minutes applying a bit of makeup and arranging my wet hair into a bun. When I emerged I found Ian upright, his hair tousled, sipping fresh coffee.

"Oh, you are a god!" I squealed and pivoted to pour my own cup of glorious java.

"Not the response I anticipated, but I'll take it." He smiled.

I grinned and took in his very cute bed-head look. "Sorry I had to wake you so early."

"No problem. I need to head home and get ready for work anyway." He fished around, searching for his shoes.

"They're over here." I pointed to the end of the bed. "Did you sleep okay?"

He slipped his feet in the unlaced Vans. "Yep, like a baby. You?"

"Best night's sleep since I moved in." I hadn't dreamt of Mr. Sexy or Kane, to my immense relief. I'd die of embarrassment if Ian heard me call out in my sleep for another man—if I did, in fact, call out in my sleep. Judging by the intensity the dreams held, I wouldn't be surprised.

"Good, glad I could help." He picked up the movie we never got around to watching. We'd been too busy discussing my ghost and—once I'd gotten over my intense embarrassment—the dreams. He'd been amused and highly curious about the new turn of events. He'd heard of dream hauntings before, but not any of the sexual nature. He promised to check into it further.

"Maybe next time."

"Yeah, next time," he agreed.

"If you're ready I'll walk you down. Maybe grab you a muffin from the café?"

"Sure." He followed me to the door.

I stopped just before opening it. "Thanks, Ian. I had a good time."

"My pleasure."

I leaned in and kissed his cheek. He winked and followed me down the stairs.

"Hey, I forgot to ask, did you finish with the results of the reading you did the other night?"

"I was going to finish up last night, but I got distracted." He grinned. "Tell you what, I can get them done today and bring you a copy tomorrow. Maybe we can finally get that dinner date in?"

"That'd be great." I smiled up at him.

"But in the meantime, you can do some research. Look for past residents of the building. See if you can find information about anyone who died here. Especially if it wasn't a natural death. A suicide, accident, murder…that kind of thing."

"Why?" I stopped on the bottom stair.

"If we find out who it is, we might have a better idea what he's doing here and how best to get rid of him."

Suddenly, I felt unsettled at the thought of my ghost's possible gruesome death. I didn't notice Kane until his irritation filled my energy field. I stiffened and turned around. "Kane?" I stood to one side, watching him.

"Jade, Ian." His eyes narrowed at Ian, taking in his appearance. Jealousy swarmed around us, and I had to hide a smile.

"You're up early," I said.

"Up late." Kane locked the door to the club. Turning to Ian, he said, "You seem to have had a late night as well."

Ian shrugged.

Kane's face stayed neutral, but his emotions spiraled out of control. Anger, jealousy and maybe even a little pain swirled together.

The pain made me pause. I put a hand on his arm. "Everything okay?" The touch sent a shiver through my entire body, and I felt him flinch slightly.

"Fine, just tired. I'm headed up to bed. See you later." He turned without another word and took the other set of stairs leading to Pyper's apartment.

"What was that about?" Ian asked.

"No idea. Come on, let's get you that muffin."

We arrived at the café just as Pyper turned the lights on.

"Good morning," I sang.

"Morning to you, too. New employee?" She gestured to Ian.

Ian laughed. "No, not today, anyway. I was promised a muffin."

"In that case, take your pick." She waved him to the trays on a rolling rack.

Ian grabbed a double chocolate and pulled out some dollar bills.

"No, no. I got it covered. Thanks again, Ian. I really appreciate everything." I leaned in giving him a big hug. "I'll call you later."

He bent down and kissed my cheek. "You better." He waved to Pyper and left out the back door.

"Oh my God!" Pyper exclaimed.

"What?"

"The schoolboy had a sleepover? Kane is going to freak." Mischief danced in her eyes.

"What? Why will Kane freak?" I asked, clocking in.

"Because, silly, he's the one who wants the sleepovers."

"Since when?" It's not like he'd asked me out or anything.

"Since the day he set eyes on you. How was it?" Curiosity and anticipation dominated Pyper's energy.

"How was what?"

"'How was what?'" she parroted. "Your night with Ian. Come on, dish!"

"We didn't have a sleepover in that way. My ghost paid me a brief visit yesterday, and I called Ian about it. He ended up coming over and stayed so I didn't freak out. We just talked and slept. It was all rather boring actually."

Her face fell. "The ghost?"

"Don't worry, nothing happened. Just a minor apparition."

"That *is* rather boring. At least Kane won't have to worry."

I laughed. "Well...he did see Ian leaving with me this morning."

Pyper joined in my laughter. "Oh yeah, this is gonna get interesting."

Chapter 8

At nine o'clock I grabbed a muffin and headed to the back for a short break. Just as I took my first bite, the back door squeaked. Kane walked in, with a calm almost Zen-like energy.

"Good morning again. I thought you'd still be sleeping," I said.

He shrugged.

"You're not stoned, are you?" I asked before I could stop myself.

His expression implied I'd lost my mind. "Of course not. Let's see what you look like after three hours of sleep."

I gazed at him, taking in his dark, wavy, fresh-from-the-shower hair. He looked as if he'd just had a full night's worth of sleep. "You look great. I was referring to your mood."

Pleasure and a heavy dose of desire flowed from him as his lips turned up in a half grin. "Great, huh?"

I nodded. With full knowledge of his attraction to me, my bravado came out in full force. "Every woman's dream."

He paused, studying me. "Even yours?"

"Maybe." I met his eyes. His energy remained steady, like a cool stream.

He moved closer, stopping just in front of me. "Who else do you dream about, Jade?"

My breath caught as my pulse sped up. I was outclassed and not experienced enough for this game. But that didn't stop me. Smiling, I raised an eyebrow. "Unfair question, Kane."

"Maybe, but you're the star of my dreams these days. I'm just wondering if Ian has a role in yours, or is he a distraction?"

His mocha eyes transfixed mine. The breath left my lungs as I sat motionless, mesmerized.

"The star?" I asked when my breathing resumed. "Who are the supporting characters?"

"Unfair question."

"Then you don't need to know who else has roles in mine." I smirked.

He narrowed his eyes, and a predatory grin broke out on his face. He leaned in close to mine and whispered, "I'll find out." Before I could respond he retreated out the back door.

"Wow."

I slowed my steps as I entered the club, unsure if I wanted to see Kane or not. Okay, I wanted to see him. Who wouldn't? But after the morning's interlude I didn't know what to say. I took a deep breath and knocked.

A muffled, "Come in," answered.

I made my way inside.

"Jade, what can I do for you today?" Charlie asked from behind the desk as I flopped into a folding chair across from her.

"I was looking for Pyper." Or Kane, but my stomach got jittery just thinking his name. "Have you seen her?"

She shook her head. "No, I think she actually went to get some sleep."

"Really? I didn't think she ever slept." I fiddled with the notebook in my lap. "I'm glad to hear it. I was hoping to research some documents, but since she isn't here I guess I'll come back." I stood up, but Charlie held her hand up in a stop motion.

"Hold on. I have access to records. What do you need?"

"Would it be all right if I take a look at who might have rented my apartment in the past? Do they have those records?" I filled her in on Ian's suggestion to try to identify the ghost.

"It's like a mystery." Charlie got up and headed to the door. "Come on, the files are in the storage room."

I followed her into the hallway. She stopped outside the room where I'd gotten my used furniture and fumbled with a ring of keys.

"There are files in here as well?" I didn't remember seeing any.

Charlie nodded. "There are now. They used to live in one of Pyper's closets until you took some of that old furniture."

We walked in, turned the light on, and found a mound of bankers' file boxes stacked next to the door, barricading us from the rest of the room.

"I guess she was in a hurry," I said and coughed from the disturbed dust. "Thanks Charlie, I can take it from here."

She sat in an old thread-worn chair and grabbed the box closest to her. "I can help." Opening it up, she pulled a stack of papers out.

"You don't have other work you need to do?" I didn't want to get her into trouble.

She shrugged. "Sure, but helping you is a lot more entertaining, and I can hear the phone from here if anyone calls."

"Okay, thanks," I said, pleased to have some company.

I couldn't get around the large pile of boxes to dig out another chair, so I flopped my butt down right on the floor. Charlie smirked. I shrugged as if to say *oh well* and pulled the nearest box to me. As I searched through the piles I said, "I didn't know you worked in the office. Did you get promoted?"

"No. I just help out Pyper sometimes. She does way too much, as I'm sure you know. I don't mind, and I get along with the girls. Or most of them, anyway," she said sheepishly.

I raised my eyebrows.

"A few are exes." She chuckled, rolling her eyes. "Never date a coworker."

"Okay, I won't date you." I smiled innocently.

"Damn."

"It's your rule."

"I'm willing to break it." Charlie leaned in and leered before chuckling.

"I'll keep it in mind." I giggled. The girls around here could do worse than Charlie. Glancing at the paper in my hand, I asked, "Do you have any others that date back a little farther? These are all from this year."

Charlie shook her head. "I don't know if Kane will have those records."

"Really?" I said, surprised. "It looks like he keeps everything." I waved to the mountain of boxes in front of us.

"He does. This is all from this year alone."

"Where are the rest?"

Charlie glanced up, dusting her hands off. "These are it. Didn't you know? Kane just bought this place last year."

I stopped scanning the papers and gave her my full attention. "No. For some reason I just assumed he and Pyper have had this place for a while now. Have you been here longer than that?"

"Wow, Jade, you really don't know the scoop, do you?"

I shook my head. "Apparently not."

"Did you know Pyper's been managing this place for about five years?"

I nodded.

"Pyper is very dedicated to the girls, and last year the owner started demanding some *new* services, if you know what I mean."

I didn't know, but I could take a guess. So I nodded again, getting really curious.

"As you can imagine, Pyper didn't take kindly to that suggestion, so she basically told him to shove it. He didn't like that too much and one night, the two of them got into it. Pyper was giving him a piece of her mind. Roy, the former owner, got a little physical. Kane was here and laid the guy out flat."

"Really?" My mind flashed back to the night Kane removed Dan from the club. Enjoying the mental image, I smiled to myself.

"Oh, it's like that, is it?" Charlie gave me a rueful smile.

I giggled nervously and felt my face flush. "What happened after Kane knocked the guy out?"

"Roy had Kane banned from the premises and threatened to press charges. He went to the police and everything. Pyper was a mess, threatening Roy daily. Can't you just see her, that tiny body standing in the office doorway, telling Big Old Roy how she was going to remove his balls with her bare hands? He would stand there, six feet, two inches tall, always with a cigarette hanging out of his mouth. She shot daggers at him with her eyes, and he'd growl at her. But she never backed down. We use to joke that if Roy went missing, Pyper would be the prime suspect." Her grin widened. "We used to pray for it, actually."

"Why didn't she just leave?" I couldn't imagine staying in such a toxic environment.

She shrugged. "He was determined to turn this place into a whorehouse. Pyper was determined to protect the girls."

I stared up at her, blinked, and asked the question I was dying to know. "This place has never been more than what it seems on the surface?"

Charlie tilted her head. "It depends on what you mean by 'what it seems.'"

I shrugged. "Just a strip bar."

She smiled a wide devilish grin. "You have no idea what goes on in a regular strip bar, do you?"

The heat burned my neck. I shifted my eyes away toward the back of the storage room. "No, not exactly. But I can imagine," I said as she hooted with laughter.

"God, you are something else. How did you ever end up working here?"

Unashamed, I said, "Pyper asked me to."

She nodded thoughtfully. "Me too."

My eyes widened. "You didn't, I mean, uh, you don't work here for the benefits...?" Shit. I'd probably just offended her. Convinced my head would burst into flames from embarrassment, I stared at the file in my hand.

There was silence for a few beats. When I glanced in Charlie's direction she threw her head back and laughed until the tears streamed down her face. Gasping for breath, she said, "Christ."

I raised my head and let out the breath I'd been holding. "I'm glad you find me so humorous."

Finally pulling herself together, Charlie wiped her eyes with a tissue I handed her from my purse. Still smiling, she reached out and grabbed my hand. "I'm so glad Pyper found you." Her touch was light and friendly. "And no, I didn't take the job for the benefits," she dragged out the word "benefits" for emphasis. "But it's a nice perk." A cat-like grin took over her face as her pale green eyes sparkled.

I sent her a tentative smile and squeezed her hand before letting go. "I'm sorry. Sometimes I can be a little bit blunt."

"A little bit? That's an understatement if I ever heard one. Don't worry," she added, seeing my frown. "When you spend your whole life surrounded by women, a little directness is a great thing."

"Uh, thanks." We fell silent as we shuffled through the piles in front of us. Then I remembered. "You were telling me how Kane came to own this place?"

"That's right, you distracted me." She set the papers in her hand to one side. "But I have got to get something to drink first. You want anything?"

Nodding, I gave her my standard chai tea order and grabbed the next box as she strode out the door. I spent ten minutes going through more employee files. I knew everyone in the stack except the last one. It read: *Charlene Keller; Lead Server.*

"Huh, I wonder who that is. Charlene, Charlene." I pictured all four cocktail servers standing up against the bar. My mind locked in on Charlie leaning against the back counter, giving them instructions, and I started to laugh. Feeling slightly dense but amused, I put the file aside and spotted one more box a few feet away.

I stood, dusted off my rear and sat in Charlie's chair. Out of nowhere, agitation coursed through my veins. Where was this coming from? Gritting my teeth, I tried fruitlessly to build my defenses back up. The poison completely took over, burning a trail as it filled my soul with gut-wrenching hate. I doubled over and slid out of the chair. As I lay on the floor shaking, the venomous emotions began to fade.

Mentally bruised, I forced myself to my feet, glanced at the last remaining box, and ran. The storage door slammed behind me. I propped myself against the hallway wall and took deep calming breaths to collect myself. *Whoa.* That was creepy. I'd never come across a piece of furniture as emotionally charged as that one. It made me want to sage smudge myself. With a shudder, I headed to the café in search of some more uplifting emotional energy.

Charlie was standing at the counter talking to Pyper when I entered The Grind. Charlie handed me my chai and after a long sip, I let out a loud, "Ahh."

"Oops. I must have been longer than I thought," Charlie said.

"No, not that long. I just needed a break." I turned to Pyper. "How about you? I could help out here if you need me to."

Her smile didn't reach her dark, tired eyes. "No, you've worked enough today. I have it covered."

"Isn't Holly here?" I asked, craning my head to look in the back.

"Sure." Pyper glanced toward the tables in the front. "She's interviewing someone."

I spotted her sitting with a pretty brunette.

"College girl?"

Charlie nodded and turned her head toward them. "Fresh potential." Her term for possible lesbians.

Pyper laughed, and I rolled my eyes.

"Come on, Charlene." I tugged her arm. "You were helping me with a project, if I recall."

Pyper snickered as Charlie's eyes widened in surprise.

"You shouldn't have left me alone with the files for so long if you didn't want me to find out your real name," I said.

"Shit. Don't ever breathe a word of this." She fell into step beside me.

I laughed then nodded toward Pyper as we walked back into the club. "I thought she was sleeping."

"Me too. I told her we'd take care of the café and she should go back up, but she said she couldn't sleep, so she figured she should be useful." Charlie raised her hands, palms up. "I don't know what else to do, but she sure looks like she needs some rest. If I didn't know better I'd say she was on speed. But that isn't her style."

"If I was Pyper, I'd have to take speed to keep up with what she does. I don't know how she handles it all without having a psychotic episode."

"Me either."

"I'm done looking at those files for now," I told Charlie as I dropped into the folding chair in front of the desk.

"Did you find anything useful?" She picked up the phone.

I shook my head and waited for her to retrieve the messages. After she hung up I said, "But I still want the scoop. How exactly did Kane end up owning this place?"

"More than just idle curiosity?" She eyed me with her eyebrows raised.

I gave a noncommittal head shake.

"You could do worse."

"I don't have anything going with Kane."

"Not yet," she said.

When I didn't respond, she shrugged and told me the story. The police had shown up at Kane's door with questions. He cooperated, and the DA decided it was frivolous and not worth his time to pursue the charges. Roy filed a civil suit and then promptly told Kane he would be willing to settle out of court and let the whole thing go, as long as the price was right. Considering there were more than a handful of witnesses who saw Kane throw the first punch, a civil suit wasn't looking so good in Kane's favor. No one saw Roy threaten and hit Pyper—that happened in the office. It was after Kane saw Pyper and the bruises that he went after him. So Kane offered to settle, apparently for a very generous amount. The only stipulation on Kane's part was Roy had to sell the place to him as part of the deal.

"Had Kane been trying to buy the place prior to that?" I asked.

Charlie shook her head. "I don't think so. At the time he was still working for some financial company. He just turned all the reins over to Pyper. It's the best thing that ever happened around here. She's a great boss."

I nodded.

"But then a few months later she opened The Grind. I didn't know it at the time, but the building next door was part of the deal."

I'd been focused on the bit of information pertaining to Kane and him not being the strip club lord I had imagined. I felt as if a weight had lifted off my heart, and I smiled.

"What?" Charlie asked

"Nothing. I'm just glad things worked out."

The imprint of Kane's kisses lingered on my swollen, tender lips. I stretched, enjoying the ache of well-used muscles. What the hell? Talk about realistic. I must have acted out a majority of the dream in my sleep. My temperature spiked as a few memorable scenes reeled through my brain. Thank goodness I didn't have a roommate. At least, not a live one.

I scanned the room for any intruding ghosts. All was quiet and apparition-free.

Lying back, I ran my hands the length of my naked body, still tingling with tiny aftershocks from the wicked ways it felt like Kane had touched me. Yep. Definitely the best, most realistic dream ever.

As intense as dreaming of Kane had become, what I found more surprising was how I felt at the beginning of my dreams when I was with Mr. Sexy. I felt safe, loved even. I knew it should have been creepy, considering the ghost factor, but it wasn't. It was…comforting, until he vanished and Kane took over. Dreams of Kane were anything but comforting. Intense. Hot. Naughty.

The mental image of Kane, bare in only his skin, sent new heat to all the right places.

There was only one thing to do. Take another cold shower. The thought had me shivering, and I opted for coffee instead.

As I sipped my java and checked email, my phone rang. No one called me this early. Ever. Not even Gwen when she could somehow tell I was awake. Crap, this could only be bad news.

"Hello," I said cautiously after recognizing the number to The Grind.

"Thank God. Jade, it's Pyper. Holly just got sick, and I had to send her home. Is there any way you can come work with me through the lunch shift?"

Bad news, definitely. If I worked today that would be six days in a row at the café.

"Jade? You there?" Pyper asked.

"Yeah." I sighed. "I'll be down as soon as I can."

The morning flew by in a blur, with long lines of caffeine-deprived tourists and locals alike. Pyper and I worked straight through the morning, and when she finally told me to take a break I almost kissed her with relief.

With my calves screaming from standing in front of the espresso machine, I made a quick getaway to the back room. Unfortunately, the one office chair was piled high with files and invoices. I groaned and opted to sit on the much-less-cluttered countertop. Pyper really needed to hire a professional organizer.

I dug into my daily muffin, washed it down with an iced latte and leaned against the cupboards with my eyes closed. My back ached. I made a mental date with my tub.

The swinging door to the front of the café creaked. "Just a few more minutes, I promise," I said.

"Take as long as you need," a deep, husky voice replied.

My eyes flew open, spotting Kane moving toward me. Where had he come from? I jolted up out of my slouch, preparing to leap off the counter, but Kane blocked me, making it impossible. His eyes roamed over my body, as if taking inventory. My stomach fluttered, and I said a silent thanks I was sitting when my knees turned to jelly. Damn.

"Can I help you?" I asked in a stiff, formal voice.

"Sure, any time." He moved in close.

"Uh, I mean, do you need something? Now?"

"Yes, I do." He leaned in with his right arm holding his weight on the shelf over my head.

I tried to form the word *what*, but as his face came closer I lost all rational thought. Wanting to taste him, to feel his lips on mine, I closed the distance between us and was rewarded with the slightest brush of a kiss. Kane's warm lips lingered on mine while his free hand caressed my neck, sending a shiver down my spine. The kiss swiftly turned heated as our lips parted with urgency. He tasted faintly of mocha and cinnamon. I pressed closer, anxious for more.

My mind stopped working altogether, and I let myself get lost in the delicious intensity of his expert mouth. Unaware of how it happened, my arms and legs somehow wrapped themselves around his waist. He pressed his hips closer, pushing me up against the cupboards.

His excitement became apparent in more than the bulge pressing against my jeans. Intense need, exactly as I dreamt the night before, took over my senses. My blood boiled, and I ached to feel him, all of him. Desperate to regain control, I pulled away.

He took a step back, smiling a devilish grin. "That wasn't exactly what I meant, but thanks all the same." He held a sleeve of coffee cups in his right hand. "I stopped in for a second, and Pyper asked me to get these."

I tilted my head and spotted the inventory of extra cups. *Shit.*

Stunned by my recent actions, I sat silent as he gazed at me.

"Kane! What are you doing back there?" Pyper called from out front.

He looked toward the door and then back at me. "We'll finish this later."

My breath caught as I started to tremble. That's what I was afraid of.

"Ouch! Son of a bitch," I yelped.

"Jade, are you all right?" Casey, the studio manager, called from my door.

"Fine. Just burned my arm. Wasn't paying attention." I'd been replaying that kiss in my mind. Again.

Sighing, I tossed the glass piece I'd been working on in a bowl of water and reached for the aloe plant. I hissed as I dabbed it on.

"Careful," Casey said then went back out front.

I stared at the three mandrels in my water bucket. Resigned, I turned the kiln off. I wasn't getting anywhere. I'd planned on spending most of the afternoon in the studio working on a few orders. Plus, beadmaking usually was a great distraction. Not today, though. I just couldn't get Kane, that kiss and the dreams out of my mind.

Giving up, I decided to run errands instead and headed for the market.

An hour later I set the grocery bags on my counter. My pants started to sing, causing me to jump. While shoving perishables in the fridge, I grabbed my phone and immediately dumped a bag of oranges on the floor. "Hello?"

"Hey there, stranger," a masculine voice said as I scrambled to gather the rolling fruit.

"Ian?"

"Yep. Ready for tonight?"

Cradling the oranges in my shirt, I stood and eyed the calendar pinned to the wall. I hadn't noted any plans. "Tonight?"

"Dinner? The ghost readings report?" He prompted.

"Of course!" *Idiot!* How could I forget? Thoughts of Kane, his lips, and that hard body, had rattled my brain.

"Great." He sounded relieved. "I just called to find out if seven is okay?"

"Sure, sounds good. See you then."

Chapter 9

After a shower, reapplication of my makeup and a thorough blow dry, I smiled in satisfaction. My strawberry-blond hair had just the right amount of wave, making it appear sophisticated, instead of my usual messy-casual look. It had been a long time since I'd been out on an actual date.

I checked my watch. Still a half hour until Ian arrived. With time to kill, I settled in at my desk and went to work listing new beads in my Etsy store.

I'd gotten two new items uploaded when the knocking started. "Come in; it's open." The door creaked. "Is it seven already?"

"No. What happens at seven?"

Startled, I whipped around, knocking my elbow on the edge of my bead tray and sending all my glass creations scattering to the floor. "Damn it!" As they rolled across the hardwood I dropped to my knees, gathering as many as I could before they disappeared under the couch.

"Sorry, didn't mean to startle you." Kane crouched, his face now eye level as he helped me. A faint trace of stubble shadowed his jaw.

I fisted one hand, resisting the sudden urge to caress the roughness. "What are you doing here?" I stood and dumped the beads back in the tray.

"What's happening at seven?"

"Huh?" An image of our last encounter at The Grind made my brain short-circuit.

"You were expecting someone at seven?" He rose and handed me the last of the runaway beads.

Right. "Ian's coming with results." I walked to my fridge, searching for something to do. "Do you want something to drink?"

"Sure. Guinness?" He sat, making himself comfortable. "You weren't going to call me?"

"Why?" I passed him the beer, grabbed one for myself and took the other end of the sofa.

He glanced at my high-heeled feet then looked at the ceiling. "To meet with Ian."

I shrugged. "I didn't realize you wanted in on the meeting."

"It *is* my building."

"Okay, okay. You're here now. Stick around, and you can get the results. By the way, why are you here?"

"Just being neighborly," he said with a wry smile.

"Oh?" I wiped my sweaty hand on the old fabric of the arm rest. "Are you my neighbor this evening?"

He nodded, his smile transforming into a grin. "Looks like it."

My heart sped up as I imagined him shirtless in bed. Last night's dream flashed in my mind. I swallowed and studied my beer.

"I stay over a few nights a week, when I work late." His gaze dropped to my lips. Longing and anticipation swirled around me in a dense fog, pulling me toward him as if I'd been lassoed.

My throat went dry. "I know, you told me."

A light film of sweat broke out on my neck as he licked his lips, leaned in and whispered, "Jade."

A rapid knock on the door broke my gaze. Jumping up, I took four steps and opened the door. Ian stood leaning against the door jam, holding a pink, long-stemmed rose. He held it out. "Good evening."

"Uh, hi, Ian. Thanks." I took the rose and stepped back, revealing my house guest. Biting my lip, I waved him in. "You know Kane."

Ian nodded. "Hello."

Eyeing the rose, Kane raised one eyebrow and leaned back on the couch. "Someone let you in the building?"

A good question, since my buzzer didn't go off.

"I ran into Pyper out front," Ian said.

"Kane just stopped by," I explained as I rooted around for a vase. Coming up empty, I poured out my beer and used the bottle instead. I set the rose next to my computer and buried my nose in the blossom, inhaling its sweet aroma. "Thank you. It's beautiful."

He smiled. "You're welcome."

Kane stood, staring at me for a long moment. Then he walked to the door. "Sorry, didn't mean to intrude." He was gone before I could reply.

"What was that about?" Ian asked.

I shrugged. "No idea." Other than Kane realizing Ian and I had a date. I suppressed a sigh.

"So," Ian paused. "Anything new to report about your ghost?"

"No."

He studied me and raised his brow in question. "No new dreams?"

"More dreams—same content." I'd already told him they were of the sexual nature. He didn't need anything else. "The dreams are harmless anyway, so I guess it isn't too important." Except it was creepy to think of him invading my dreams, especially since while I was having them, I wasn't creeped out at all. The whole thing was twisted.

"They might be an important clue as to why he's here. Would it be too awkward to tell me about them?"

I frowned. How could sex dreams be interpreted in any other way than wanting sex? "Can we get to that later?" I stalled. "I'm dying to know the results you got."

"Sure." Ian's face lit up as he sat down on the floor and spread files all around him.

I laughed. "Very professional."

He grinned. "Take a look at this." He handed me a photo of my apartment.

"What am I looking at?" I peered at it, seeing nothing unusual.

"Now look at this one."

I gasped. "Oh, is that him?" The same scene reflected back at me, only this time I was in the photo with a silver outline of what looked like a person standing next to me.

"I'd say so. Here are the rest." He handed me a small stack. "Remember I told you all we got were some EMF readings here in your apartment?"

I nodded.

"I'd sent this out to be developed and forgot to pick it up. The digital didn't capture what the manual camera did, so we thought we didn't have a shadow image. But now we have the proof. Isn't that great?"

All of the photos without me in them were imageless, and all of the ones with me had a silvery outline image. "I guess." I frowned. "Does this mean he follows me around?"

"Maybe." Ian passed a chart of numbers to me. "From the photos it looks like he might, but we have no way to tell if he leaves the apartment or not. It's possible he has more energy when you're around, causing the outline." That scenario didn't make me feel any better.

He pulled out a chart. "See here?"

Two columns of numbers were lined up side by side. "Uh-huh."

"Look at how the numbers don't seem to change much."

"Okay." I had no idea where he was going with this.

"The numbers are a reading from an EMF detector. It reads the electromagnetic field. We use it to pick up paranormal activity. Do you follow?" Ian glanced up.

"I think so. These numbers are telling you there's paranormal activity?"

"Yes. That's the theory anyway. These numbers here—" he pointed again, "—are in the range of four to six. That's the area we look for. These charts are the readings from before you entered the room and after. See how they don't change a great deal?"

"So they didn't change a lot, which means he was likely here but stronger when I entered the room?"

"Exactly." Ian beamed, no doubt pleased I'd caught on.

"That's better than the alternative. I'm not crazy about being stalked by a ghost."

Ian shrugged. "It's possible he does follow you sometimes. These are just the readings we got that day."

"Not what I wanted to hear. I'm going to assume he stays here in the building." It's what I wanted to believe and let's face it; the scientific readings hardly seemed, well, scientific. "Did you get any interesting readings in the club?"

Ian started bouncing on his heels, going from excited to downright giddy. "Oh, yeah. Look at these."

More photos. Again, pictures of the empty club, then pictures of my silver shadow and me.

"Now look at these." He handed me a third stack.

"Wow, that's weird. Pyper has a shadow too, but hers is a darker gray. Is that a different ghost?"

Ian shrugged. "I'd bet it is the same one."

"Even though the outline is a different color?"

"Yes, ghosts take their energy from those around them, so he would appear different depending on whose energy he's feeding from."

I nodded. Being in the position to feel and sometimes see people's energy, I perfectly understood his explanation. "Okay, but why would he be following both of us around?"

Ian shook his head. "Good question. Maybe he thinks she's sexy."

A sudden bolt of jealousy struck me. I'd come to think of him as my ghost. He invaded my dreams with love and devotion radiating off him each night. So why was he following Pyper around? I knew it sounded crazy, but his emotions were doing a number on me.

Snap out of it, Jade. This is a ghost you're thinking about. Just a dream lover. A very sexy dream lover.

Kane's face flashed in my mind, and suddenly I felt like an idiot. Here I was sitting with Ian, my date, and I was jealous of Pyper over a ghost and thinking of Kane.

I put the whole thing out of my mind. "All right, that's enough ghost talk for now. You ready for dinner?" I asked.

Ian checked his watch. "Yep, our reservation is in twenty minutes." He got up and held a hand out to me.

"You brought me here because it's haunted?" I sipped from my wine glass and looked around Muriel's, the famous restaurant Ian had brought me to.

"You haven't heard the story?"

"No." I glanced over my shoulder as if I expected a ghost to appear.

Ian laughed. "A lot of the restaurants are said to be haunted. It's unavoidable with the sordid history of New Orleans."

"I bet," I said. "Have you done scientific measurements on any of them?"

"I'd love to, but no, I haven't had the opportunity." He lowered his voice to a whisper and leaned in. "When I choose a restaurant I always pick one rumored to be haunted, hoping for a sighting."

A shiver ran up my spine. That was the last thing I wanted after my recent experiences. "Do you ever see any?"

"Nothing definitive, but there have been a few occasions that made me wonder." Ian's eyes got big and sparkled with excitement.

"Ever see anything here?" I bit my lip and glanced around again.

"No, but I love coming to check it out. It's said the guy who built this house lost it in a poker game. Before he turned his home over, he hung himself here. People say he still haunts the place. I'd love to get a glimpse of him." Ian craned his neck, studying the exposed inner courtyard.

"See anything?"

"No. Not yet." He twisted around to check behind him toward the front lobby.

I set my almost-empty wine glass down and signaled to the waiter for more. Great. Just what I needed. A ghost-hunting expedition. A small sigh escaped my lips.

When the waiter came back, I had him leave the bottle.

Ian spent the entire meal giving me a verbal ghost tour of the supposed hauntings in the French Quarter. By the time dessert was offered I'd had enough. It was a rare evening when I wasn't tempted by cheesecake. But I didn't want to continue watching Ian crane his neck, waiting for something unusual to happen. People were starting to stare.

"Ready to go then?" he asked, signing the check.

"Sure. Where to?"

"Frenchmen Street. Let's walk." He held out his hand.

I took it and stifled a groan. I didn't mind walking, really I didn't. In fact I liked it, except when I have my sexy date heels on.

After seven blocks a blister had formed on my left toe, causing a mild limp.

"Are you all right?" Ian asked.

"Oh sure, just not the best walking shoes." I grimaced. It was my own fault. Nobody drives in the French Quarter. I made a mental note to buy more sensible shoes. *Yeah, right.*

Embarrassment washed over him. "I'm sorry, Jade. I didn't think about that. We'll take a cab back."

"Sounds good."

"You're gonna love this place," Ian said when we finally made it to the front of a club. "It's one of the best places to hear music and maybe catch a ghost sighting."

Great, just what I wanted to hear. "More ghosts?"

"You never know." Ian took my arm and led me to a table in a corner. After we placed our drink order, he scooted his chair closer and leaned in. "This is nice, right?"

"Sure." The music was slow and soulful, successful in bringing people's emotions to the surface. Mostly they were pleasure-based, but sadness also worked its way in. I put my guards up, wary of being worn down.

Ian slid his arm around my shoulder, letting his fingertips caress my arm. I closed my eyes, enjoying the music and the sensation. This date might still be salvageable.

"Did I tell you how beautiful you look tonight?"

Opening my eyes, I smiled. "Thank you. You're looking pretty good yourself." Ian had dressed in all black. Black pants, black button-down shirt and black Converse shoes. It worked for him, highlighting his blond hair and clear blues eyes, now staring intently into mine.

"You are the first woman I've taken out who really gets me," Ian whispered in my ear.

"Oh?"

"Uh-huh. Most of them don't understand the ghost thing."

"As in, don't believe? Maybe they just don't have any experiences with them?"

Ian tilted his head. "Probably. But it's more than that. You accept me for me. That's rare, you know?"

I did know. More than I could explain. I nodded.

"Most women I meet can't accept my passion is ghost hunting and not climbing the career ladder. It must be because you're an artist. Your living isn't exactly conventional either."

I laughed. "No, it isn't. But that can't be rare in New Orleans?"

Ian moved a lock of hair from my eyes. "No. Not really. There's something a little bit different about you. I haven't put my finger on it yet. But I like it. I like it a lot."

Heat rose to my cheeks, making me grateful for the dim lighting.

Ian brushed his fingers along my jawline then tilted my face toward his. As he leaned in his eyes flickered slightly toward the stage. "Oh my God!"

I followed his gaze. "What?"

"Do you see them?"

"Who?"

"The two people on the left? The woman and the man? There's a faint outline of them."

I squinted, searching the stage. I didn't see anything. "I only see smoke."

Ian frowned as he glanced at me.

"Sorry," I said. Though I wasn't. While I understood Ian's excitement, ghosts were not on my list of things I wanted to experience. Enough was enough.

"It's all right. Maybe they'll appear again."

For the next two hours Ian stared diligently at the stage, only speaking to relay tales of previous ghost sightings at the club. After catching me covering up a yawn, Ian reluctantly paid our tab and had the doorman call us a cab.

The ride didn't take long, and within minutes, we pulled up to the corner of Bourbon Street closest to Wicked. As usual, Bourbon Street was barricaded, with the street party in full swing.

"Looks like a busy night," Ian said, helping me out of the cab.

"Looks like it."

"I'll walk you to your building." He put his arm around my waist, guiding me as I hobbled on my blistered feet.

When we reached the building entrance I stopped. "I think I'm safe from here."

"Oh, okay then." His disappointment penetrated my defenses.

"Thank you for the nice evening. Dinner was excellent." At least, the food and wine was.

Ian smiled. "You're welcome. Maybe we can do it again sometime."

"Sure." I pulled the door open. "Goodnight, Ian."

He leaned in, and I automatically turned my head slightly to the left. The kiss landed on my right cheek.

"Night," I said again. "I'll talk with you soon." Before he could say another word I scooted through the entrance door, pulling it closed behind me. Thank God that was over.

"Have a nice date?"

I jumped. "What the hell are you doing? Spying on me?" I glared at Kane.

"Why would I do that?" He backed up in front of the stairwell, effectively blocking me from going to my apartment.

"No idea. But why else would you be skulking in the hallway?"

"I'm not skulking." Kane crossed his arms, a mix of irritation and amusement floating around him.

I rolled my eyes.

"How long have you been dating Ian?"

"I'm not dating Ian." What the hell? Who did he think he was? I tried to move past him but he put his arm out, blocking me.

"You just went on a date with him. That's dating where I come from."

"Fine, I'm dating Ian." Irritated, I flung a hand out, gesturing to the stairwell. "Can I go up to my apartment now?"

"I didn't picture you with a guy like that." Kane's eyes stayed level with mine.

"You were picturing me with guys?" I smiled, my irritation replaced by smug satisfaction.

"No."

"Okay, sure." My smiled blossomed into a grin. "Excuse me, but these feet are ready for some pampering, so if you'll kindly move—"

"This was, what, the second date?" Kane asked, still blocking the stairwell.

"What? No. The first," I said, caught off guard.

"Huh, I must have been mistaken."

I smirked, remembering the night Ian stayed over. "Why are you so interested?"

"I'm just wondering why." He shrugged.

"Why what, exactly?"

"Why you're dating *him*?"

"Because he asked." I pushed past him and paused for just a moment. "Not that it's any of your business."

Chapter 10

Sitting at my computer, I took a big bite of my freshly made omelet. My hangover specialty. I wasn't nauseous, so I knew it wasn't really a hangover, but I'd woken up with a headache. Maybe the smoke in the jazz club caused it. More likely, it was Ian and his nonstop ghost hunting. Or possibly the latest dream I'd had—but I didn't want to think about it.

I went for a second cup of coffee, leaving my breakfast on the desk. As I poured the drink, a loud knock sounded on the door.

Checking the peephole, I bit my lip, took a deep breath and opened the door. "Good morning, Kane."

"Morning."

"What'cha got there?" I eyed two paper coffee cups and a pastry bag.

He held a cup out.

I inhaled the sweet honey spice of chai. "You're my hero!"

"Mission accomplished." He set the bag on the counter.

"Breakfast, too?"

He nodded.

I picked up the bag and peeked inside. "Chocolate muffins? That's not breakfast, that's dessert. You're sweet, but my breakfast is right there." I pointed to the desk, trying to behave.

Kane looked to my omelet then back at me. "Aren't you going to share after I brought you a chai?"

My gaze shifted from the plate to the muffins, and I shrugged. "Sure." If I was going to be polite and eat the muffin he brought me, I needed to save some room.

I grabbed another fork, returned to my desk and cut a line through the middle of the omelet. "That half is yours."

"Don't trust me?" he asked with mock surprise.

After claiming a spot on the couch, I gestured for him to join me. "Nope."

Kane's eyes crinkled as he laughed. Damn, that was sexy. My heart melted.

Lost in my own thoughts, I missed what he was saying. "Huh?"

"You forgot your chai."

"Oh yeah, thanks." I grabbed the cup and a muffin and reclaimed my seat. "What brings you by this morning?"

"The ghost report."

Damn it. Why did my life have to be all about the ghost? I sampled my chocolate muffin, and then relayed the information I'd learned from Ian.

"The ghost is attached to Pyper too?"

"I don't know. He apparently likes her since he showed up in her photos."

"I better tell her." Kane got up, taking the plate to my sink.

"All right. See you later." I waved from the sofa.

He lifted one eyebrow. "Trying to get rid of me? And after I brought you breakfast?"

"Uh, no…I just thought you said you were…never mind."

"Do I make you nervous, Jade?" Kane walked toward me.

"No." I stood up, concentrating on the cinnamon flakes in his eyes.

"You're sure?"

"Yes."

"In that case, have dinner with me tonight." His voice held a bit of a challenge.

"What makes you think I don't have plans?"

"Considering you ditched your date last night without inviting him up, I'm not too worried." However, nervous energy radiated off him like static. If I hadn't had my special ability I'd be thinking he was a smug bastard right about now.

My lips turned up in a little smile.

"Is that a yes?"

"I'm thinking it over," I said, enjoying myself.

"Hmm, let me convince you." The nervous energy vanished, replaced by determination and confidence. He leaned in, eyes locked on mine. I stood motionless as one arm wrapped around my waist, pulling me close. He bent his head, bringing his lips inches from mine. I'm pretty sure I stopped breathing.

His lips brushed mine while his free hand trailed down my bare neck. My body shivered against his, and he chuckled softly. Closing my eyes, I focused on the nerve endings, which sent electric shocks through my body.

"Tonight at eight," he whispered.

"Okay."

His lips clasped my lower lip, sucking almost painfully, until a small moan escaped my throat. At the sound he crushed me to him, tongue exploring. I molded my body to his unyielding frame, desperate to be closer. The passion of my nightly dreams sparked a fierce intensity, propelling the aching need deep in my center.

He pulled back. "Eight it is."

"Huh?" I looked up, dazed and breathless.

"I'll pick you up at eight for dinner."

"Right. Dinner."

Kane leaned in, brushing a soft kiss over my cheek. "Thanks for breakfast." Then he left.

"Holy Jesus." I stared at the door. A flash of light to my right startled me. The apparition grew into the shape of a person, glowed a bright gold, turned red, then melted into a blob on the floor before finally evaporating.

Leaning back, I put a hand over my eyes. "This is too weird."

Feeling like I was being watched, I headed to the bathroom, brushed my teeth and took off for the studio.

Sweat trickled down my back as I fumbled with the key in the doorknob. "Damn it! Come on." Glancing at my watch, I groaned. Only twenty-five minutes until Kane was due to pick me up.

I'd been grateful for the distraction of the weekly beadmaking class earlier that day. Thank God Bea had been there. Her energy calmed me just enough to be able to teach the class successfully. I really wanted to know how she did that. Maybe I should have taken her up on her invitation. When she'd asked me after class to join her for lunch I'd turned her down. I'd already committed to helping out a fellow glass worker in the hot shop making paper weights and goblets. It had been the perfect thing to get my mind off my ghost and my upcoming date. Unfortunately, I'd completely lost track of time. No way was I going to be ready by eight. Kane would just have to be patient.

At the thought of him I practically swooned. It's a damn good thing I'd been busy all day. If it hadn't been for that I'd be ready to explode by now. Who was I kidding? I was a walking time bomb, and just the thought of him lit my fuse.

But first I needed a shower. Maybe a cold one. I taped a note to the door, telling Kane to come in and wait in case I didn't hear him knocking.

Grabbing my favorite green cotton skirt and a black tank top along with my favorite bra and matching thong, I headed to my bathroom, thinking I'd be quick. However, removing the hair from my legs proved to be more important. My quick bath turned into a longer grooming session than normal.

Stepping out of the shower, I spied the Honey Dust. Unable to resist, I applied it all over with a silly grin on my face. After I was dressed, I poked my head out of the bathroom and spotted Kane relaxing on my couch.

I smiled. "Hey there."

"Hey yourself. Mighty risky asking me to let myself in while you're in the shower, don't you think?" His lips turned into a sly smile.

"No choice in the matter. Sorry I'm running late. Grab yourself something to drink out of the fridge. I'll be out in ten." I winked and shut the door. Twenty minutes later, my hair and makeup done, I strolled out of the bathroom.

Kane stood up, gave me an approving glance and kissed my cheek. "Nice. Ready for dinner?"

"Definitely." I took his hand, and we walked toward the door. As I was closing it, a gust of wind kicked up and slammed it hard. "Oh!" I said, startled. "Must have left the window open." I turned the key in the lock. "Let's go."

Kane fell in step behind me. "No, you didn't."

"Didn't what?"

"Leave the window open. I closed it while you were getting ready. It looks like a storm might blow through, and I didn't want you to forget about it." He opened the door to the street for me.

I stopped in the middle of the doorjamb. "You did? Damn it. That's twice today."

"Your door slammed like that twice today?"

"No." I turned around to face him. "My ghost made two appearances. I don't think he likes you much."

"Huh?"

"He appeared after you left this morning, and apparently just slammed the door on us."

"Did you call Ian?" Kane frowned, unhappiness flowing from him.

"No. I was busy and forgot." His unhappiness dissipated, replaced by relief. I stared at him, confused. "You don't want me to call Ian?"

"No, not right now, but if you need to fill him in on the details, I can wait."

"No, no. I'll call him tomorrow." And broach how I could get my ghost to be less active. So far Ian seemed to be all about *more* ghostly action. I was tired of it.

"Good." He took my hand and guided me through the crowd of tourists on the side walk. The streets were crowded, and we didn't talk again until we reached the Bourbon Street Seafood House. He spoke to the hostess, who smiled brightly at him. A moment later we were seated.

"That was impressive," I said, scanning the large line of hungry patrons waiting for a table. "Do you have a standing table or something?"

He laughed. "Not really. Though I do know some of the staff and depending on who's working, I can sometimes get seated more quickly."

I glanced over his shoulder at the attractive brunette taking care of another party. "How do you know her?" I took in her tight, black dress and instantly hated her for the slim, curvy figure it showed off. I frowned and studied the menu in front of me.

"Who?" He followed my gaze as I looked up. Spotting the woman in question, he said, "Just an old friend. I've known her for years."

I nodded, trying to appear unconcerned. But I wondered just how good a friend she was and exactly just how much of her he knew. I mentally shook myself. First, I had no claim on this man, though it was becoming clear to me I wanted one, even if my head screamed it was a bad idea. Second, he'd done nothing to warrant my irrational jealousy.

"Oysters?" he asked.

My lips twitched. "I hear good things about oysters."

He grinned back. "Never tried them yourself?"

"There's a first time for everything."

We sat in silence for a few minutes, and then I asked him about his college days. He told me he went to LSU, which was where he met Pyper. He regaled me with wild stories of their college adventures. Mostly they were about Pyper. She'd changed personas as often as she changed boyfriends. And girlfriends, for that matter. In their sophomore year Pyper came out of the closet. In her junior year she went back in and, finally, by senior year announced there wasn't a closet and dated both men and women.

"And you two were best friends through all that?" I asked, my curiosity getting the better of me.

"Pretty much."

My eyebrows rose, and he shrugged. I guessed that was all I was getting. "How did you meet?" I asked.

"She was my neighbor in the dorm our freshman year. She befriended my girlfriend at the time. Eventually they became an item, and I was left in the cold, shunned by the two most beautiful women in the class," he said in a matter-of-fact tone.

"No!"

"Yep. It's okay. I had my eye on someone else anyway."

An hour and a half later, full of oysters, grilled redfish, crab and a shared bottle of wine, Kane paid the bill and led me back onto Bourbon Street. Music blared from nightclubs, drowning out the chatter of the mass of people making their way up and down the street. Kane took my hand, guiding me down a side street away from the crowds. "Would you mind taking a walk?"

The wine had relaxed me considerably, and my hand tingled in his. Even my blistered toe didn't hurt. "I'd love to."

He led me down Iberville Street and turned left on Royal. We strolled along, appreciating the architecture and window-shopping the art galleries and antique stores closed up for the night.

I stopped, studying one building. "Do you ever wonder how the balconies manage to stay in place?" I pointed to the one in front of us. "Look at that one. The balcony is slanted down, and it's just held on by what looks like L-brackets."

He chuckled, putting his arm around my waist. "I try not to think about it."

"Good plan." We walked a few more feet, his arm still around me. I wondered how the buildings themselves managed to stay upright. Many of them dated back to the eighteenth century and if you looked close enough, you could see the buildings leaning slightly one way or another, or in some cases leaning drastically in one direction. I assumed the buildings themselves held each other up, since they were mostly all connected with shared walls.

My attention shifted to Kane's hand, which had moved to the small of my back. He stopped beside me, and I did the same, closing my eyes for just a moment to take in the comforting sensation. Kane turned and steered me ninety degrees, causing my heel to stick in the cracked sidewalk.

"Ouch," I yelped, buckling.

Kane's quick hands steadied me and kept me from falling. "I'm sorry. Are you all right?"

"I think so." I put my foot down, testing the weight on my ankle. Grimacing, I lifted my foot, only applying pressure with my toes. "I don't think I can walk anymore." At least, not in high heels.

Concern reached my consciousness before I turned and found it etched on his face. "Sprained?"

"Probably. I need to get some ice on it. Can you call a cab?" I leaned into him.

He reached down and easily lifted me up into his arms. I wrapped my arms around his neck, feeling weightless and very feminine pressed against his chest.

"Uh, okay, but you don't really think you can carry me all the way back to my apartment, do you?" As romantic as it was, even he couldn't possibly sustain carrying me that far.

He smiled down at me, "No, just a block." He took off in easy strides.

"Where are you taking me?"

"You'll see."

He stopped in front of a beautiful, deep gold Victorian home, trimmed in brick red. I sighed wistfully. "Who lives here?"

He lowered me gently, my body grazing down the front of his. I stood on the top step, both of my hands on his chest. Heat radiated. Leaning toward him, I stumbled and his arms came around me, steadying me once more. "Careful," he whispered, his breath warming my ear. My eyes unfocused as his lips brushed against my cheek.

"Come on." He produced a key.

Regaining my senses, I asked, "You live here?"

Nodding, he opened the door and nudged me inside. "We need to get you off your feet."

I'd forgotten all about my ankle.

The home was a shotgun double. I mentally calculated the cost of such a place in the French Quarter. As I added up the zeros, my chest tightened. I realized I was holding my breath and slowly let it out. I'd known on some level Kane was a man of means, considering he owned a club and building on Bourbon Street. But for some reason seeing his beautiful home made me feel inferior. I'd never had more than just enough to pay my modest rent.

Shaking off the ridiculous feeling, I took in my surroundings. Typical shotgun doubles were originally a type of duplex. The front had two doors, but this place had one covered in shutters, with access to only the left side. It had been converted into a single. The story goes, the homes are named shotguns because a person could open the front door, fire a shotgun and the slug would sail out the back door without ever hitting any walls. My first glimpse told me this was true. I could see straight through the living room, dining room and kitchen, clear to the garden in the back. Each room was separated by an archway, carved away in the dividing walls. To the right was what I supposed were bedrooms.

"This way." Kane led me into the pale yellow kitchen and pointed to an island in the middle. "Have a seat."

I sat, undid my strappy heel and inspected the damage. Not too much swelling, but enough that it would be sore for a few days.

Kane handed me ice wrapped in a towel. "Here, I'll get you something to drink."

I waited while he poured a couple glasses of wine. "Trying to get me drunk?"

He grinned. "No, but since no one's driving…"

"No driving, but walking on this foot, especially while drunk, is likely to permanently maim me." I picked up the glass anyway.

"I hadn't planned on you walking anytime soon."

"Oh, and what were you planning?" I gazed at him through lowered lashes.

"Dessert."

'Dessert?"

"Cheesecake, actually." He pulled a cake plate out of his refrigerator and set it on the counter.

"Oh my God. I think I'm in love." Cheesecake, wine and Kane all in the same room. I hoped I wasn't drooling.

Kane paused, mid-slice, and raised his eyes to mine.

Panic seized my brain. "With cheesecake…and wine. I mean, I love both. I'm not in love with it. Obviously." I cleared my throat. Someone had taken over my mouth. "It's an expression."

Kane's eyebrows rose steadily through my stammering, then his lips quirked as he dished up two plates. *Shit*. That's me, the stunning conversationalist. My eyes stayed glued to the dessert, even as he handed me a fork and claimed the stool next to me.

"Cheers." Kane raised his glass.

"Cheers." I risked a peek before taking a sip, and then reached for the cheesecake. "Yum, this is wonderful."

Kane watched me, leaving his plate untouched.

"Aren't you going to eat?" I asked.

"Eventually. It's more fun to watch you."

I smiled and began licking the dessert off the tip of my fork. His gaze dropped to my mouth. Slowly I wrapped my lips around the morsel, careful to get every last bit of creamy goodness. Satisfied I had his full attention, I brought a fresh forkful to his mouth and stopped breathing as he used his tongue to mimic my movements. What I wouldn't give to be that piece of cheesecake right then.

"You're right." I swallowed, trying to clear my dry throat. "That was fun." My skin prickled with the current of desire sparking through him. Suddenly my whole body pulsed with aching need. Mine and his.

"Jade," he said, his voice a few octaves lower than normal as he gently pulled me from the chair, sending shockwaves to my most sensitive places. His strong muscular arms wrapped around my waist, pulling me tight to his heated body.

It was too much. Too fast. Everything pulsed. The tender flesh of my neck. My taut nipples. Between my thighs. And he'd barely touched me. I closed my eyes and took a deep breath, intending for some sort of calm, but failed miserably as his fresh rain scent overwhelmed me. An exquisite tremor ran the length of my limbs, and a small moan escaped my throat as it reached my core.

"God, Jade, I've been dreaming about this for days." Kane pushed me against the counter, his lips hungry and searching as they met mine.

Somewhere in the depths of my mind a wry laugh echoed. If he only knew. Pent-up passion exploded and all coherent thought vanished when I ran my greedy hands over his rippled stomach and the concave of his narrow hips.

He pulled back just enough to break the kiss. Passion smoldered in his rich chocolate eyes as we held an intense, agonizing gaze. His unguarded raw emotion was like nothing I'd experienced before. Desperate need and hunger overpowered something more vulnerable; an aching desire to know me, all of me, and to be known. To love and be loved. It changed everything. My heart swelled and broke all at once as I recognized the familiar ache. An ache I'd buried long ago.

I reached up, tracing the smooth edges of his freshly shaved jawline. A tiny shiver raked over his skin, transferring to me as he gently nuzzled a trail of kisses down my bare neck and collarbone. I tilted my head, reveling in the tender moment, until his hands found my hips and he yanked me tight against his hard length. Desperate to be closer, feel more, know more, I lifted my injured leg over his hip and pressed into him.

Kane grasped my thigh, pulling it higher, and ran his smooth hand over my silky skin. His mouth assaulted my neck, nipping and sucking, while his merciless fingers teased the sensitive area of my hip and upper thigh. I writhed between him and the counter and buried my hands in his thick wavy hair, holding on as his thumb inched closer between us toward my heat.

Kane's kisses turned feather-light and moved up my neck. He paused and whispered, "I want to see you. All of you."

A new shock of desire rocked my core. All I could do was nod.

In one swift movement he lifted and cradled me against his broad chest, striding from the kitchen to a nearby bedroom. Careful of my foot, he lowered me gently and stepped back, staring with burning intensity.

I licked my lips and struggled to maintain balance in the midst of unsated tension.

"I want to see you," he said again.

Delicious pain raged in his psyche as he held himself back. He was savoring this moment. It made it that much sweeter. I wasn't wearing much, just a skirt and tank top over my bra and silk thong, but I took my time lowering the zipper until the skirt fell, pooling around my ankles.

His searing gaze fell just below the hem of my tank top. I struggled to maintain an appearance of calm. Overly heated and wet, I wanted nothing more than to drag him to the bed and wrap myself around him, until everything touched and he'd buried himself inside me.

Instead, my fingers danced around the edges of the cotton tank until he lifted his eyes, silently begging me to continue. Slowly I flattened my hands, gathering the fabric with my thumbs as they moved up over my flat stomach. I paused, cupping my full breasts, watching him as he watched me.

His eyes narrowed as my fingers inched together, pinching one nipple until it stood erect beneath the lace fabric of my bra.

His control, already pushed to the brink, waivered and pressed against my consciousness. A second later it shattered. I quickly pushed my tank over my head, freeing my arms to wrap around him as his mouth clasped on my breast, sucking painfully, deliciously through the thin lace until I cried out.

"My turn," I gasped and pulled on the button of his jeans, rushing to push them over his hips. He tore his attention away from my nipple long enough to divest himself of his shirt and kick the jeans aside.

"No fair," I whispered as his teeth scraped my other breast.

"Hmm?" he mumbled into my flesh.

"I didn't get to—oh!" His hand had slid its way between my thighs, pushing past the satin fabric. One long finger massaged the slick flesh, gliding into my opening. My knees buckled.

He caught me as a chuckle rippled from his satisfied half-smile. It took him just a moment to free us both of the rest of our garments, and when he laid me back on the bed our bodies melded together in the inferno, pressing, needing, clawing. Desperate to feel his silky flesh inside me, I opened to him, begging with my body to be consumed.

"Not yet." He pulled back, his body trembling with effort. "Not yet."

Slowing the pace, he inched his way down my flesh, lips brushing and nipping, until finally he reached my center. His tongue, hot and greedy, sent ripples crashing through me. I whimpered in approval and felt his pleasure wrap around me. Every sensation, touch and emotion intensified. Seconds later his fingers plunged into me. I gasped, clenched the cool sheets, lost in the tide until ripples exploded, electrifying every inch of my being.

Moments went by as I lost myself in the pleasure-filled haze of my orgasm. Then suddenly, I was brought abruptly back with the shock of Kane's unyielding passion to take me. Now. Poised above me, his hands grasping mine, our eyes locked. I lifted my hips in answer.

His eyes never left mine as he reached for a condom. When he entered me, slowly, he relished in the sensation. Locked in his energy, I savored his pleasure of each new shock as we inched together until our hips fused as one. We held still for a long moment. Then our energies merged and I no longer knew where I started and he stopped.

Our bodies moved in rhythm, picking up the pace, faster, higher, deeper. The tension built in hot, urgent waves spreading to my limbs. I cried out with each thrust until suddenly my body spasmed. With a strangled moan, he buried himself in me. I wrapped myself tightly around him, letting the explosion take us together.

Some time later, lying snuggled in the crook of Kane's arm, my body liquid and tranquil, I kissed his chest lightly. A small tremor ran through his body, and suddenly my soul was wrapped in tenderness and a fierce emotion I could only describe as love. The emotional energy was Kane's. I felt intrusive and self-conscious all of a sudden and glanced up to find him gazing at me, intent and thoughtful.

"What?" I whispered.

"You feel it, don't you?"

A chill that had nothing to do with the air-conditioning rippled through me. Had he sensed my ability? Sadness settled in my chest. I wasn't ready to lose him. I'd bared too much. Trying hard to keep it light, I nipped his lower lip and replied, "The magic?"

"Yes, there's magic." He kissed my temple and ran his hand the length of my arm. "I've known that since I first met you, but I don't think you have."

Relief replaced my fears and I smiled. "I may not have known it, but I've certainly felt it." I demonstrated my feelings by pressing into him as my hand roamed lower, wrapping around his silky shaft, already firming to my touch. He let out a small, strangled moan and pulled me on top of him.

"If you keep that up, you're likely to kill me," he said, deftly putting on another condom then sliding into me.

"If you keep that up, I may never leave."

His hands found my hips, holding me to him as he lifted his lips to mine. "Deal."

When we'd had our fill of each other, we lay content and motionless in each other's arms. I closed my eyes, listening to Kane's breath steadily deepen as he fell effortlessly into sleep. Sighing softly, I snuggled beside him and let the night take me.

Chapter 11

Intruding anger slammed into me. An intense sense of betrayal sent an arrow of pain straight through my heart. I gasped, struggling to breathe. Jealousy filled my being, joined by disbelief and shock. Mr. Sexy stood in front of me, shaking with fury, tears of disappointment in his eyes. A cry ripped from my throat as white-hot splinters of fire shot through my belly, shattering my soul.

"Jade! Jade, wake up. Come on baby, wake up."

The voice was far away and muted. Through the blur of sleep-filled eyes, my brain registered someone hovering over me. I cringed, curling into myself.

"There you are," he said, his voice tight.

"Kane," I said softly.

"It's all right now, just a dream. It was just a dream." He gathered me to him.

Still full of pain, the tears flowed hot and steady, turning into racking sobs. Kane held me for a long time, murmuring, "I'm here. You're safe."

I concentrated on those strong arms encircling me and held on until the tears subsided and the raw, stabbing pain in my soul eased to a dull ache. Snuggling closer, I pressed my cheek to his chest and whispered, 'Thank you." Sniffling, I added, "I'm sorry."

Kane handed me a tissue from the box on the nightstand, while he stroked my back. "Sorry for what?"

"This." I waved a hand around my face. "Not a great way to end the night." I pulled away, suddenly self-conscious, and wrapped myself in the sheet.

"Morning, you mean." He nodded toward the pre-dawn light filtering through the open window.

"Oh."

Kane leaned in and tilted my chin up. Catching my eye, he gave me a small smile. "This isn't how we're ending the morning. Go ahead and take a shower. I'll make us some breakfast." He kissed my nose lightly, pulled on his jeans, and wandered out of the room.

I let out the breath I'd been holding and fell back onto the bed. What kind of a woman was terrified and reduced to tears by a dream? God, I was an idiot. Emotionally empty and physically battered, I swung my legs over the side of the bed and hobbled off to the bathroom, careful of my still-sore ankle.

Scrubbed and pink from the shower, I made my way from the bedroom to the kitchen. I spotted Kane sitting in the breakfast nook at the back of the house. A full wall of windows and French doors led out into a lush courtyard. I stopped at the open doors, taking in the soft morning breeze and vibrant colors. Orange honeysuckle covered one wall, and the large red blossoms of a hibiscus bush bloomed just outside the door.

Kane came up behind me and rested a hand on my shoulder. I leaned into him as his arms came around my waist. Comforted by his touch, I let my mind go blank and willed my soul to soak up his energy. He projected a steady calm, but I could feel it masking nervousness and maybe a bit of weariness. Well, who could blame him? My mind clamped down on the emotional radar. I was intruding and didn't want to know what else he was feeling.

"You should eat before it gets cold. I made omelets." Kane stepped back and pulled out a chair for me.

"You did?" I looked at the table for the first time. It was set with a pale yellow tablecloth and a slender vase in the middle, holding pink and white stargazer lilies. "Are those from your courtyard?"

He nodded and settled into the chair next to me.

"They're gorgeous. Your place is wonderful." And I meant it.

The ceilings were at least ten feet high with crown molding. All the rooms except the bathroom and kitchen had original, wide-planked pine floors, recently resurfaced and gleaming in the morning sun. The nook looked like a picture I'd once seen in an architectural magazine. A bay window was on the left outside wall, complete with a window seat. To the right an adjoining sun room, separated by a double-opening archway, was furnished with indoor white wicker, lots of green plants and a vibrant painting of the French Quarter. I could happily make that one room my home.

"This is delicious," I mumbled after the first bite. My omelet was full of fresh tomatoes, mushrooms, chives, avocado and swiss cheese—just the way I like it. "You remembered."

Kane winked and poured me a cup of coffee from the carafe on the table.

"Thank you," I said after taking a sip. "Everything is wonderful."

"You're welcome." As he gazed at me, his smile vanished, and he suddenly became very interested in pushing the eggs around on his plate.

What happened? Was he having second thoughts? Who wouldn't after my emotional outburst? I suppressed a sigh and shoved a forkful of omelet in my mouth.

"Jade." Kane brought both arms down on the table and turned to look me dead in the eye. His determined expression caused me to pause mid-bite. "Who's the man in your dreams?"

I choked. "What?"

"The one you dreamed of last night. Usually powerful dreams like that feature people you know."

"What makes you think I was dreaming of a man?"

Agitation radiated off him, ripping holes in my emotional armor. "Let's not play this game. I know because I saw him."

"What? You saw my ghost?"

His eyes went wide, surprised, and he straightened. "The ghost? The one Ian's been hunting? He's the one you've been dreaming about?"

I set the coffee cup down, furrowed my eyebrows and asked, "How exactly did you know about my dreams?" Had he spoken to Ian?

He didn't say anything, his face hard as he stared me down. "Ian told you?"

He shook his head and frowned. "You told Ian?"

"He's the ghost hunter. Of course I told him. If it wasn't Ian, then who told you?" No one else knew.

He blew out a breath, and pushed his uneaten breakfast away. "You did."

"What! No I didn't." I knew without a doubt we hadn't had that conversation. "I certainly would remember—"

Kane held a hand up. "You told me in your dreams."

I gaped, too stunned to talk.

"I have something to tell you," he continued, focusing on something over my shoulder.

"Clearly." My voice held a slight chill.

He raised his determined eyes to mine and held the intent stare for a long moment. I was sure he was searching for my soul. "Have you heard of dreamwalking?"

"Yes, that's when you travel in your dreams, right?" Gwen's best friend Annabelle, back in Idaho, swore she traveled all over the world in her dreams. Her descriptions and tales were so vivid and entertaining, it was easy to believe it was possible.

"Yes, for some people. My dreamwalking is a bit different."

Torn between curiosity and aggravation, I pushed the food around on my plate until, finally, curiosity won out. "Okay, tell me about *your* dreamwalking."

"When I was little, I had very vivid dreams about people I knew." He shook his head, rose from the chair, and started pacing the kitchen. "Not about people, really, but more like dreams from their point of view. They were always people I was close to, so

I figured it was natural to dream of them and their emotions."
He paused. "As I got older the dreams changed, became more intense, and I was able to watch from the person's perspective. Or I could interact in the dream, like a character in a movie."

A slow ball of uneasiness grew in the pit of my stomach. I leaned back in the chair, picked up the coffee, set it back down, then asked in a whisper, "You dreamwalk my dreams?"

He took a deep breath and nodded.

"Oh, God." I stood up, turned and strode out into the courtyard. I walked to the far end, stopping at a fountain with a stone fleur-de-lis spouting water in a steady stream. Kane's footsteps scraped on the bricks behind me, but he didn't say anything.

My face burned, no doubt the color crimson. Unwilling to face him, I continued to stare into the clear pool in the fountain basin, wishing the ground would open up and swallow me whole.

"I'm sorry, Jade," he said softly. "I know it's an intrusion, and I'm sorry for it. But I—"

My temper broke, and I turned on him. "Stop. Just stop. How could you? Do you have any idea of how violated I feel right now?"

His eyes squinted as he frowned. "I can imagine. But I thought you felt it."

"Felt it? Of course I felt it. You were making love to me in my dreams. It wasn't just me dreaming it. *You* were there? Participating?" The last of my words were barely audible as my voice broke. My own anger and humiliation pressed a heavy weight on my heart.

His eyes turned sad and a small tinge of pain reached me. "Something like that."

Pushing past him, I grabbed my purse from the counter, ran through the house and out the front door.

The tears gathered quickly. Blinking hard, I tried to hold them back and disappeared around the nearest corner. I prayed he wouldn't follow me. As I hurried down the street, I realized unless I went to Kat's place, he would be able to find me. And I couldn't go to Kat's with Dan there. "Damn!"

Nowhere to go but home. Maybe I could just lock the door and pretend I didn't exist.

Ten minutes later, I limped passed Pyper's red VW Bug and stopped in front of my building's entrance. I hoped she was at the café and not just inside. Careful to make as little noise as possible, I slowly pulled the heavy door open and peeked in.

"Who are you sneaking up on?" a voice whispered from behind me.

I let go of the door and jumped. It slammed with a loud thunk. "Holy shit!" I turned, finding Pyper standing behind me, with a twitch of a smile.

"Sorry, didn't mean to scare you." Her smile grew then faded as her brow creased in concern. "What happened?"

"Just a fight," I muttered, waving a hand to signify unimportance.

"Uh-oh, what did he do now? You're talking about Kane, right? The big date was last night?" She rolled her eyes at my nod. "Men can be so dense." She whipped her key out and reopened the door. "It couldn't have been all bad though, if you're just getting home." Her gaze roamed down the length of my body to my feet. Her lips turned into a teasing smile. "Forget your shoes again?"

I grimaced and moved past her, making my way up the stairs. With my ankle starting to throb, I grasped the railing and took my time, trying not to think about what must be glued to the bottom of my feet after walking barefoot through the French Quarter.

"Hey," Pyper called as she bounded up the steps. "Really, are you okay?"

I gave a slight nod, unlocked my door and turned around. "Did you know Kane dreamwalks?"

Pyper's eyes widened then narrowed. "Is he dreamwalking you?"

I nodded, fiddling with my keys.

"Damn."

"You knew of this special gift?"

"Yeah." She studied me, searching for something, but I didn't know what.

"If you don't mind, I'd like to be alone for a while." I tried to close the door, but her hand stopped me. We stared at each other for a few moments until I lost my patience. "What?"

She pursed her lips. "Look, I know you're upset and believe me, normally I would never stick my nose into anyone else's relationship, but I think you have to know this." She paused.

I waited.

"If Kane is dreamwalking you, it's serious."

I let out a mocking laugh. "Serious? No kidding, talk about invasion of privacy." A heavy dose of guilt rocked me. Invasion of privacy. The same thing I'd done to Kane—spying on his emotions. The same thing I'd done to Dan for years and never told him. No wonder he'd felt so betrayed and hurt when I'd finally revealed my gift. I stumbled backward into the apartment and sat heavily on my worn sofa.

Pyper followed. She sat next me and took my hand. "No, Jade. I meant his feelings are serious. From what I know of Kane, he doesn't dreamwalk on purpose, at least not these days. So, if he walked your dreams, it's because of a deep connection to you."

"Has he done it to you?"

She broke eye contact and grimaced, then nodded. "It's been a long time, though."

"I see," I said with a hint of ice in my voice. "Then you know how it feels." She opened her mouth to speak, but, spurned by irrational jealousy and inner turmoil, I cut her off. "I'd really like it if you left me alone now."

I felt the sting of my words penetrate her tough exterior. She stood and walked to the door. "If you need to talk, you know where to find me."

"Pyper?"

Holding the doorknob, she glanced back at me.

"I'm sorry. I just need to process this."

"It's okay. I understand." The door shut softly behind her.

Somewhere deep inside, a nagging voice told me I was over-reacting. Nothing Kane had done was worse than what I'd done to him. I'd spied on his emotions. He'd been an active participant in my dreams. Either action was a huge intrusion.

But damn, my dreams were so personal.

As if his emotions aren't. I snorted loudly and clenched my fists in frustration.

The worst part was I didn't know how much my desire for Kane was based on my own feelings or a result of what we'd done while he dreamwalked me. I'd always desired Kane. I had since the first day we'd met. But in the dreams I'd experienced a passion I'd never known, escalating that desire into something I couldn't resist. Now I knew Kane himself had influenced at least some of that without me knowing.

It made me feel used and manipulated.

Is that how Dan had felt after I told him I could sense his emotions?

I'd spent my childhood ostracized by my peers for knowing things I shouldn't. One doesn't make friends easily when teachers force you to tell on other students by reading which ones have a guilty conscience. My only defense was to keep my gift to myself and try to be as invisible as possible. But the damage had been done. I'd been labeled the town freak.

That changed when I'd moved to Boise shortly after I'd lost my mom. I'd shut off that part of my life completely, vowing to never tell anyone about my gift. Only one person knew: Kat. She'd lived for a short time in the small town I was from and had known me before I lost my mom. She'd said she thought my gift was kind of cool, and we'd become best friends then and there.

When Dan had come along I'd kept my vow, especially after he'd saved Kat and me from the horrors of that foster home. I hadn't wanted him to know I'd experienced everything he'd felt that night. At the time, it had seemed too much to bear.

But when he'd proposed years later, I found myself unable to accept until he knew the truth. I'd known he'd be upset. I'd lied to him—for years—too locked up in my own fears to trust him.

At first he'd scoffed, unable to believe I had such a gift. Then he'd spent three days grilling me on the status of his emotional energy. Finally I'd snapped, and explained in great detail everything he'd felt the day he'd proposed. The information had rocked him to his core.

He'd definitely been hurt, but I'd been shocked to feel deep-seated twinges of disgust and horror. All the rejection of my childhood had come roaring back. And a week later when he'd slept with someone else, I'd sensed it immediately. His intense satisfaction at hurting me had ended us then and there.

I'd hated him for it. But now, I had to stop and wonder what I'd done to him. He'd always said he'd loved me because I understood him in ways even he didn't always recognize. He'd believed in soul mates and often said how lucky he was to find me. Had he thought I'd done anything to manipulate his emotions? I couldn't change what he was feeling, but I could read them and use them to my advantage.

Did he feel used? Betrayed? The same way I felt with what Kane had done.

The guilt weighed heavy on my soul. Suddenly, I had to get out of my apartment.

Ten minutes later, the tension in my shoulders eased slightly when I sat behind my work bench in the studio. It was exactly what I needed, and I'd be safe from any unwanted company. Ready to be immersed, I turned the volume on my iPod to high and then lit my torch.

It must have been late afternoon by the time I finished the last bead of the day. The air conditioner had been no match for the June heat. I was soaked in sweat, but I was calmer. Mission accomplished. After cleaning up, I splurged and called a cab. My ankle needed a rest.

Chapter 12

Emerging from the bathroom in old, faded jeans and a T-shirt, I crossed the room to shut the window. I pulled the latch closed and jumped at a sudden movement. Kane stood in front of me.

"Feeling better?" he asked through the glass.

"Jesus, Kane. What the hell are you doing here?"

"Sorry. I didn't mean to startle you." A thin thread of appreciation reached me.

I scowled. What exactly did he appreciate? My fresh-from-the-shower look? My hands curled into fists. It was a damn good thing glass separated us. For him, anyway. "How long have you been here?"

"A while."

I narrowed my eyes.

"Can you open the window?"

Feeling the urge to deck him, I ignored the request. How dare he intrude on my private space? "Did you come in while I was in the shower?"

He shook his head slowly. "You weren't here. I waited."

I laughed humorlessly. "Figures. What? Used your landlord key?" That meant he'd been on my balcony the whole time I'd been home. I felt violated all over again.

He nodded.

"Bastard." I spat.

"No argument here."

Anger boiled in my belly as I glared at him.

"Jade, come on. It's starting to rain. Could you let me in so we can discuss this?"

A couple of fat raindrops splattered on the window. Then the skies opened up into a typical New Orleans afternoon downpour. A twisted sense of satisfaction grew from my aggravation as I watched the water stream down his face. Fully intending to leave him there, I started to close the curtain.

Then the first booms of thunder rumbled.

"Oh, all right!" I couldn't be responsible for him being struck by lightning, could I? "Wait right there." I pointed to the wall closest to the window. "Do not drip on my computer." After he toweled off, I shoved a folding chair at him. "You can sit here."

He moved toward me.

"No. You're only allowed to sit there, or else you can leave."

Stepping back, he sat.

"What exactly are you doing here?"

"I was thinking you need a security latch on your door. Keep the underbelly out."

"Are you the underbelly?" I turned in surprise at his comment.

He shrugged. "Strip club owner. I make my money off of naked women. Most people would consider me one of the underbelly. So yes, I guess so. Couple that with invading the private dreams of the women around me, and I think the jury would reach a unanimous conclusion."

I raised a suspicious eyebrow. "Women?" My voice rose higher than usual as anger coiled tighter. "Are you invading other women's dreams these days as well?"

"No, just yours lately."

"Lately. Lucky me." I snorted. "Who else has had this pleasure?"

"You know Pyper and I are old friends." It was a statement, not a question, but I nodded. "She's my closest friend. The thing is, the closer I am with someone the more likely it is I'd unconsciously slip into his or her dreams. I've learned over the years how to stop it, or to step out of the dream when it happens. I haven't found myself in one of Pyper's dreams in a few years."

"A few years?" An unwelcome image of him and Pyper together, intimate, in a dream flashed through my mind. I frowned and pushed it away. He'd just said they were friends. It could have been a dream about flying to the moon for all I knew.

He nodded.

"Wait," I said, as my brain started to function again. "You said you learned how to step out of dreams. *Why* exactly didn't you step out of mine? Didn't you think what you were doing to me was a huge invasion?"

He looked pained.

"Not only that, but you seduced me in my dreams, letting me think it was my own subconscious. God! You had me thinking I have feelings for you. I feel like an idiot for jumping into bed with you."

"You do have feelings for me," Kane said softly. I opened my mouth, a string of expletives poised on my lips, but his raw emotion stunned me into silence. Regret, shame and a trickle of loneliness punctured my defensive wall. "You do, and I have feelings for you." His voice was low and rough. His vulnerability wrapped around my soul, and suddenly the spark fizzled from my anger. I still hated what he did, but I knew without a doubt it had been done with passion and something close to love. Even if it was wrong and twisted.

Overwhelmed, I stared into his eyes and for once didn't feel like melting. "I thought I did, but…I need time to process."

"I know." Kane got up, moving toward the door.

"Where are you going?"

"Home. I thought I'd give you space."

"Space later. Right now I have more questions about your ability." He wasn't getting out the door until I had answers.

Kane cleared his throat and reclaimed the chair. "Okay."

I sat on my couch, facing him. "Tell me how it works. You said you just find yourself in other people's dreams, and you can step out of them. How?"

He took a moment, seeming to process my question, then leaned forward. "It's easier if I realize a dreamwalk is going to happen. Then I can clear my mind and consciously will myself to 'stay at home' in my own head, if you know what I mean."

I didn't but nodded anyway, encouraging him to continue.

"It takes a lot more effort to step out of a dream. I have to realize I'm there and leave. It's sort of like when you're dreaming and you realize it's a dream and wake yourself up. Of course, if I *want* to dreamwalk it's pretty much the opposite. I envision myself in a person's dream and will myself to go there."

"You do that often?" I said, in a more accusatory tone than I meant to.

A weak smile lit his lips. "No. I haven't consciously dream-walked since college."

I bit back a snarky reply and continued with my interrogation. "You said you accidentally walked in both Pyper's dreams and mine."

He nodded.

"Anyone else?"

He didn't say anything at first. I started to get nervous. It wasn't really any of my business and I didn't have a right to ask, but I was anyway.

"An ex-girlfriend," he finally said.

"Holly?"

He jerked back and shook his head. "No. Holly and I have never dated. Where did you get that idea?"

A bit of tension eased out of my shoulders. I shrugged. "I saw you two talking once and just had the idea in my mind. Sorry, it's none of my business."

He raised his eyebrows. "Isn't it, though?"

My heart squeezed at his question, but I ignored it. "What did Pyper and your ex-girlfriend do when they found out you were invading their dreams?"

He winced at my tone. "I didn't do it on purpose, you know."

Softening, I moved closer to him on the sofa. "No, I don't know. Explain it to me."

He got up, pacing. Back and forth he strode, gathering his thoughts. Finally he stopped. "Pyper knew what it felt like when I was in her dreams. If I had to guess, I'd say you have an idea of what that means, even if you didn't know it when it was happening."

I thought about that. Yes, I did know. There were times when I dreamt of Mr. Sexy and suddenly Kane was there, as real in my dreams as he was in life. Heat inched up my neck, reaching my face as the intimate scenes flooded back. Then the emotions. The implications of what he felt for me were a lot to process. I decided to not think about it at all until I had time to examine what it meant. I cleared my throat. "Yes, I felt you." My voice seemed far away, a little detached.

He nodded. "I thought you did. Pyper knew in much the same way."

I blanched.

He caught my look and laughed. "It's not like that. It never has been." Taking two steps, he reached my side and took my hand. "I know I've violated your trust, but please believe me when I say there is no one else."

Tears welled in the back of my eyes, and I did my best to blink them back. I didn't know what to say. Yesterday I would have been thrilled to hear Kane say I was his one and only. Now I didn't know what I wanted.

I shifted, pulling my hand out of his. The love I'd felt the night before was now shadowed in pain. My rejection was hurting him just as much as he'd hurt me, Overwhelmed, I steered the conversation back to the dreams. "So what did Pyper do to stop you from invading her dreams?"

Kane sat back on his heels and ran a hand through his hair. "There are a few precautions one can take to keep others out of their head, but it wasn't necessary for her to do that. I worked harder on keeping my distance. It usually only happens when something intense is going on or my defenses are down. Once we started working so closely together, the dreamwalking began. I just strengthened my defenses, and it stopped." He sighed and in a husky voice said, "This time my defenses have been blown away. Everything I've done to try to stop the dreamwalking with you has failed. I'm sorry, Jade." With his shoulders hunched, he looked miserable.

Fighting the urge to reach out to him, I asked. "How long?" As he lifted his face, I clarified. "How long have you been fighting it?"

He grimaced then said a little sheepishly, "A few days."

The dreams had been going on quite a bit longer than that.

"I know it doesn't mean much, but I really am sorry. I know it's an awful thing to do. I just…" His face turned a rather dark shade of maroon. "It's just, I enjoyed your dreams…unless *he* was starring."

"Jesus, Kane," I said. Irritated and embarrassed, I got up and moved to stare at the rain.

"It was driving me crazy." He followed me.

"I told you to sit in that chair or leave."

Ignoring my statement, he stepped in front of me, locked his eyes on mine and stared. Golden glints sparkled from rich chocolate irises.

He reached out and stroked my cheek. I clasped my hand over his, wanting to stop the motion, but Kane took it as an invitation and leaned in. Just as his lips met mine, lightning flashed and a loud crack sounded, jolting us apart. Another bolt struck, illuminating a dark shadow darting up the walls. It circled us then hovered over my computer.

It grew larger, glowed red and flew at me as if to attack. I screamed in terror as my insides ripped apart, just as they had in my dream the night before. Falling to my knees, I clutched my stomach, gasping for breath.

The apparition disappeared just as the tray with my glass beads rose in the air. "No!" I shouted as I watched them tumble out and rise toward the ceiling, hovering high above our heads. Kane knelt next to me, his arms covering my shoulders and head protectively.

"Get off," I huffed, pushing him away. Jumping up, I took a deep breath and said in my most commanding voice, "You put those beads down right this minute. I won't stand for your scare tactics. How dare you treat me this way!" My voice echoed off the walls, slightly muffled by the thunderous storm. The beads rotated, inched higher then fell.

"Gently!" I yelled. Just before they would have crashed, all of them came to a sudden stop, less than an inch from the floor, and tumbled softly.

I stood in the center of the room, my chest heaving. The next thing I knew, Kane grabbed my hand and tugged me out the door.

"Where are we going?" I gasped, trying to clear my head.

"Out of here," Kane said, his voice muffled.

He was right in front of me but I couldn't focus. His lips moved, but I had trouble hearing him. "What did you say?"

"I said, you need to be somewhere safe. Let's go."

Too tired to protest, I weakly muttered something about clothes.

Kane positioned me outside the door. Through a distorted hazy consciousness, I watched him open my drawers and throw some garments in a bag. In seconds he returned and picked me up. That's the last thing I remember.

A chatter of voices pulled me from my slumber. Disoriented, I sat up and, through blurry eyes, I spotted rich, heavy velvet drapes. Pyper's apartment. Again. I needed to get out of this habit. The silver crescent moon shone through the window. How long had I been here?

"No, she isn't going back up there tonight," Kane said.

"Isn't that up to her?" Ian said.

"Not when she's passed out."

"I'm up," I said from the doorway, leaning against the jamb to steady myself.

"Honey, are you okay?" Pyper rushed toward me, led me over to the couch and gently pushed me down. "I'll be right back." She disappeared into the kitchen.

Ian and Kane both turned toward me.

"Go where?" I asked

"Nowhere," Kane said.

Ignoring him, I turned to Ian. "Where do you want me to go?"

Ian frowned. "I know you're wiped out, but if you have any energy at all, the best thing to do—if we want more clues—is to go back up to the apartment. I need another reading with you." He glanced in Kane's direction. Reluctance penetrated my awareness when he added, "and Kane too."

"No," Kane said.

Pyper appeared with hot tea and a few cookies. "Here, honey, this should help."

"Thanks." I took a bite, sipped my tea and looked over at Kane. "I can speak for myself."

"Of course you can," he said. "But I'm still not going to let you go back up there." His voice was tender now, losing some of the authoritative edge he'd used with Ian.

With a faint smile, I asked, "Let?"

He shrugged as he raised his hands, palms up. He glanced at Pyper, found no help, and then sat on the sofa.

"Anyone care to fill me in on the details I've missed?" I glanced around at each of them.

Kane spoke up. "You haven't missed much. You passed out. I brought you here and called Pyper, who then called Ian. Ian's been here for about an hour. We've been discussing a course of action to rid you of your ghost."

"An hour?" How long had I been asleep?

"You've been here for about three hours." Pyper patted my hand. "We didn't think you'd suffered any physical damage, judging by what Kane said, so we let you sleep. Does it hurt anywhere?" She peered at me, checking for nonexistent bruises, I guessed.

I smiled at her mothering. "I'm fine. Just feel like my insides have been ripped to shreds, is all."

"Really?" Ian's eyes went wide. "Did it happen upstairs?"

I nodded.

"Can you tell me exactly what happened?" He dug around in his canvas bag and pulled out a notepad.

"Do we have to do this right now?" Kane sounded impatient. He slid toward me on the sofa and brushed the hair out of my eyes. "You don't have to do this now, you know."

I caught Ian watching me. He was also doing a fair job of suppressing the jealousy that had bubbled up when Kane touched me. With a grim smile at Kane, I said, "I know, but somehow I think I need to get this out."

He let out a long breath then acknowledged my statement with a nod.

"Kane told you what we saw?" I asked.

"Yes, but I'd like to hear it from your perspective." Ian made small fast circles with his ballpoint pen, trying to get the ink to flow.

"Okay." I launched into my version of the events. Ian scribbled intently as I recounted the haunting. When I got to the part when the shadow disappeared, I paused. "I felt like something in my gut shattered like the red image. Not like a stomachache or anything like that. More like my soul was being torn into individual little pieces. It happened just like that in my dream last night, too."

Ian took in a sharp breath.

Kane clasped his hand over mine. "Damn it, Jade. The ghost is haunting your dreams. You aren't just dreaming about him."

"Right, I told you that this morning."

"No, you said you were dreaming about him."

"No, you interpreted it that way."

"Jade—"

"Can you two work that out later?" Pyper said.

Kane sighed and leaned back. "Fine."

Ian finished scribbling some notes then looked up, focusing for a second on my hand clasped in Kane's. "This is very unusual, especially considering the sexual content."

"I thought you said ghosts haunting dreams weren't unheard of," I said.

Ian leaned forward. "They aren't, but I've never heard of someone being attacked in one. That, plus the intimate nature, makes me uneasy."

Ian's troubled expression unsettled me more than his words. "So what do we do now?"

"I have a few ideas, but I'd need to get you back up there—"

Kane let out an audible grunt, cutting Ian off.

"—when you think she's up to it," Ian finished, eyeing Kane.

"It's not up to him to decide." Feeling smothered, I lowered my voice. "Look, Kane, I know you want to protect me, but this is something I have to deal with. I have a feeling the longer it goes on, the worse it's going to get. I need to do what I can, even if I have to endure more encounters with the ghost. Plus, he invaded my dream at your house last night. I'm not so sure location matters anymore. If Ian thinks he can help, I need to trust him."

Kane searched my eyes for a moment, kissed my hand and said, "Okay."

A tiny bit of weight lifted from my heart. I squeezed his hand before letting go.

"All right then. I've already got my equipment set up, and John is monitoring the readings. Let's go." Ian tilted his head toward me as he moved toward the door. "I'll have her back as soon as possible. I know she needs to rest, but I don't want to miss the chance of getting a reading so close to the event."

I stood, trying to shake the dizzy feeling, and followed him. When I glanced back, I found Kane on my heels.

"I'm going also."

"I don't think…" Ian paused when Kane's face darkened.

"Don't think what?" I asked.

"I'd rather get a reading with just you. It's more scientific," Ian said. Kane's irritation poked at me as Ian continued. "From what I've heard, this ghost is really only interacting with Jade. I don't want to introduce any other elements until I get a clean reading with her."

"But you said earlier you wanted a reading with both of us," Kane countered.

"Yes, but Jade first, then you," Ian said.

Kane continued to look unconvinced.

I sighed and waved at Pyper, "A little help here?"

"Come on, Kane, I'll entertain you while they're up there." Pyper grabbed his arm and led him to the couch.

I strode out the door with Ian close on my heels. When I got to the stairwell of my own apartment, I stopped dead in my tracks and stumbled forward as Ian barged into me. He reached out a strong arm and grabbed me around the middle just before my head bashed into the railing.

"Oh, sorry, Jade!" Ian turned me toward him. "Why did you stop?"

I gave him a weak smile. "Just nervous." Nervous was putting it mildly. My knees started shaking, and my heart felt like it would beat right out of my chest. I took a few deep breaths and grabbed on to the railing.

Ian took my arm and patted my hand. "It's all right. Really, I've seen a fair number of odd paranormal occurrences. I know what to do if something happens." He lifted my chin and looked straight in my eyes. "I won't let anything happen to you. It'll be all right. I promise."

I nodded and let him tug me up the stairs. We stopped just outside my door.

"Now, when we go in, don't say anything until I ask you to. I'm going to walk you around the room then onto the balcony while I take readings. Okay?"

I nodded my agreement and followed him inside.

The investigation was set up in much the same manner it had been during the first recording. Candles burned in a circle around the room. A video camera was set up just to the right of the door, along with an old-fashioned tape recorder. John had two cameras around his neck, a 35mm and a digital camera. He had told me digitals were the preferred choice, but ghosts were known to mess with electronics, causing them to fail. Just like last time. The 35mm was the camera that caught my ghost image.

Ian steered me to the middle of the room, holding my arm, keeping me close. He cleared his throat and began to speak. "Lord in heaven, please protect us, your children, from harm and possession. We only seek knowledge and not destruction. Amen." He smiled "Ready?"

I gave him a small nod.

"Dear earthbound spirit of apartment 3-A. We are here seeking only information and do not wish you harm. If you so choose, please allow us to communicate with you."

John handed Ian a small electronic device. Holding it under candlelight, he scribbled a reading in a notebook. He took my hand and walked me slowly around the room, focusing on the electronic readings. The continuous click of the camera cut through the silence as John snapped photo after photo. The conditions with the candlelight were dim. I wondered how he'd get any decently lit pictures without a flash.

After the third circle I started to get dizzy and was relieved when Ian led me to the balcony. "Stay out here for a minute. I want to get some more readings, and then I'll have you come back in."

I sat down in my chair to wait.

Ian stepped back inside and let out a loud yelp. I scrambled to my feet and poked my head in the window.

Ian grabbed my shoulder. "Get in here!"

A queasy feeling rolled through my stomach as I scanned the room. I saw nothing out of the ordinary. It looked just as it had, except for the expressions on the two men's faces.

I stepped in, confused. Ian held up a hand, gesturing for me to wait. John stood in the corner using the 35mm camera, clicking over and over again in rapid succession. He paused to reload and then nodded at Ian.

Ian, standing just to my left, put a hand on my arm and whispered, "Talk to him."

I took a shaky breath, let it out slowly and opened my mouth. No words came out.

Ian, seeing my struggle, asked, "Have you spoken to him before?"

'Yes."

"If you gave him a name or title, use it now."

"Damn," I muttered under my breath. "Oookay. Hello, Mr. Sexy."

John chuckled quietly from across the room. I shot him a dirty look, but he didn't seem to notice. He was still busy snapping away. Click, click. Click, click.

I focused on talking to my ghost. "It's been an eventful day, has it not? You must have used a lot of energy picking up all of my beads. Thank you, by the way, for setting them down gently." The candles flickered a few times then burned bright again.

I glanced at Ian. He nodded his head enthusiastically, encouraging me to continue.

"Thank you for the acknowledgment. I assume that was you, flickering the candles?" The candles flickered again, a few of them blowing out entirely. "Yes, I know you're there. I wish I knew your real name." The flame on the candle closest to my bed went out.

"Yes, I know it's you in my dreams." I stopped, at a loss for words. My skin started to warm, and something soft wrapped around my shoulders. Even though I was sure the gesture was meant as a loving one, hair stood up on the back of my neck. "Is that you? Did you wrap a blanket over my shoulders?" My knees started to tremble and, not trusting myself to stand any longer, I sat on my couch.

"Keep going," Ian said softly.

I closed my eyes and concentrated. "I wish I knew who you were and why you're here. I get the feeling you don't know you're a ghost." The warmth slid from my shoulders. I shivered. Unwilling to give up, I asked, "What happened to you? Can you tell us? There's a recording device over by the door. If you stand close to it, we might hear you. Please, we want to help."

"Jesus!" John jumped suddenly from his spot near the recorder and scooted closer to Ian.

"What the hell—" Ian started, but was cut off by the door opening suddenly, with Kane striding in.

"You've got to get down to Pyper's apartment," Kane announced, grabbing Ian's arm.

"What? No. We're just getting going here." Ian glared at Kane. "It's best if you leave."

Ian's face contorted in pain as Kane gripped harder. "No. Pyper's in trouble. You need to go, now."

"In trouble? What happened?" I demanded. Not waiting for an answer, I ran out the door, took the stairs two at a time and was on the ground floor before I realized no one was following me.

Chapter 13

A minute later I burst through the apartment door and found Pyper sprawled out on the floor. Falling to my knees by her side, I placed my palm on her chest. My hand rose as she took in a breath. The dread in my gut eased slightly.

"Thank God. Pyper? Can you hear me?" She didn't move as I smoothed her hair back from her closed eyes. Her skin burned. I ran for a cold wet cloth. Once I started to mop her brow, her eyes flickered open.

"There you are," I said. "Welcome back."

"Jade." Her eyes filled with tears. "Is he still here?"

"Who? Kane?" My voice was low and, I hoped, calming, though my heart was beating hard enough to leap right out of my chest.

She shook her head, tears streaming down her temples.

"It's all right now. Shhh. It's all right." I moved to cradle her head in my lap and stroked her hair.

Pyper's breath came short with silent sobs. She turned her face into my shirt and held on while her body shook. I continued to whisper soothing words until finally she stopped and was silent.

A muffled sound came from her buried face.

"Hmmm?" I said.

"Thank you," she said in a hoarse voice. She sat up across from me.

I handed her the cloth and gave her a small smile. "No thanks needed. It's what friends do."

She tried to smile back but failed, turning her head toward the window.

I got up and headed to the kitchen. I didn't notice the shaking until I grabbed the tea kettle. After filling it and placing it on the burner, I ran my still shaking hands over my arms. Pyper wasn't the type of person to break down. I didn't think anything else could unnerve me more. Searching through the cupboards, I found a new bag of mint Milano cookies. After arranging the cookies on a plate, I set it on a tray along with the tea and headed back into the living room. Pyper sat curled up at the end of the couch.

I set the tray down and handed her a mug. "Here, drink this."

She took the mug but neglected to take a sip and stared into the contents. After a few moments, I held out a cookie. "This might help."

She glanced up but sat unmoving.

"If you don't want it, I'm eating it. This is not the time to turn down chocolate."

She made a move for it, but I bit into it before she could grab it.

"Bitch," she said, but it lacked any heat.

I smiled sweetly and handed her another from the tray. She took it before I could snatch it back, and we nibbled the cookies in silence for a few minutes. Finally, I asked, "If you weren't asking about Kane, who were you asking about?"

She ran her fingers along the rim of her cup then looked up meeting my eyes. "The man I've been dreaming about."

My head jerked back, causing me to spill my tea. "Shit!" I tried to mop it up with a napkin, but a small dark spot stained the cream sofa.

"Don't worry about it." Pyper waved her hand in a dismissive fashion. "I know the owner." She tried to smile, but it came out more as a grimace.

I shook my head and said something about getting it cleaned. After putting the tea cup down to avoid further disaster, I turned to give her my full attention. "You're dreaming of someone, too?"

She nodded, fear flashing in her eyes. It wrapped around my chest, making me wheeze. I took shallow breaths and tried to conjure up as much calm as I could to combat her energy. When the air flowed freer, I asked, "Do you know him?"

Her confusion, fear and anger seeped through my protective calm. Clamping down on my barriers, I shoved her emotions and my own mounting anger aside and concentrated.

Pyper shook her head. "I don't actually see him. There aren't any details, just a shape, so I don't know who it is."

"Can you tell me what happens in your dreams?" My stomach did flip-flops. Was it the same ghost as Mr. Sexy? My hands started shaking again. I didn't really want to know what had happened to cause her breakdown, but I knew I needed to hear it.

Pyper focused on her tea cup again. "He torments me, almost every night, or day. Whenever I try to sleep."

My fists curled. "How?"

"I don't know how to explain it exactly." Her voice shook a little and I took her hand, squeezing it lightly. "It's like…well, like I'm being physically beaten, but I'm not."

I nodded and waited for her to continue.

She screwed her face up in concentration. "In the dreams I can feel myself being hit all over, but the brunt of it is my stomach and my face. My arms feel pinned down so I can't defend myself. I *feel* the pain. I literally feel it so intensely, I think I must cry out in my sleep."

I shivered as the hair stood up on my arms.

"When it's over I feel empty. And bruised. Only, when I wake up, I'm not bruised at all. Then I think it's just all in my mind, the pain, you know? "

"I think so." Her experience was very much like my own dreams of Mr. Sexy, only most of the time he brought me pleasure. It wasn't until recently that he'd brought physical pain, and it didn't sound the same. Mine was more of an emotional hurt, not an actual beating.

I thought about what she said for a moment. "What happened tonight that sent Kane to get us?"

"Hey, where is he?" Pyper glanced around.

"I have no idea," I blurted. "He came in raving about how we needed to help you. I took off and the rest of them stayed in my apartment."

Pyper drew her eyebrows together and frowned. "That's odd." I thought so too, but didn't respond. "Well," she continued, "Kane and I were just sitting here talking and I felt so safe being here with him, I curled up and went to sleep. I haven't been sleeping well lately."

"I can imagine." I felt a small twinge of guilt as I remembered actually enjoying Mr. Sexy in my dreams.

"I guess I thought with Kane here, things might be all right." Her face paled. "But I was wrong. It was the worst attack yet. I woke up screaming and ran."

She plucked at the couch cushion. "I guess I was disoriented and panicked. Kane started yelling at me to stop so he could help me. I froze. When he got to my side and put his arms around me, there was a light that flashed. Lightning, probably." She squeezed her eyes closed and shuddered. "Then I suddenly started to burn from the inside out. I guess that's when I passed out." Her eyes fluttered open and found mine. "The next thing I knew, you were sitting next to me."

"Oh my God, Pyper." I squeezed her hand harder and said in a very small voice, "This is my fault. I'm sorry."

"What? Your fault?" Her shock penetrated my defenses.

"I don't know if it's my fault exactly, but I've been having somewhat similar dreams. Maybe if I'd shared the extent of them we could have figured something out so this didn't keep happening to you."

"If I understand correctly, you're having sex dreams. Those are nothing like mine."

Her flat, cold stare made me flinch. "No, the content isn't the same. You're right." I stopped, rubbed my eyes. "What I mean is, mine seem so real. They feel just as real as yours do. When I wake up I can still feel the effects of the lovemaking." My face burned hot and I turned away, embarrassed.

"Okay, maybe, but what does that mean?"

"I know, or at least I think I know, that the person in my dreams is the same as the ghost in my apartment. What if the same ghost is invading both of our dreams?"

"If that is true, why would he torture me and have sex with you?" Her eyes narrowed, piercing me.

"I don't know!" I threw my hands up. "How could I know? He's been hurting me too, lately. And with the similarity, it could be a link." I paused as my words triggered a thought. "You said this attack was the worst one yet, right?"

"Yeah. Why?"

"Kane was with you. The two times I was attacked, Kane was with me."

We stared at each other until Pyper leaned back and in a low, controlled voice asked, "You think Kane has something to do with this?"

A thread of anger, combined with protectiveness, entered my consciousness. I rushed to reassure her. "No. I don't. But maybe he's a trigger for the ghost."

"I'm sorry." She moved to sit next to me. "You're right that he could be a trigger, but the ghost hurts me when Kane isn't around, too."

"I know. It just seemed like too much of a coincidence."

She nodded agreement then jumped to her feet. "I'm tired of being the victim. I wish there was something we could do. Like confront the bastard."

"We can," I said, surprising myself. "We can call him out like we did that first day in my apartment."

"Now?"

"Yes." I said in a firm voice, not feeling at all as confident as I sounded.

She studied me for a long moment and gave a quick nod.

I moved to the middle of the living room. Pyper joined me and clasped my hand in hers.

"I think we should both call him at the same time. Do you have a name you refer to him as?" I asked.

"Mr. Evil," she said in a matter-of-fact tone.

I couldn't help it. I burst out laughing.

"What?" She frowned.

"You'll see," I said trying to contain myself. "On three, then." With a nod from Pyper, I counted backwards from three.

On one I called out, "Mr. Sexy," just as Pyper called, "Mr. Evil."

Pyper turned her head toward me and grinned briefly. Another flash of lightning shone through the uncovered window. Pyper flinched, tightening her grip on my hand. Her face went chalk white. Her terror rippled through me as if it were my own. "No, please don't," she whispered.

I turned my head frantically from side to side, seeing nothing. She shook violently.

Panicked, I yelled out "Mr. Sexy! Stop this right now. Do you hear me? I need you to stop this!" I concentrated hard on gathering as much energy as I could from my being. A tight ball formed in my stomach. It grew rapidly like an inflating balloon. When I mentally pushed the force from myself the lights flickered off and on, off and on. The tea tray vibrated on the coffee table, and a dark shadow appeared right in front of the two of us. A light breeze tickled my skin and ruffled my hair.

And suddenly there was Mr. Sexy, standing in full view in front of us. He looked at me, turned around and put his arms out wide. The flickering and shaking stopped, and all that was left was a light tickling breeze.

Trembling, I turned to Pyper. I felt the tension run out of her and her death grip loosen. But she didn't let go. The color returned to her face, and a rush of gratitude and relief oozed from her into my awareness.

"It's all right now." I stared at my ghost and reached my hand out, slow and tentative. The air felt hot and thick, even though I could hear the air conditioner blowing just over our heads.

The ghost lowered his arms, turned back to face me and just as my hand was about to reach his outstretched one, the door flew open with a bang. He vanished into a dark shadow and disappeared. "Damn it!"

Kane, Ian and John barged into the room. Equipment filled their hands and hung from straps around their necks.

Kane shot me a weary glance as he strode toward Pyper.

"Where have you been all this time?" I asked.

"Dealing with your ghost." He stopped in front of Pyper. "Are you okay?"

"I think so." She turned to me. "Thank you, Jade." Her arms wrapped around me. She hugged me hard and whispered, "I'll be right back." She moved toward her bedroom. I thought I saw a single tear roll down her cheek.

I watched her disappear through the door then turned on Kane. "What the hell are you talking about? The ghost was *here*." Kane raised his eyebrows and Ian's eyes went wide. "At least for a little while, anyway."

Ian didn't question me. He said something softly to John, and the two of them went about setting up equipment around the room.

I grabbed Kane's arm. "What did you mean? What happened after I left?"

"What happened here?" he said at the same time.

"You first," I said, poking him in the ribs. "It must have been something compelling to keep you away when Pyper was passed out on the floor."

"Passed out?" His voice rose and he turned in the direction of Pyper's room. "She was screaming just like you did last night. I couldn't get her to come out of it. I thought—"

"She's all right." My heart squeezed with his pain. "What happened?"

Kane led me to the couch and tugged me down to sit next to him. "When you left, I followed you."

"No—"

"Yes. I did. At least, I tried to."

My eyebrows pinched together, causing a wrinkle just above my nose.

He reached his hand out to smooth it. "Don't do that. You'll give yourself a headache."

I frowned, in no mood to be teased. "Go on."

"I was right behind you when you left. You ran out the door. I turned to follow you, only Ian yelled for me to stop and I hesitated. Both of them, Ian and John, went crazy taking pictures." He shook his head. "I thought they'd gone mad. I couldn't see anything, so I turned to follow you. Only…well, when I tried to go out the door, it was blocked somehow."

"Blocked? With what?"

He shrugged. "I have no idea. I couldn't see anything except you turning the corner at the end of the stairway. I called out. Didn't you hear me?"

"No, I didn't. How could the door be blocked by nothing?"

"You've got me. Ian said it was the ghost's energy keeping us trapped in the room. It was hot, like fire. I could get right up next to it and feel nothing, but as soon as I tried to go through I'd burn."

I gasped. "How did you get out?"

"Right after the lightning struck, the doorway turned bright orange then dissipated into thousands of tiny particles and flew down the stairs."

My heart started hammering again. "Then what did you do?"

"Came here, obviously." He took my hand and held it lightly in his own.

"Here." My voice was weak and my head swam. "You said it broke right after the lightning?"

He nodded.

"Shit." My skin went cold and the gooseflesh came back. "I called him. That's why he left." My voice shook. "Well, we both did, actually." I tilted my head toward Pyper's room.

Kane's face turned red. I could see him try to control his anger. "Why would you do that on your own? One or both of you could have been seriously hurt."

I threw my hands up in frustration. "Because we're both sick of being out of control. I guess I figured if we called him, we might have the upper hand."

"And did you?" He looked skeptical.

"In the end, yes I did." I smiled with satisfaction and filled the three of them in on what happened.

When I finished, Ian stopped his frantic recording of my account, put his notebook down and looked at me thoughtfully.

"What?" I asked.

"I was just thinking about the timetable of events. It seems we were encountering something in your apartment at the same time something was going on with Pyper when Kane came to get us."

"Can a ghost be in two places at once?" It seemed unlikely to me.

Ian scratched his chin, pursed his lips and said, "Not that I know of. At least, I've never heard of such a thing. But if it's the same ghost—"

I cut him off. "It is. I saw him materialize in front of me. I recognized him."

"I know, I heard. What I was going to say is, if the same ghost has connected with both of you, I wonder if he can be in one person's mind, while physically somewhere else. Like in Pyper's mind, while interacting with you in your apartment. That would take a lot of energy. More than I've ever encountered."

Kane and I started asking questions at the same time. Then a movement caught my eye. I glanced up to see Pyper, emerging from her room. She'd changed into tiny black hot-pants and a large gray sweatshirt.

"What the hell are you wearing?" I asked in disbelief. "You're not going to work at the club after all of that, are you?"

She rolled her eyes. "What am I supposed to do? Sit around here and waste my life waiting for more abuse?"

"Make her not go," I demanded, turning to Kane. "She's in no shape to be dealing with the club. Take her home or out to eat or something, but do not let her go to work."

He patted my hand like a father would his daughter. "Of course I won't let her work. Pyper, are you insane?"

"I hear that's up for debate." She flipped her pink hair over her shoulder and headed for the door.

Kane leaped up from the couch, scooting in front of her. He folded his arms over his chest and stared her down. "Charlie's there. She's got it covered."

Pyper narrowed her eyes, pointed her finger and walked right up to him. "You cannot keep handing everything off to Charlie, Kane. It isn't right." She stabbed him in the chest. "That girl deserves a raise and a promotion based on how much you take advantage of her."

"Done," he said.

Pyper took a step back, clearly not ready for that. "You gave her a raise and a promotion?"

"Not yet. But I've been planning to."

"Oh." Pyper backed off. "But you better give her a bonus or something for time already served."

Kane looked up, as if to ask God for help, or patience. "Fine. Just stay here until we're ready to go." He strode off toward his part-time room.

"Go? Go where?" She turned in his direction and found John staring at her ass, camera pointed and ready. "Jesus, just take the damn picture already." She stripped off her sweatshirt, revealing a black lace push-up bra, and posed, sticking her ass right in John's face.

I covered my mouth to hide the laughter bubbling up. John's face went beet-red as he stood, staring.

"Hurry up. I'm freezing." Pyper reached around, snapping her fingers in front of his eyes a few times.

John quickly snapped the picture, then retreated to Ian, who made no effort to hide his laughter on the other side of the room.

Kane cleared his throat and gestured to Pyper. "If you want to put some more clothes on, the three of us—" he nodded, indicating me, "—should get some food." His tone of voice made it more of an order than a statement.

"What's wrong with my outfit?" Pyper cooed from the chair.

Kane rolled his eyes, and I shrugged.

"Oh, all right." She bounced off to her bedroom, clearly feeling more like herself.

"Would you mind if we stayed to do more readings?" Ian asked.

"Fine," Kane answered. "Stay as long as you like. The girls can stay at my place."

Kane glanced at me in question. Despite my earlier concerns that he might be a link with the pain the ghost was causing, I nodded in agreement. I wasn't up for an argument, nor did I want to be alone.

Chapter 14

With a promise from Ian he'd call sometime the next day, we left in search of food. An hour later we sat at Kane's table with takeout from the Gumbo Shop. The conversation was nonexistent, as the three of us sat pretending to be absorbed in our meals. Letting out a barely audible sigh, Pyper picked up her plate and carried it into the living room, where she curled up in the overstuffed chair. I wanted to do the same but decided she might like a bit of time to herself.

I looked up to find Kane watching me intently. I gave him a weak smile and asked, "Wine?"

Without saying a word he rose, grabbed a bottle of red and two glasses from his wine rack. A small pop sounded, causing Pyper to look our way. Kane held the bottle up in question, but she shook her head and went back to moving the etouffee around on her plate. After handing me a full glass, Kane set the bottle on the table, sat down next to me and focused on my face as he sipped.

"Thank you." I raised my glass slightly.

He gave me a small nod, still staring.

The heat rose to my face as I examined the blackened swordfish on my plate. It was one of my favorites, but it sat untouched. "Stop," I said in a low voice.

"Stop what?"

Whipping my head up, I looked him straight in the eye. "You know damn well what. Stop staring at me like that."

"Am I making you nervous?"

"No."

"If you say so."

I glared at him.

Kane scooted closer, bringing his face mere inches from mine. "I wanted to get your attention."

"There are easier ways."

He shrugged. "This was a pretty low-level effort for me."

My eyes slanted. "Now that you have my attention…"

"I just wanted you to know. What we started last night and this morning isn't over." He brought his face so close, I could almost feel the smooth silk of his lips.

I jerked back. "No? I don't think that's for you to say."

"I do. I know there's something different about you. I just don't know what yet."

A chill ran up my spine. "You mean, apart from my ghost-attracting abilities?"

He took his time before he spoke. "No, Jade. This isn't about your ghost. I can sense your energy. I don't know how to explain it, but even if I can't see you, I always know when you're around."

The statement couldn't have surprised me more. It hit me hard as if he'd punched me in the gut. "You do? How?" Mortified, I gnawed on my lower lip, suddenly very interested in my hands now lying in my lap.

I risked a glance, catching his eye.

He shrugged. "I don't know. I just feel it. Probably the same way you feel me while I'm dreamwalking."

"Does this happen with anyone else? Can you sense Pyper?"

"No. I've never experienced this before. It's something special about you."

I stood up and carried my dishes to the sink. How could I possibly tell him about my own abilities? I knew my invasion of his privacy was just as bad as his dreamwalking, but I'd told myself I didn't do it on purpose. Of course he'd said he didn't either, he just didn't do anything to stop it. Well, neither had I. Worse, I hadn't even wanted to, until this morning when things got too intense. My stomach knotted, making me glad I hadn't eaten much.

Overcome with emotion, my eyes filled. I blinked rapidly, trying to keep the tears at bay.

Kane walked up behind me. "Jade, are you going to tell me about it?"

"I'm sorry," I said, so low even I could barely hear it. I turned around, realizing he deserved an honest answer. But I just couldn't tell him. The last person I'd told was Dan, and that had turned out disastrous. In my heart I knew Kane was different. He wasn't likely to cast me aside. I just wasn't ready to face what I'd done, especially after how I'd reacted to his confession. "I really am sorry. I just can't talk about it right now." Unable to hold it back, a single tear fell down my cheek.

Cupping my face with his palm, he caught the tear with his thumb. "There's no need to be sorry," he said softly. "We'll talk later. It's all right."

The tenderness made the tears flow fast and hot. His arms wrapped around me, pulling me close. For the first time all day I felt safe. My world narrowed to all things Kane. His fresh scent. The hand gently stroking my hair. The way he held me, patiently waiting until my tears were spent.

Finally I removed myself and made my way to his bathroom. After a long, hot shower, I changed into a T-shirt and a pair of Kane's boxers and returned to the living room.

The two of them were huddled together, talking quietly. The image gave me a small jolt, reminding me how close they really were. I was in danger here and didn't know how to stop my growing emotions. They both said they were just friends, and I didn't have any reason to think otherwise, but my rational mind wasn't convincing my inner jealous woman.

Not wanting to interrupt, I tried to make my way quietly to the guest bedroom.

"Where are you going?" Kane asked just as I was about to open the bedroom door. Caught. Damn.

I put a smile on my face before turning around and said, "To bed. I could really use a good night's sleep."

"In there?" the two asked in unison.

"Uh, yeah. Is that a problem?"

Kane gazed at me with an intense look, while Pyper glanced back and forth between the two of us.

Kane turned to Pyper. "And where are you sleeping?"

"Here, I guess." She patted the couch cushions and failed at the attempted smile, resulting in a smirk.

'No," I said quickly. "You can sleep in here." I pointed to the queen-sized bed through the now-open door. "I don't mind sharing. As long as you don't snore." I teased.

Pyper lifted her eyebrows, questioning Kane.

He stared at the ceiling. "It's college all over again."

"Huh?" I asked.

Pyper giggled and punched his arm. "Get over it already." She turned toward me. "I dated one of his ex-girlfriends in college."

"Dated? More like stole," Kane said.

"You can't steal someone from someone else, Kane," Pyper replied.

"Close enough."

"Umm…" I didn't know what to say.

"Don't worry. I haven't hit on a girl in ages, and I'm not going to start with Jade." Pyper turned to me. "I don't mind sharing if you don't."

"Not at all." I waved as I turned toward the room.

'I'll be right there," Pyper called.

"Take your time. Once I'm asleep there's no waking me up. I closed the door behind me and crawled into bed.

The dream came on in a vibrant cascade of soft white light. My awareness floated somewhere near the ceiling, giving me a clear view of the room. There I was, snuggled up with a pillow, Pyper curled up next to me. Beautiful light illuminated both of our faces. We looked so peaceful. The light was like a protective layer of warmth and love. As my awareness drifted back to my body I spotted Mr. Sexy at the foot of the bed, keeping a watchful eye over us. The last thing I saw before I drifted back into unconsciousness was a small reassuring smile from him.

I woke, feeling thick and groggy. The sun was doing its best to shine through the shade on the window. Blinded with sleep, I stumbled to the bathroom to complete my morning ritual. When I'd finished I found Pyper sitting in an armchair in the corner, waiting.

"Morning. The bathroom is all yours." I shuffled over to the bag Kane had packed for me the day before and found a blue cotton skirt and form-fitting white tee. He couldn't have done better if I'd given him a list.

"I had a dream," Pyper said, still sitting in her chair.

Her words triggered the memory of my own dream. I stopped rummaging through my bag and sat on the bed opposite her. "And?"

"I slept better last night than I have in weeks. The dream was full of warmth and light. I felt safe, protected even." She gave me a small smile.

I frowned. It made no sense. This was the ghost that had hurt both of us. "I had the same dream. Did you see anyone in it?"

"No. Why, was Kane there?"

I shook my head. "No. Someone else." She tensed. Should I tell her? I bit my lip, then decided she had a right to know. "Our ghost was there, but all I sensed was him protecting us." Her face went white. "Both of us." I added reassuringly.

"Why?"

"I don't know. I really don't, but you felt it just the same way I did. It didn't feel threatening, did it?"

She shook her head.

"It's definitely odd, but better than the alternative, right?"

She plucked at the blanket. "I guess."

"Then let's consider it progress." I stood, not wanting to dwell on it any longer. "Did Kane make something to eat?"

Her lips quirked. "Yes. I don't know what you did to him, but I never got breakfast before."

"Well, *I* didn't steal his girlfriend." I winked and headed for the door. When I glanced back, she stuck out her tongue. I was still chuckling when I found Kane.

"Sleep well?" he asked, giving me a light kiss.

I nodded. "You?"

"No."

"Really? After all that happened yesterday, I'd have thought nothing could keep you up."

"Nothing but the knowledge of the two of you sharing a bed." He gave me a rueful smile and I rolled my eyes.

"Men."

Later that day, Pyper and I worked late closing down the café. I was covering for Holly, who'd been working extra while we played ghost hunter.

"He's coming at five?" Pyper asked, referring to Ian.

"Yep. When he called, he said he wasn't finished analyzing but wanted to share what he had."

"Did you tell Kane?"

"No." That would be counterproductive, since I wanted to avoid him. I still hadn't found the nerve to be honest with him. And as each hour passed, my anxiety about it grew.

"Okay, I'll give him a buzz and let him know."

Great. "I'll just go get cleaned up and meet you back here in about fifteen."

"Sounds good."

I heard the phone ringing as I unlocked my door. "Coming!" I called, as if someone could actually hear me. By the time I got in and picked it up, I'd missed it. "Damn."

The message was from Kat, wanting to see when we could get together. We'd been playing phone tag ever since I'd found her note and gift card. I'd forgiven her after having some distance and did want to see her, but didn't think I'd have enough time to spend on a proper conversation since we hadn't actually spoken in a few weeks. I made a mental note to call her back later.

I changed my clothes and took a few extra moments to reapply my makeup. Just because I wanted to avoid Kane didn't mean I had to look like a slob. On my way back down I grabbed a six-pack of beer and a bottle opener. Something told me getting results sober was a bad idea.

Once inside the café, I took a seat between Ian and Pyper and popped the cap on my Guinness. "Anyone?"

Pyper grabbed a bottle. Kane got up and poured himself coffee.

"Not yet." Ian passed out a pile of graphs and charts to each of us. "Let me get through this first. Does everyone have this sheet?" He held up a color-coded chart.

We each nodded.

"Good. This graph here shows the level of assumed paranormal activity when Jade was in her apartment. Do you see how it spikes when she speaks?"

The graph peaked in several places. "All of these are only when I was talking?" I asked.

"Yes. Except for here at the end of the chart—it peaks higher than any of them. That happened right after you left the room to find Pyper."

"When we were trapped in the apartment," Kane said.

"Right." Ian said.

"This just confirms my ghost was in my apartment and stayed there when I left." I shrugged. This wasn't anything we hadn't already suspected.

"Yes it does. But what's more interesting is this." He pulled out a second graph. "This one is the readings from right after we found the two of you in Pyper's apartment."

The graph was similar to the first, but had about twice as many peaks as the first one.

"Each peak is when either Pyper or Jade spoke, but no one else." Ian eyed my beer.

I held it up, offering, but he waved me off.

"So, the ghost is…what? Giving off energy when either Jade or I speak?" Pyper asked.

"Yes. He's responding to your voice or energy. The only other time we see a spike is when he trapped us in the apartment." Ian held up another graph. "Now, check this out. This one is after you both left for the night. Not only are there no peaks, but there isn't any paranormal activity at all."

"This was from Pyper's apartment?" I asked, looking it over.

"No, both. Your apartment too."

"You're saying he's only present around either me or Pyper?"

"From what we have here, yes. But we can't be totally sure. I wish we'd thought to get a reading of Pyper while we were getting that first reading with you. It would answer some questions."

"What questions?" Kane asked.

"I'd like to get a reading on both Pyper and Jade at the same time, but in different areas of the building. We don't have a clear idea how Pyper could be haunted in her dreams, while Jade is interacting with him at the same time. If I could get some more readings—"

"What would happen in these readings?" Pyper asked, cutting him off.

"Pretty much the same as what we did with Jade. We'd take readings and have each of you speak to him to see the response."

"What exactly will that accomplish?"

"It'll help us understand what's going on," Ian said.

"So?" Pyper asked.

Ian pursed his lips. "So, don't you want to know what's going on?"

"No." Pyper stood up. "I want him to leave me alone. Will answering your questions make him stay away from me?"

"Uh…" Ian cleared his throat. "I can't say, really. It might give us some insight on when and why he attacks."

"Haven't you been listening? He attacks me every time I sleep, with the exception of last night. If you don't have a solution for getting rid of him permanently then I'm out." Pyper grabbed her beer and stalked to the back room.

"Ian," I said. "Do you know how to exorcise a ghost?"

He rolled his shoulders. "To be honest, I've never had a case this intense. Usually we just ask the spirit to back off and it does. Mostly I've been just recording information and trying to understand it." He paused. "This case is really intriguing and I didn't stop to think about how it's affecting the two of you."

Perfect. All this time, I'd been putting my trust in him as the experienced ghost hunter, and he didn't have any better understanding about what to do than we did. "Last night I pretty much demanded he stop hurting Pyper, and he did. Do you think that did the trick? He did leave her alone last night." I met Kane's eyes when a mixture of worry and gratitude radiated from him.

"Maybe. Only time will tell." Ian stood up, grabbing his papers. "In the meantime, I'll try some of my contacts about what else can be done if need be."

"Okay, thanks."

He reached over and gave me a tight hug and left.

Jealousy rolled off Kane, but his face never changed. I hid a smile as I drank the rest of my beer.

"I'd like it if you and Pyper stayed at my place for a while," Kane said.

"Are you thinking of a threesome? 'Cause I got to say, I'm not into that sort of thing."

"No." He rolled his eyes. "I'd just feel better if you were both nearby where I could keep an eye on you."

"The apartment here is close enough." When he opened his mouth to speak again I cut him off. "Look, Kane, I appreciate the thought. Really, I do. But I'm not afraid of the ghost. After Pyper was attacked yesterday we realized he's only attacked me when I've been close with you." I paused. "Maybe it's better if we have a little space and see what happens."

He opened his mouth, closed it, then nodded.

"All right then. Beer?" I held one out.

"No thanks." He got up and walked out.

Heaving a huge sigh, I picked up the remaining bottles and went to find Pyper.

"Hey. Want to come back to my place and get stupid drunk?"

Pyper straightened and grinned. "That's the best invitation I've had all month." She eyed the bottles. "But we'll need more than what you've got there. Let's make a stop in the club."

Chapter 15

A rhythmic pounding entered my awareness. I rolled over, groaning. What the hell? I heard a muffled voice, shot up in bed and winced when I banged my elbow while fumbling with the light. Once fully awake, I realized someone was banging on my door.

"Jade? Jade? Open up."

"Hold on. Just a sec." Hastily wrapping my naked body in a short robe, I took the four steps to the door and opened it to find Pyper. Dark circles rimmed her red, puffy eyes on her pasty white face. "Are you all right?" I asked, pulling her in.

She clutched a thin cotton robe and in a small voice said, "He's back."

"Fuck."

She nodded and curled up on my couch in a fetal position. "The last time I slept was here."

I sat on the arm of the couch next to her, recalling when we'd swiped booze from the club and stayed up half the night giggling. "That was four days ago."

She gave a small incoherent sound before closing her eyes. "It's hot in here."

"The air conditioner isn't working."

"You should tell Kane." Her voice was weak, barely a whisper.

Pyper was right, of course, but since I was avoiding him I was suffering in the heat. Stupid, yes. But I was willing to wait it out a little longer. I got up and pointed my rotating fan toward her. Then, reaching for a pillow, I gently lifted her head and placed it under her. She snuggled into it and sighed. I stayed perched next to her until I heard the deep rhythmic breathing of sleep.

Standing next to my open balcony window, I gazed down at the moonlit courtyard. Why was he tormenting her? Since the day I had physically called him, Mr. Sexy had only appeared in my dreams to watch over me. In a comforting way though, not a creepy stalker way, as if he was protecting me. I think I should have been creeped out, but I wasn't. I actually felt comforted and safe.

I checked on Pyper once more then pulled on a tank top and cotton bikinis and crawled back into bed. Too hot for covers, I stretched out on the top sheet and closed my eyes.

I woke to the smell of fresh coffee. "Yum. You can stay forever."

"If I'd known it was that easy, I'd have made you breakfast in bed weeks ago."

My eyes flew open. Kane stood next to me with a coffee mug. With a glance, I found my tank top had shimmied up, just barely covering my breasts. *Crap.* I jumped up, barely missed knocking the cup out of Kane's hands, and put on my robe.

"I liked the other view better, but this is nice too." He held the cup out to me.

"Did you say something about breakfast?" I took the coffee, avoiding eye contact.

"I brought bagels. It's too hot to cook. Why didn't you tell me the air wasn't working?"

I shrugged and moved over to the counter. "Where's Pyper?"

"She went down to the coffee shop. She asked me to bring you breakfast as a thank you."

Noticing for the first time the bright sun shining through the window, I whirled around to look at my alarm clock. Seven a.m. "Oh, thank God. I still have an hour."

"'Til what?"

"I have a class to teach. Thanks for coming by and for the breakfast, but I really need to get ready to go." It wasn't going to take me that long to shower and get dressed, but I didn't want to be alone with him. I still needed time to sort out my emotions, which were running rampant at the moment.

So were his, but I was trying to block them out. It was overwhelming. While he was cool and calm on the outside, desire raged on the inside. And feeling it was having a profound effect on my willpower.

Not waiting for Kane to leave, I locked myself in the bathroom and turned the shower taps on high. When the cold water hit my body, I think steam actually radiated off me.

Ten minutes later I emerged, wrapped in my tiny robe. I kicked myself for not remembering to take clothes into the bathroom. There just wasn't enough material, considering all the sparks flying around. Peeking around the corner, I found an empty room. Relief rushed over me as I realized Kane must have left. As I sat on my bed, a note on the nightstand caught my eye.

Jade, I will see about getting the air fixed or replaced today. You should have called as soon as it stopped working.
K.

I frowned, feeling slightly ashamed. I should've called. I should've been more gracious this morning as well. Vowing to behave better, I dressed quickly and grabbed the bagels on my way out the door.

Holly was busy taking orders, while Pyper handled three different coffee drinks at the same time. The line of customers snaked right out the front door. Grabbing an apron to help them out for a bit before my class, I jumped in next to Pyper and packed grounds into the espresso machine as fast as I could.

"Is it always this busy on Saturday?" I asked.

"Yes." She gave me a grateful smile. I was happy to see the circles under her eyes were lighter, though not gone. One night of sleep wasn't going to make up for missing days.

I smiled back and filled three cups full of ice to finish off the iced café au laits I was working on.

Within twenty minutes the line worked its way down to something manageable. I stepped into the back to hang up my apron and by the time I returned, Holly's posture had relaxed and she was smiling at something Pyper had said.

"What's up?" I asked.

"Pyper was just telling me she spent the night with you last night." She gave me a sly knowing smile. "I didn't know it was like that."

Huh? What was she talking about?

Pyper reached over and lightly smacked her on the back of the head. "No! I slept on her couch after waking her up in the middle of the night. Besides, she has a thing with Kane. Where have you been?"

"Kane?" She turned to me, wearing a startled expression. "Sorry" she said. "I didn't know." Turning on her heel, she walked purposefully into the back.

"What was that about?" I asked Pyper.

She shook her head. "No idea."

"Feeling better this morning?" I wanted to ask about the events of the last four nights, but customers kept streaming through the door.

"Yes, better. I don't usually need much sleep, but I do need *some*." She bagged up a few muffins and passed them to a waiting customer.

"Uh, Pyper?" I edged my way closer to her. She looked up and I asked, "Do you think you should tell Ian he hasn't left you alone?" I didn't think he would have any answers, but I didn't know what else to do.

Her shoulders slumped. "He'll only want to do more readings." Just then, two couples walked in the door. She stepped back to the register, ready for their order.

She had a point. Last I spoke with Ian, he still didn't have a plan to help us exorcise the ghost. I'd have to call and light a fire under him. In the meantime, I'd ask Bea if she had any ideas. Any witch worth her salt would know something about ghosts.

I checked my watch. Eight o'clock. Time to get to the studio. I grabbed my purse and stopped next to Pyper, putting a hand on her arm. "You're welcome at my place anytime."

She nodded slightly and put on a bright smile for her patrons. "What can I get y'all today?"

My stop at the café left me with no time to spare. I arrived at the studio just as Bea and two other students strolled up. My master plan of speaking to Bea about the ghost would have to wait.

The class started out just as fun and easygoing as the previous ones, until my mind started to drift back to Pyper and the ghost. I've always been a good teacher since I can sense frustration, disappointment, satisfaction, and the like, which allows me to provide the feedback needed to fuel a student's learning. But only if I'm paying attention.

"Damn it!"

I focused on Sandy, who was almost completely concealed in a haze of purple. I blinked. What the hell is that? She was surrounded by a bubble of gas-like substance, turning the color of eggplant. Frustration pulsed in time with the bubble, moving like a beating heart. Looking around, it was clear no one but me, and possibly Bea, saw it.

I glanced at Bea, who just smiled and nodded her head in Sandy's direction. Abandoning my post at the other end of the table, I moved closer to the gas cloud. It parted and swirled like a fine mist when I walked up behind her. "How's it going?"

"Argh! Terrible. I just can't make this stringer of glass do what you showed us and now my bead is ruined."

"Let's see." I took the metal mandrel out of her hand and inspected the bead. Green blobs of glass had been smeared haphazardly over one end. "Okay, here's what we can do. Cover up this part with some more white."

She took the mandrel back and started adding some glass to the end I'd indicated.

When she got the section covered, I said, "Now, melt it in nice and smoothe, and roll it out in a barrel shape."

Intent on her task, Sandy did as I said. The gas faded, but not completely.

"But now the bead is bigger than the other one I made."

"So? Just finish this one and make another smaller one, and you'll have a pendant and an earring pair."

"Oh! Cool." She smiled and continued to shape the bead in the flame.

I watched as she rolled the warm glass on a graphite surface. "Next, take that green vine stringer." I pointed to an extra-thin strip of glass. "Bring it as close to the flame as you can without melting it. Remember, it's so thin it'll melt before you actually put it in the flame."

I waited for her to find the spot. When she did I added, "Get your base bead good and hot. Hot enough that it glows orange. That's it. Get your stringer in that magic spot you just found. There you go, touch it to your base bead. Now move the bead, keeping your stringer in that sweet spot. See how the heat of the bead combined with the radiant torch heat melts the stringer? That's what gives you control. Excellent! Nice job!"

The other four students clapped as Sandy held up her bead, with perfect scrolls of vines wrapped around it.

"Wonderful, Sandy!" Bea cheered.

The color around Sandy shifted to very pale lavender and then dissipated.

"Nice," I said. "Now add some dots for flowers, and you're all set."

"Thanks, Jade." Sandy picked up some pink glass, intent on completing her bead.

With the rest of the class happily melting away, I caught Bea's eye. Her white light energy engulfed me, warming me to my toes and leaving me with the impression she'd just given me a mental hug. Cheered, I moved toward one of the other ladies to give more instruction.

When the clock struck twelve-thirty, everyone begged to stay a few more minutes. Feeling pleased and content with their progress, I obliged the request and sat down to finish the wire wrapping of last week's beads.

Just as I finished, white light surrounded me. I looked up. "All done, Bea?"

"For today. Great lesson."

"A little unusual, don't you think?"

"Really? Looked pretty normal to me." Bea watched the last of the students file out.

"Are you trying to tell me you didn't see the purple gas cloud?"

"No. I saw it. I just wanted you to see it."

I stood up. "Why?"

"I wanted to get your attention." Bea took out her keys. "Will you join me for lunch today?"

"Yes." I grabbed my purse and followed her to a sleek Toyota Prius. "Love your car."

"Thanks."

"Did you manufacture the purple gas, or...?"

Bea smiled. "No dear, I just fixed it so you could see it. It wasn't gas, it was her aura."

"And you did something to make me see it? How does that work?" I squinted as her white light grew brighter, making my eyes water. "Stop. I'm going blind over here."

The light faded to more of a soft glow. "Auras feed off energy, and mine is pretty strong after all these years. I can enhance them. Only people with gifts like ours can see them. You just needed a little help."

Gifts like ours. Maybe lunch wasn't such a great idea.

Bea slowed in front of a large Greek revival home in the Garden District, complete with a black iron gate. She hit a remote attached to her visor, and the gates swung open.

"You live here?" I gaped.

She nodded and turned into the circular driveway, passed the main house and pulled up to what is known as a carriage house. In a previous life it would have housed horses and a carriage. She pointed. "This is where I live. The property is family-owned, and my cousins live in the house. I prefer a little privacy."

Following her up the walkway, I breathed in the sweet fragrance from the lush gardens. "This is paradise."

"As close as I'm going to get, I suspect." She unlocked the door. "Come in."

The inviting, pale yellow room had a garden stenciled on one wall and traditional antique furniture. A table sat off to the left, in front of a smallish kitchen painted bright white with glass cabinets.

"It's gorgeous," I said.

Thank you, I painted it myself." She nodded toward the garden stencil. "Are you hungry?"

"Very. Let me help you."

"No need. I have a salad made up. I just need to dish it out on plates. Why don't you go outside and enjoy this lovely day on the porch?" She gestured to a door off the back of the kitchen. "I'll be right out."

The porch was screened in with three large ceiling fans, a must for the heavy summer heat. I sat admiring the small garden and smiled when I noticed a beautiful golden retriever curled up in a patch of shade.

In no time Bea emerged with a large tray of salads and freshly squeezed lemonade.

"This looks wonderful. Thank you," I said.

"You're welcome. Thanks for coming to visit. I have wanted to talk with you for a while now." She took a slice of bread.

"What about?"

She forced a smile. "My brother."

I furrowed my eyebrows together. "Your brother?"

She nodded, her smile still plastered on her face. "Yes. I wanted to know how he's been treating you."

Putting down my fork, I stared at her. "Who's your brother?"

"Robert Wilson. Or Bobby is what I called him." Bea's smile faded into a sad wistful expression.

"I'm sorry. I don't know a Robert or a Bobby." I had no idea where she was going with this. Maybe she was confused.

"You do. You just didn't know that's his name."

"Who are you talking about?"

She picked up her lemonade glass, took a long sip and carefully placed it on the table. "Have you ever known a ghost before, Jade?"

A shiver shook my body as her words sank in. "Known? No, but I've seen one."

Bea nodded. She held her hand up indicating I should wait and then disappeared into her house. She returned, holding a silver picture frame. "Do you recognize this man?"

I gasped. "That's my ghost." I took the frame from her, studying it in detail. There he was. My Mr. Sexy, standing next to a much younger-looking Bea. "When was this taken?"

"Over thirty years ago." Her eyes stayed on the picture. "That was just before he died."

"Thirty years ago," I said in a soft voice. I looked up. "How did you know?"

Her eyes rose to mine. "Bobby followed you out of The Herbal Connection that day you came in."

Setting the frame on the table, I leaned back. "He followed me?" My eyebrows raised in disbelief.

"Yes. I knew right away you had a gift. I just wasn't sure what it was."

"You think ghosts are my gift?" Maybe she didn't know about my other talent.

"Oh, it's one of them, but not the main one." Her smile returned, only this time it looked natural.

"And?"

Ignoring my question, she picked up the photo. "Is he treating you well?"

"Um, he's been…interesting." How could I tell her about what he did to Pyper? Or me, for that matter.

"Interesting?"

I shook my head. "Never mind. Why did he follow me?"

"Because of your energy, of course." She said it as if talking to a simpleton.

Like that cleared things up. "Has he done this before?"

"No. For thirty years he's been a presence in my life as a spirit. Mostly he hung out at the shop, as he seemed to enjoy the interaction with people. That day you walked in I knew you were special, but when Bobby followed you out...well, I just needed to find out more about you."

"And that's why you signed up for my class?" I asked, making the belated connection.

"Yes."

"I thought it was a bit of a coincidence." I glanced at the photo again. "Why me? I've never collected a ghost before."

"Well," Bea paused, "As I said your energy probably attracted him."

"But—"

"And the way you look."

"The way I look?" I frowned.

Bea got up. "I'll be right back." She disappeared into the house.

I set my fork down, pushed the plate away and got up to pace the garden. Why did the ghost choose me? Surely I wasn't the only one with interesting energy to ever walk into The Herbal Connection. Was there something about my particular ability that attracted him? Rounding a corner, I eyed the large golden retriever bounding up to me.

"Hi, cutie pie." I smiled and reached down to pet it. Just as I thought I would connect with its head, it vanished. "What the hell?" I jumped up, looking around.

"What is it?" Bea came around the hedge.

"Where did the dog go?"

"What dog?" Bea frowned.

"The golden retriever," I said still searching.

"You saw a golden retriever?"

I nodded.

"Oh wow." Bea grinned.

"Wow, what? What the hell is going on?" Agitation took over.

Bea waved me over. "Come back to the table. I have something to show you."

As I reclaimed my seat she handed me another old photo in a silver frame. "Take a look at this."

"Oh my God! Who is this?" I pointed to the strawberry-blond woman standing next to Bobby.

"It's a remarkable likeness, isn't it?"

I gaped.

"That was his wife," Bea said.

"*Was* his wife? Is she—"

"She's still living, but she moved up north years ago. After Bobby died, she couldn't stand being here, so she moved to be closer to her family. I haven't talked to her in years. But you look just like her."

"I guess that explains why he attached himself to me." I felt downright creepy now. Visions of our nightly encounters flashed through my mind. Ick. He thought I was someone else.

"Now look at this." She handed me another photo. This one showed Bobby a few years younger and a dog. A golden retriever.

"No way." I set the picture down.

"I'd say it has to be him. His name was Duke, and he belonged to Bobby."

"Have you seen him lurking around?"

"No. Never." She shrugged. "But they lived in the big house, not this one."

I got up and moved around the hedge. The golden retriever was sitting exactly where I'd seen him before he vanished. "Heya, Duke." The large golden dog lifted his head in response. "So it's true." How freaking odd! Just then my pants started to vibrate. I jumped, forgetting I'd set my phone on vibrate before class started. "Oh crap." I laughed and pulled it out of my pocket. "Excuse me a moment."

Bea nodded.

I strode across the lawn. "Hello."

"Hey, girlfriend," Kat said. "Long time no see."

"Hey, yourself. Phone tag was getting old. Where are you?"

"Whole Foods, where are you?"

"At Bea Kelton's house in the Garden District."

"Who?" she asked.

"A student. She owns The Herbal Connection and asked me for lunch."

"That's, cool. I called because I wanted your help with something. What are you doing later?"

"I was planning a nice long soak in my tub." I eyed Duke as he moseyed up to me.

"Do you think you can put it off? I need something special for an order, and I want to raid your bead stash." Kat was a silversmith and periodically bought glass beads for her jewelry line.

"Sure. I don't know when I'll be home, though. I'll need to get a ride from Bea."

"You're on my way. I can pick you up."

"Perfect." I walked back to Bea, relayed the address and sat down at the table. "My friend Kat is on her way. I hope that's okay."

"Of course."

I pushed the lettuce around on my plate and for the first time that afternoon I realized I wasn't getting any of her emotions.

"Bea, what is it about this place? It's…different." I wasn't sure what to say. I was seeing ghosts, and my emotional radar was out. Not that I minded. It was kind of nice to not be tuned in.

"It's a protection ward. I like the silence."

Uh, okay. A protection ward. She had to be a paranoid witch. I started to get really uncomfortable. I'd known plenty of witches, and they scared the crap out of me. And for good reason. They were the reason I'd lost my mom.

"What's wrong?" Bea peered at me.

"Nothing. I just—wait, can you see Duke?" The retriever had moved and was currently sitting next to me.

"No. Is he here?" she asked, looking around.

"Yes." I pointed to my feet, then looked up and swallowed. "And now Bobby is sitting next to you." Did he follow me everywhere? This was too weird.

She turned to the empty chair and chanted something under her breath I didn't understand. The warm air chilled, and Bea's anxious excitement washed over me. Bobby's outline grew stronger. The golden retriever bounded up to him, tongue wagging. He reached down to pet him with a grin on his face.

I jumped again when the phone started vibrating.

"Kat?"

"I'm out front. Are you ready?"

"Yes, I'll be right there." Flipping the phone closed, I turned to Bea. "My friend is here."

Disappointment swirled around her, but her smile didn't waiver. "Of course."

I took a deep breath. "Before I go, there's something I have to ask."

She sat up and nodded.

"Does Bobby have any history of violence?"

Her brow creased. Defensiveness crept into her voice. "No. Not ever. Why would you ask that?"

Closing my eyes, I forced the words out. "He's been hurting my friend, Pyper. It happens in her sleep unless she's near me."

Fierce denial engulfed me, squeezing until I sputtered, "Bea, stop. Please."

Her energy vanished. Gooseflesh popped out on my bare arms. "I'm sorry," she said, her voice stiff. "I have trouble believing Bobby would ever hurt anyone."

I stood on shaking legs. "Thank you for having me and telling me about him."

She stared across the yard with unfocused eyes. After a moment she spoke in a detached eerie tone. "I sense the truthfulness of your words, though what you believe to be true doesn't make it so." She turned back to me. Her expression cleared. "Please ask your friend if we can meet. I'll see what I can do."

"I will. I'll call you tonight. Thank you." I gave her a tentative wave as I crossed the yard, making a beeline for Kat's car.

"Thank God you're here. That place was starting to freak me out," I said, jumping into the passenger side.

"Why?" Kat put the car in gear and drove off.

"She's a witch."

"Really? Did she tell you that?" Kat glanced my way.

"Not in so many words, but she lifted a *ward*. I know she has some kind of special powers, but we didn't talk about it." I flipped the visor down to cut out the sun. My eye caught something in the rearview mirror. I groaned.

"What?" Kat asked.

"I just inherited a ghost dog." Duke was in the back seat, his head hanging out the window.

"So, you're saying Ms. Kelton's dead golden retriever followed you home?" Kat sat cross-legged on the hardwood, pawing through my bead stash. Since I didn't have a dining table, I'd spread out half a dozen trays right there on the floor. She set a few aside and cocked an eyebrow.

"Not exactly," I said as Duke staked out a place on the couch.

"Not exactly? Do you mean you dognapped him?" The incredulous look on her face suggested she thought I was joking.

"No, he jumped in the car, and you drove him here. He followed us up the stairs."

"Are you even allowed pets?" She laughed.

"Ha-ha. Very funny." Frowning, I grabbed a beer and slammed the refrigerator door.

"Oh come on, it was a little funny. Do I get one of those?" She tilted her head toward my Guinness.

I shrugged, stepped out onto my balcony and sat down. Leaning back in my chair, I sighed heavily.

Kat appeared with a beer in her hand. "What is it?" She pulled a chair next to mine.

My eyes filled. I tried to blink back the tears. Breathing deeply, the air came in ragged, short spurts. "Oh, Kat," I whispered as tears streamed uncontrollably down my face.

She shifted and her reassuring hand closed over mine. "It's okay, sweetie," she murmured. "It's going to be okay."

"There's just so much going on. I don't think I can handle much more." I sniffled loudly. "And, now I have a ghost dog!"

Kat squeezed my fingers. "It'll be okay. Bea said she'd help. At least now you know who you're dealing with and why he's attached to you. And a ghost dog is really a great thing, the way I see it."

"Huh?"

"Well, it's a golden, and you love goldens. With a ghost dog, you don't have to feed him, walk him, pick up his shit or even clean up all that hair. You get a companion, and you don't have to worry about how long you leave it home alone, if it'll chew your favorite shoes, track dirt in the house, drool on you or get sick. You don't need a vet or need to register it. Plus, it could still be a guard dog, I suppose. At least, warn you when something isn't right."

My lips quirked as she went on. "Do you suppose he'll still want play toys? What about treats? You know how much goldens like to eat. Maybe you could get plastic doggie treats. That way he can pretend, and you don't have food out rotting. He'll want a doggie bed too, I suppose."

I chuckled. "He's already made himself at home on the couch."

"That didn't take long, did it?" She turned, looking in the window. "Is he on the right side?"

"Nope, left."

"Your couch is sagging then."

"Of course it is. It's used."

She smiled. "You're going to be okay. We'll call Ian with the new info. He keeps saying if he knew why the ghost was here it would help. Maybe this is the piece of the puzzle he needs to finally get something done."

I nodded. "I suppose I should tell Kane, too."

"Why?"

I shrugged. "Just seems like he should know."

Kat got up. "I'm gonna use your bathroom, but when I get back I want the full scoop on Kane. You never gave me all the details."

She went back inside while I dialed Ian and left a detailed message about Bobby and why he was stalking me. Afterward, I called Pyper and filled her in. To my relief she offered to relay the information to Kane.

Then I retrieved Bea's number and was disappointed when her phone automatically when to voicemail. "Hello, Bea. I've talked to Pyper, and we're both anxious to meet with you as soon as possible." I left my number and as I put my phone down, Kat reappeared.

"All right, dish," she said.

Obediently, I replayed the gory details of my short affair with Kane.

"Okay, let me get this straight," Kat said. "You're mad at him for invading your dreams?"

"Yes. Wouldn't you be?"

"With the dreams you described?" She laughed. "No."

I glared at her in exasperation. "It isn't the content of the dreams so much as the invasion."

"Kind of like how you read his emotions and don't tell him?" She raised her brows.

She was right, of course. Hadn't I already had this same debate with myself? Hearing her say it out loud only made me feel worse.

"You're going to tell him, right?" She peered at me.

I slumped, dejected. "You know why I don't tell people."

"Probably some of the same reasons Kane isn't eager to share the details of his gift." Kat leaned back, fingering the top of her beer bottle. "You need to tell him."

"But what if—"

"He's not Dan. So stop the what-ifs right this instant. You can't live your life around how Dan acted. Kane is his own person. You should give him the chance. You might be surprised."

"But I—"

"No buts. I know Dan hurt you. But you have to at least accept that part of the blame was yours for not telling him sooner."

"He cheated on me!" I said, automatically defaulting to my ingrained indignation of how I'd been wronged even though I knew she was right.

"He was hurt, Jade." She took a deep breath. "I know it was wrong. Of course it was. But you kept your gift from him for seven years, if you count the time we were all friends in high school. You've known Kane for, what, two weeks? What if this had been happening for years and he never told you? How would you feel?"

The beer turned stale on my tongue. "Awful. Betrayed. Horrified."

Kat reached her hand out and clasped mine again. "You made a mistake. It's understandable, given your history, but don't let your fears get in the way of a good thing with Kane. If he's so easily scared away, he isn't good enough for you."

I gave her a sad smile. "I really like him."

"I know, honey. That's why you need to tell him." We sat in silence for a long moment, until Kat said, "You'll find a way."

"I hope so."

She grabbed my arm and pulled me back inside. "Enough. Let's go in so I can keep rummaging through your beads."

Hours later, after Kat had left, neither Ian nor Bea had returned my calls.

Chapter 16

A variety of Voodoo dolls lined the windows of The Herbal Connection. I did a double-take and checked the store sign.

"I thought you said this was a new-age shop?" Pyper stood next to me, a skeptical frown on her face.

I'd offered to conduct a cleansing ritual on Pyper to neutralize any negative energy. It was a long shot, but at this point we were ready to try anything. "It was the last time I was here."

"Looks more like Marie Leveau's." The shop named for the famous Voodoo Priestess was located at the other end of Bourbon Street.

I shrugged. "They're probably trying to cater to the tourists."

The door jingled as we walked in, and my skin tingled with pleasure as I inhaled the strong fresh rain scent. Kane's scent. But he was back at the club, which only meant one thing. The store's 'happy place' charm had evoked it. Damn, I was in trouble.

"Do you think that cinnamon chocolate scent is a candle or incense?" Pyper asked.

"I'm sure you can get it in either." If Bea could charm a whole shop, certainly she could do something as simple as a candle. Though I wasn't sure why Pyper would need it. Clearly her happy scent was the café.

A woman at least half Bea's age clad in a chick, stylish, bohemian tunic and leggings greeted us. Now this is the kind of person I expected to see in an herbal shop. Her energy had the same lightness as Bea's, but as I tried to get a read on her emotions all I sensed was a cool void. Weird. I'd never had that happen before.

"Hi," I said. "Is Bea around?"

"Sorry, she didn't come in today. Can I help you?"

"Yes, we need a Desert Sage smudge stick." I pulled a bill out of my wallet, but Pyper put her hand over mine.

"I got it."

I smiled and turned toward the clerk. "I hope Bea isn't sick."

"I'm not really sure. She left me a note letting me know she wouldn't be here, so she either came in last night or this morning. I can leave her a message if you like."

"It's all right, I have her number. Thanks though."

"Anything else?" the clerk asked.

I shook my head.

As she finished the transaction, a small twinge of curiosity flowed from her. I reached deeper to find her emotions and was rewarded with a brilliant white light bouncing off the honey-colored hair piled on top of her head.

"Wow," I said and stepped back.

"What?" Pyper asked.

"Oh, sorry. Nothing." I bit my lip.

The clerk's energy went from white to purple and back to white as she studied me. Realization seemed to dawn and she smiled. "An empath. That explains the bright purple pulsing around you. I can see auras and," she waved her hand, "other things."

I froze. Who *was* she?

She leaned in close to me. "Your friend has something attached to her. Something dark."

"Dark?" I repeated. Did Bobby follow us everywhere?

"Really dark. The worst kind of dark. I'm not sure the smudge will work, but you can try." She looked unconvinced.

"Can you tell what it is?" Pyper turned her head, checking over her shoulder.

"I don't know. It's just black, but it isn't your aura. Yours is red, with tinges of yellow. Very dynamic."

Pyper straightened and smiled. "Really? That's so cool." Apparently her aura trumped the dark thing following her.

"Anything else you'd suggest, besides the smudge?" I glanced around the shop, hoping something would jump out at me.

"You'd be better off asking Bea. If I see her, I'll let her know you could use her advice."

"Thanks." I handed her a card. "I'm Jade, and this is Pyper."

"Nice to meet you. I'm Lailah. Come see me sometime, and I'll read your auras more carefully." She slid a card in the bag and handed it to Pyper.

I waved and tugged Pyper out of the store.

Pyper grabbed a piece of cheese pizza. "Auras, huh? Do you think that stuff is real?"

"Sure, don't you?" I sipped my lemonade. It was just wrong to have pizza without beer, but I couldn't drink and smudge and expect it to be effective.

She shrugged. "I guess I should be open to anything now. Dreamwalking, ghosts and now smudging. Why not auras?"

"Doesn't all this freak you out?" If I hadn't been exposed to all kinds of odd occurrences growing up, I'd be running for the psych ward right about then. Pyper's ability to take everything in stride left me in awe.

"No. Not really." She paused. "All right, the ghost shit does, but the other stuff, no. I think it's kinda cool. It reinforces my belief of all of us being connected. Some of us just see it better than others." Her calm energy floated in soothing waves toward me.

"How can you be so cool about it, with everything happening?"

"I don't know. Maybe it's an act." She grinned.

"It's not. I can see it isn't."

"You're that good at reading people?"

"Yes. I am." I saw no point in denying it.

"Interesting. Anything you want to share?" She peered at me.

"Like what?" I pretended deep interest in my veggie pizza slice.

"Like maybe you want to tell me what an empath is and what was going on back there?" Her eyes gleamed.

Shit. I'd been hoping with the whole aura thing, she'd forgotten that comment. Lailah pulled me out of the closet with one reading of my aura. I'd had my aura read once before and already knew it was purple. But that just means intuitive. It doesn't mean empath. How did she know?

"Come on, Jade." Pyper set her food down, giving me her undivided attention.

I took a deep breath. The last person I'd told about my gift was Dan. Look at how well that had turned out. "I guess Lailah can see people's auras."

"That part I got."

"She also said she sees other things, and apparently she saw something dark attached to you." I stalled.

"Right, I have a dark ghost following me. That isn't news. That's why I'm staying with you. What's so special about you that makes him behave?" Her eyes bored into mine.

"There isn't anything special about me!" Warped maybe. Or flawed. But not special. And certainly nothing that would keep evil ghosts away.

"That's crap, and you know it. Hell, I knew it the first time I met you. Look at Kane and how he's fallen for you. And Charlie, she's friendly and outgoing, but she doesn't respect a lot of people. And she respects and admires you, Jade Calhoun. There's something very special about you, even if you don't see it." She stopped to catch her breath. "Now, what's an empath, cause I didn't forget."

Stunned, I let her words sink in. For the first time in my life, I had a network of friends and hadn't even realized it. Something unlocked in my heart, and the last of my resolve melted. "An empath is someone who feels other people's emotions as they feel them."

"Kind of like being around a happy person can make you happy? Infectious energy stuff?"

"Yeah." I laughed humorlessly. "Only normal people get a small fraction of that transfer. Empaths, people like me, get a full force version whether we want to or not."

Pyper leaned in, giving me her full attention. Curiosity bubbled up, replaced by empathy gliding off her and swirling around my center. "So when people near you are upset, you feel their pain?"

I nodded. "And for people I have a close relationship with, like Aunt Gwen, sometimes I feel her emotions no matter where she is."

"Oh, Jade. You poor thing. Is there anything you can do to block it out?"

Her sympathy wrapped me in a blanket, and I let myself cherish the sensation. Not that I wanted to be pitied, but I'd never had someone understand that terrible part of my existence so quickly. I cleared the newly formed lump in my throat. "Yes, I can build defenses, but it's draining. And sometimes if an emotion hits me too hard, I can't block it out."

She squeezed my fingers and let go. "But you also feel joy and happiness too, right?"

"Sure. Those are great, kind of like a natural high, but that wears me out, too. Too much outside emotional energy is exhausting. Then I can't block anything, and that can be destructive." I looked down at my half-eaten pizza and pushed it away, no longer hungry.

Pyper didn't say anything and when I risked a peek, she met my eyes and said, "It's a gift, Jade. But it isn't what makes you special."

One tear rolled silently down my face.

She moved her chair next to mine and used a napkin to catch it. "Honey, I don't know what happened in your past to make you think this was something to be hidden or ashamed of—"

"I'm not ashamed."

"Okay, guarded. How's that?"

I nodded. "Guarded."

"But you're part of our family now. You must know we accept you for who or what you are, no matter what. There's no need to hide from us. Kane, me, Charlie, even Holly."

"Holly hates me." I sniffed.

"Of course she doesn't."

I raised an eyebrow.

Pyper smiled. "Hate is a very strong word."

"Right, but I don't think she sees me as part of the family."

"Well, maybe not, but she likes you better than you think." Pyper stood up. "Come on, let's get out of here and get this smudge thing done. I'm tired of my black shadow."

Two days later I stood at the cash register of the café, stifling a huge yawn.

"You look like you're ready to fall over," Pyper said.

I nodded, wiping down the counter. I'd seen my reflection in the mirror. It wasn't pretty. The smudge hadn't worked, and Pyper had taken up residence, sleeping on my couch. She was no trouble, but the dog was constantly barking at her—or, more likely, her black shadow. I'd performed a ritual to ask the dog to move on, but it hadn't worked. Without any other options, I'd been afraid Pyper would feel pressured to leave. So, I just didn't tell her about it.

"Am I keeping you awake?" Pyper stepped close to me.

"No, no." Another yawn took hold, causing my eyes to water.

"I don't believe you. I should stay at my own place tonight."

"No! That's not an option." We were stuck in a holding pattern. Bea and Ian were still MIA. We'd each called Ian, with no answer. I'd called Bea and left numerous messages. When she didn't call back, I'd stopped by her house, but she hadn't been home. Then I'd tried her shop again. Lailah didn't know much.

She'd gotten a message Bea was unavailable for a few days. In the meantime, I wouldn't let Pyper out of my sight.

"It's Kane, right? That's what's keeping you up. I know he hasn't called you or stopped by. The ass."

"No. It isn't. I asked him for space." It was true. I had asked him, and he was giving it to me. Be careful what you wish for. He hadn't even shown up in my dreams. Though Bobby was still there, watching.

"But—"

"It's the ghost dog." I cut her off before she could work herself up further. "Duke, the ghost dog. He barks all the time while you're there. He just won't stop."

"Oh." She chuckled then sobered. "I'm sorry, it's not funny."

"It's kinda funny, except I'm about to pass out."

Pyper looked thoughtful. "Do you think it would help if we had separate bedrooms? I mean, if we stayed in my apartment, do you think I'd still be able to sleep? Maybe the dog will sleep in your room with you. Do ghosts sleep?"

"I don't know about ghosts, but Duke certainly looks like he does. That dog lies around all the time." I shrugged. "I'm up for trying it, if you are. You have a lot more to lose than I do."

"It's worth a shot."

Later that night, while Pyper went to work at Wicked, I curled up in Kane's bed once again and was rewarded with the faint whiff of his scent. I hadn't realized how much I'd missed him until that moment. A hollow ache formed deep in my heart.

I closed my eyes and did my best to put Kane out of my mind. Within moments Bobby's soothing image stood before me. I don't know how long I slept before the barking started. Damn dog. I got up and followed the noise to the living room.

"Hi, Pyper." I waved.

"Did I wake you up?" Her worry seeped into my consciousness.

"No. It was the dog. I've come to collect him. Come on, Duke. Let's go." He trotted over to me and disappeared in the bedroom. "Want me to stay up until you go to sleep, just in case?"

Worry swirled around her, but stubbornness quickly took over. "No. I'll wake up fast if it doesn't work."

Too tired to argue, I nodded. "Okay. Goodnight then."

"Night."

I fell right back to sleep. Bobby watched over me as usual, with Duke lying at his feet. The bliss seemed to last for hours, until the light around Bobby brightened to a reddish glow and the calm turned anxious. I rolled over, restless and knocked my head against something hard.

"Ouch. Damn it."

"Hey," a gruff voice said. "Are you all right?"

Kane's distinct energy engulfed me. "Was that your head?" I asked.

"Yes." He ran his hand lightly over my skull. "No large bumps. I think you'll live." He wrapped his arm around my shoulder and I snuggled in closer.

"Good." I closed my eyes hoping for more sleep, but his intruding desire snapped me awake. "Wait, why are you here?"

"There's a storm raging and rather than take a cab home, I decided this sounded much nicer."

"But you're avoiding me."

"I was giving you space."

"And now?" I sat up.

"Now I'm not giving you space." He pulled me back down into his arms and crushed my lips with his.

Shocked, I didn't move, but when I felt his tongue searching I kissed him back with just as much intensity. His heart pounded against my breast. I pressed closer as his desire overpowered all my other senses. That alone was enough to send my blood pumping.

Kane rolled me over, trapping me beneath him, hands everywhere. My thoughts jumbled, and I wanted nothing but him.

"God, Jade, I've missed you. I've been—"

A high-pitched screaming sounded through the wall.

Kane froze.

I pushed him off of me, jumped up, ran to the other room and yelled, "Pyper! Wake up, honey, wake up!"

Her screams stopped, and a second later her eyes fluttered open. "There you are."

"Jade. What happened?"

"I don't know, sweetie. You'd been sleeping for a while, but then you just started screaming. Can you tell me anything?"

Kane brushed my arm as he moved to sit next to Pyper.

"I don't know. I was feeling peaceful, like I always do when I sleep at your place, then all of a sudden the calm disappeared and hell took over." She clutched the covers to her chest. Kane reached out, running a hand over her leg.

I joined him on the edge of the bed. "I dreamt of Bobby and the dog and had the same peacefulness. Then right before I woke up it got tense and uneasy."

"Right after I joined you in the bed?" Kane asked, his eyes crinkling with worry.

"How long had you been there?" I asked.

"I'd just gotten there when you knocked me on the head." He turned to Pyper. "I'm sorry."

"Why?" Pyper looked from Kane to me.

I slumped. "The ghost has a problem with me and Kane, ah, getting close."

"Oh." Realization dawned in her eyes.

"This has got to stop!" I jumped up and paced. "We can't wait around until Bea and-or Ian shows up. We don't even know if they can help."

"I've been thinking about that," Pyper said. "I wonder if Lailah might know someone or be able to do anything."

"I don't know. When we asked her about it she said our best bet was to ask Bea." I flopped back onto the bed.

"It's worth a try," Pyper said.

"It is. In the meantime, why don't the two of you stay here? I'll take the other room." Kane got up to leave.

"Won't work. My ghost dog likes to bark at Pyper. He's doing it right now. I won't get any sleep." I glared at the door where Duke stood.

"I guess it's the couch for me then." Kane kissed me on the forehead and left.

Back in Kane's room alone, it took me a long while to go back to sleep.

The next morning, Pyper and I walked the short distance to The Herbal Connection.

"Hello," Lailah sang from the back of the store. "Are you here to get your auras read?"

"Thanks, but not today. We're here about something else," I said.

"The black thing still following your friend?" Lailah frowned, studying Pyper.

"Yes," Pyper said.

"We haven't been able to get a hold of Bea, and things are getting out of hand. We were hoping you might have some suggestions for what to do, or know someone else who might be able to help us."

Lailah focused on Pyper. Her white light energy took on a gray hue, and then shone bright white again when she looked back at me. She bit her lip. "I don't know. That shadow is really strong, and it's not going to be easy to get rid of. I know a way, but I'd feel a lot more confident if Bea were here to help me."

"Do you know when she's coming back?" I asked.

Lailah shook her head. "No. In fact I haven't heard from her at all, which is really weird."

Pyper stepped up next to me and put her hand on Lailah's arm. "Please try?" A small twinge of desperation seeped from Pyper.

Then something odd happened. Lailah seemed to absorb it, change it somehow, and sent it back as a stream of calmness. She'd physically changed Pyper's distinct energy. I could siphon energy, or send my own as a sort of suggestion, but I couldn't change it.

"How did you do that?" I asked.

"You felt that, huh? Just one of my gifts. I'll show you some-time. Right now I need to prepare for getting rid of this jackass tormenting Pyper here."

"Yes!" Pyper pumped her fist in the air.

"Don't get too excited. It won't be pleasant. So be prepared." Lailah turned to me. "I'll perform the ritual, but we'll need a fourth person. A female. Females have more power with this kind of thing. Do you have someone you trust?"

"Sure." I knew Kat would come if I asked. "But she doesn't have any powers."

"If she's female, it's enough." Lailah grabbed a note pad and started scribbling. "We need to do this as close to midnight as possible, and outside. Do you have a place we can meet for this?"

"Yes," Pyper said. "We have a courtyard between Wicked and The Grind. You know where they are, right?"

Lailah nodded, still writing.

I handed her my cell phone number. "Give us a call when you're out front, and one of us will come get you. Do we need to do anything special to prepare?"

"Nope. I'll take care of everything."

When we got back to our building, Pyper headed to her apartment and I went to mine. I called Kat and invited her to a girl's night in, leaving out the part about needing her for a ritual. Okay, so I felt a little guilty, but I wanted to feel her emotions while I told her about it in person. If she had any hesitations, I'd have an easier time navigating how to convince her.

My heart sank. Talk about being a hypocrite.

Chapter 17

Kat showed up right before nine. "Where's Pyper?"

"Working down in the club. She'll be here before eleven." I poured two glasses of wine. "Did you eat?"

"Yes, but snacks are expected on girlfriend night." She took a glass. "So chop up the cheese and whip out the olives or whatever it is you have stashed aside."

Laughing, I pulled out a cheese plate from the fridge. "I'm way ahead of you."

"Gouda!" She put a piece in her mouth, closed her eyes and groaned in ecstasy. "Man, this is good."

"Glad you like it. And here's dessert." I set another tray next to it.

"Oh my God! I want girlfriend night at least once a week. Dark chocolate, strawberries, and what are these?" She held up a small round chocolate ball.

"Chocolate-covered blueberries."

"Damn, Jade. You'll never get rid of me now." Kat filled a plate and sat back.

"Good, cause I have an ulterior motive for bringing you here."

The cheery contentment surrounding her faded to suspicion. "What? What are you gonna make me do?"

"Not me. Lailah." I grabbed my wine glass and told her about the day I'd met Lailah, my confession to Pyper and the upcoming exorcism.

When I finished my speech, Kat cast a sideways glance as she popped a few chocolate covered blueberries in her mouth. "Now that Pyper knows you're an empath, did you tell Kane?"

After everything I'd just told her, that's what she focused on? "No."

Kat washed down her chocolate with a gulp of wine. "You better do it soon before someone else does."

"What? Are you going to tell him?"

"No. But word spreads. You know that."

I frowned, knowing she was right. "Fine, I'll tell him. Happy?"

"Yes. Now, what exactly have you signed me up for? An exorcism?" Her expression told me she thought I'd lost my mind.

"Lailah said she might be able to get rid of the ghost. She needs three other women to help with the ritual." Feeling her questions rise, I raised my hand in a stop motion. "I don't know what or how. She did say it wouldn't be pleasant, so if you don't want to do it, I need you to tell me."

Her suspicion faded to weariness. "Is she a witch?"

"I really don't know. What I do know is Pyper is willing to try just about anything to be free. Kat, it's horrible. I can feel her pain when she gets attacked." I shuddered and whispered, "It's awful."

Kat sighed, still filled with weariness, but she said, "All right. If it helps Pyper, I'll do it.

I grabbed her and gave her a hug. "Thank you. I'm sorry I didn't tell you on the phone."

"Don't worry about it." She refilled her wine glass. "Let's get down to the really important stuff. Like where exactly is tall, dark and yummy this evening?"

I smiled. "He's working at the club. We can go down there if you want."

"Uh, yeah! Let's go."

We ran into Charlie at the bottom of the stairs. When I told her we were headed into Wicked, she shuffled us through the employee entrance and led us through the crowd. Once we reached the bar she waved a couple of dancers off the bar stools, making room for us.

"You didn't have to get up," I said to the tall, gorgeous, barely covered blonde in front of me.

She winked, smiling. "When the boss says move, you move. Enjoy yourself." She turned and sat in the lap of a man sitting at a nearby table.

"You got promoted!" I stood on the bottom rung of the stool, leaned over the bar and wrapped my arms around Charlie.

"Yep, and a nice raise, too." Charlie hugged me back, holding on a little longer than really necessary. Her eyes sparkled as she released me, and I laughed.

Kat reached over and gave Charlie a quick hug. "Congrats!"

Watching them, I jumped off the stool, lost my balance and stumbled backwards, crashing into someone. Mortified, I turned to apologize and stopped midsentence. Hate crept up my spine, shattering my defenses. I took a step back.

"Dan," I said.

Kat whirled in surprise. "Hey! I thought it was poker night." She put her arm around Dan's waist and kissed his cheek.

His eyes went wide with shock and then he scowled. "What the hell are you doing here? I told you I didn't want you hanging out with that freak."

"Dan." Kat warned and backed away. "Don't talk about Jade that way."

Ignoring her, Dan glared at me. "Why did you have to bring her to this slut palace? Again."

"She wanted to come," I said.

"Like hell. You talked her into it, you cheap bitch."

Kat leaned in, poking Dan in the chest with her finger. "Do *not* call her that. And don't you dare tell me who I can and can't hang out with, Dan Pearson." She took a few steps forward, forcing him back. Her anger, mixed with confusion, took over, pushing all of Dan's hatred right out of my awareness. "What the hell is wrong with you?"

Dan grabbed her wrists and yanked her aside. As he moved toward me, Kat regained her footing and jumped between us, stopping him.

"I'm warning you, Kat, get out of my way," he said.

"Or what?"

"Or you'll get what's coming to you." He grabbed her shoulder, trying to yank her sideways, but Kat swung her forearm up and knocked his arm away. Before he could say another word, she reached up and slapped him. Hard.

"Don't ever touch me like that again," she seethed.

"Excuse me. Is there a problem here?" Kane suddenly appeared next to me.

"It looks like Kat has it under control," I said.

Kane glanced at Kat, and then focused on Dan. "That may be true, but I recall banning this individual from the premises." He stepped around Kat and dodged the swing Dan threw his way. "You'll want to calm down now."

"Fuck you. I won't stand for a pimp telling me what to do," Dan yelled and lunged forward.

Kane sidestepped him and kicked. He caught Dan in the rear, sending him sprawling into a couple of stools. Dan crashed to the ground and groaned as he rolled to his side.

Kane signaled to one of the bouncers. When his backup appeared and hauled Dan to his feet, Kane leaned in and said, "I thought we had this conversation before, but let me inform you one more time. Stay away from these premises. Stay away from Jade, or I'll find a way to have you arrested."

"I never touched you. Good luck making that stick." Dan winced when the bouncer yanked his arms back.

Kane shrugged. "True, but I have a bar full of witnesses who'll say you attacked one of my girls. Now move."

Kat turned to me, holding her wrist. Her face was etched in disbelief. "What just happened here? Who was that?"

My anger at Dan turned to sympathy for her. It was the first time she'd seen that side of him. Worse, it wasn't just that she'd found out her boyfriend had turned into a first-class asshole, but he was also one of her closest friends. I knew exactly how she felt.

"I don't know," I said sadly. "But he behaved in much the same way the last time he showed up here. I tried to tell you."

She furrowed her brow. "Damn, Jade. I'm so sorry. I was pretty drunk that night. I didn't remember a lot of what happened, just that you and Dan were arguing and then he told me…well, it doesn't matter what he said. He obviously lied about it."

"I'm sorry," I said. But thank you, Jesus! She'd finally seen Dan at his worst.

"You have no reason to be sorry. This is Dan's problem. And now mine, obviously."

"What are you going to do?"

She blinked back tears. "Tell him to move out, I guess."

"I'm sorry. I know it's hard." I took her hand. "And I'm sorry we let him come between us."

Kat pulled me into a hug. "I know, honey. So am I. Don't worry. You won't have to deal with him anymore." She dabbed at her wet eyes and forced a smile. "What's a girl got to do to get a drink around here?"

I smiled, gave her another hug and turned to Charlie. "This girl needs a drink. But better make it a diet Coke, minus the rum." I flashed Kat an apologetic smile. "We can't be drunk when Lailah shows up."

"Anything for that bad-ass girl. I wouldn't want to be on the other end of that stabbing finger and lecture." Charlie winked at Kat and filled two glasses with ice.

Just as I pulled out a ten to leave on the bar, Kane appeared beside me. "You know," he said in a husky voice, "there are perks to being the owner's girlfriend."

"Like what?" I held the bill out for Charlie to take it.

She glanced at Kane, hesitating.

"Like, free drinks." He lowered my arm.

Leaning toward him, I lowered my voice. "I wasn't aware I was your girlfriend."

"You are if you want to be." He watched me, maintaining a casual appearance. No one would have guessed the nervous hopefulness churning beneath his cool exterior.

I wanted more than anything to say yes. "Can we talk about it later? Tonight." I'd told Kat I would tell him, and I meant it. I needed to have it all out on the table before we moved any further in this relationship.

He searched my eyes and smiled at whatever he saw there. "Sure. Come find me when you're ready."

I slipped the bill I still held into the tip jar. "Thanks for taking care of Dan. Again."

He winked and took off into the crowd.

"Whoa. Is it suddenly hot in here or what?" Kat said, fanning herself.

"Shut up." I laughed as we made our way to an empty table, drinks in hand.

Kat sat and took a sip of her drink. "Damn, this would be much better with a heavy dose of Bacardi."

"Sorry. We already had a glass of wine. Drinking and messing with spells is a really bad idea." I slide my chair next to her and held my glass up. "A toast to ridding Pyper of her black shadow, and to me finally coming clean with Kane."

"Amen to that." We clinked our glasses together. "I don't know if there's any hope for the ghost stuff, but judging by the sparks between you and that man, I'd say you don't have much to worry about."

I prayed she was right.

Kat turned her eyes to the stage. "Can you believe how in shape these girls are? Look at her climb that pole using just her hands."

I watched along with her, until Kat plunked her drink down and started inspecting her wrists.

"You should keep icing them. It really helps," I said.

"A margarita or two would numb the pain faster." She smirked.

"Lush." I chuckled and gazed around the room, searching for Kane. Instead, I found the creepy angry guy, still sitting alone in his corner with that unlit cigarette in his fingers. Deep satisfaction and anticipation reached me as my eyes locked on his. A shiver ran through my body, causing my hands to start shaking.

"Kat, I think we should go get Pyper now."

"Already?" She tried to read her watch in the semi-dark room.

"Yes, now." I stood up, leaving the unfinished diet coke behind and took off to find Pyper, pulling Kat behind me.

"Pyper?" I called, while walking into the office.

"She went upstairs to change." Kane's voice made me jump.

"Damn it, Kane. Don't startle me like that."

"Sorry, didn't mean to." He stepped out from behind the open door. "I was putting some files away."

I half-turned to face him.

"What's wrong? Your face is pale. Did something happen?" He started for the door.

"No, nothing. I just…one of the guys out there gave me the creeps."

"Is that all?" Kane shrugged. "That's what we get in the strip club business, a bunch of creeps. Like that ex of yours."

"Right. Well, I better go get Pyper. Lailah will be here soon."

"Okay, sure." Kane searched my face. "Be careful. I'll see you later." He pulled me closer and whispered, "I've become rather fond of you."

I took a breath and cleared my throat. "I will."

His lips came down and brushed mine lightly before he let go.

I stumbled out of the office and stopped in front of Kat, who was patiently leaning against the wall.

"Holy shit, that man is hot. You better lay claim to him before someone else does." She craned her neck, trying to catch a glimpse of him in the office.

"Stop it. Let's go." Together we made our way up to Pyper's apartment.

At eleven thirty, Pyper strolled through my apartment door.

"Where is she?" I asked, looking behind her for Lailah. Pyper had left minutes earlier to let her in the building.

"Downstairs talking with Kane."

"Kane? Do they know each other?"

Pyper avoided my glance and stared out the window. "Yeah. I should have made the connection before. Kane dated a girl named Lailah for a while, but I never met her." She shrugged. "He said she had special talents, but you know I always assumed he meant in the bedroom."

Kat let out a loud giggle, but stifled it when she caught the look I gave her.

"Great." I sat heavily on the edge of my bed.

Kat got up from my desk and sat down next to me. "What's up?"

"Just tired."

She put her arm around my shoulders, giving me a small squeeze. Just then Kane and Lailah walked in. Their mutual affection reached me, stabbing me in the heart. She gazed up at him, smiling, while Kane chuckled at something she'd said. He sobered as his eyes found me, his face and emotions unreadable. How did he do that? I'd always been able to read his emotions before.

Standing up, I walked over to Lailah. "It's pretty close to midnight. Don't we need to get started?"

"Oh! Yes. Sorry. I got distracted." She smiled at Kane. "We need to get to the courtyard. Kane, you stay here. We'll be back." She gestured to us and headed back through the door.

The three of us filed out after her with Pyper in the lead. When we reached the courtyard Pyper asked, "Why does Kane have to stay back?"

"The goddess will only speak to her daughters," Lailah replied.

"We're calling a goddess?" I asked.

Lailah ignored my question. Trepidation settled over me as I wondered what the hell we were getting ourselves into. I hoped she was speaking in symbolic terms. Literally calling a higher being meant opening pathways. And when that happened, you never knew what was coming.

"Over here, girls. We have a lot to do, so please do as I say," Lailah said.

We nodded in unison.

Lailah's easy smile was replaced by a fierce concentration. "Pyper, take all of the candles out of my bag and light each one. Jade, I need you to draw a pentagram with the chalk. You know how to do that?"

"Sure. How big?"

"Pretty big." She walked in a large circle to show me. She stepped off to the side, and I went to work on the border, using the dim candlelight Pyper was busy creating.

"What can I do?" Kat asked.

"Help Jade. It doesn't have to be perfect, just a five-point pentagram enclosed in a large circle."

I hurried my motions as Kat knelt on the courtyard bricks opposite me, filling in the lines of the pentagram.

"So, Lailah, are you like a witch or something?" Kat asked.

"Or something," Lailah said.

Both Kat and I looked up, staring at her. Oddly enough, Pyper kept her head down lighting candles.

"Pyper, after they're done with the pentagram, put the white candles on the outer circle, then put the blue candles on the points where the pentagram intersects." Lailah pulled various herbs from her bag.

Pyper nodded and continued with her work.

Kat glanced at me, and jerked her head toward Lailah. "Or something?"

"Kat," I said in a low voice, not wanting to offend the one person who might be able to help.

"It's all right." Lailah sniffed one of her herbs. "I'm not a witch. I'm a low-level Angel. I sense things other people can't, and I can utilize some Wiccan-type spells to my advantage."

"A low-level Angel?" Kat said, each word rising.

Lailah flashed a genuine smile. "That's the reaction I usually get. I'll explain more later. Right now we have work to do."

I sensed Kat having difficulty containing her curiosity, but she kept quiet until we finished the pentagram circle. "Low-level Angel?" she whispered to me.

I shrugged and whispered back, "That's new to me, too."

Pyper never once registered she heard the exchange between Kat and Lailah. She stood a small distance apart from the three of us, waiting.

Finally, after studying some notes, Lailah looked up. "I need the three of you to stand in the middle of the blue candles in a small circle with your hands linked."

We each stepped carefully over the ring of lit blue candles and faced each other. I held my hands out and warmth spread to my center as I grasped the hands of my two friends. Suddenly everything felt right. Like we were supposed to be there together. I smiled, feeling for the first time this might actually work.

"Good. Just like that. The three of you stay linked until I tell you it's time. Then each of you will need to move across the blue candle plane, into the space I'm in. Got it?"

We all nodded.

"Now, I just need to do this last thing before we start." She stepped outside of the white candle circle and began to chant in a language I didn't understand, while dropping a trail of crushed herbs. Once she'd completed three rotations around us, the chanting stopped, and she stepped back over the white candles into the circle.

"What should we expect?" I asked.

"I don't really know. No spell is ever the same twice. I'm going to call on the goddess for help to dispel the spirit. It'll be her will as to what happens after that. The idea is to trap the spirit in that circle you are in and to get the three of you out before he can hurt anyone."

Panic radiated off Pyper.

I squeezed her hand in assurance. "I'm not letting go."

She nodded and looked straight ahead, her eyes wide.

Lailah stood directly in my sightline and, for the first time that evening, I noticed she wore a deep plum velvet cloak with gold trim. How had I missed that? Then the vision of her gazing with dreamy eyes up at Kane filled my head. I scowled.

"It's very important that each of you keep a positive attitude through this ritual, or else there could be severe consequences." A twinge of irritation jabbed me right between the eyes.

Startled, I followed it to Lailah's piercing stare. Damn. I hated that she could read me. I bit my lip, took a large intake of breath and willed my irritation away as I exhaled.

Pyper relaxed her hand in mine, and I noted the easing of the tension lines around her mouth. Gathering energy, I projected what I hoped was calm in her direction. A little help couldn't hurt.

Kat squeezed my hand, getting my attention. Her posture wasn't exactly relaxed, but she didn't look like she wanted to run away either. I squeezed back, grateful for the support.

"This spell works primarily off of intentions. I need each of you to focus on trapping the spirit in the circle. Jade, your energy is the most suited for this type of thing, due to your empath abilities, so your intentions will carry more weight. You said you've seen the ghost?"

"Yes. Lots of times."

"Good. Form a clear picture of him in your mind, and use all of your energy to bring him to the circle."

"Isn't he already here? Can't you see Pyper's dark shadow?" I asked.

"Yes, her shadow is there, but once we start the spell anything can happen. Just keep focused."

I nodded and closed my eyes, concentrating.

"I'm going to start now." Lailah's light energy circled us as she walked the perimeter of the circle. "I need each of you to stay silent and focus. Expect anything from rain to sunlight to intense heat or extreme cold. Like I said before, I just never know what will happen."

I looked up at the clear night sky, spotted the familiar yellow Louisiana moon and gave a little shudder at the unknown yet to come. I snapped my mind back to the mental picture of Bobby and focused on the brick closest to the center of our inner circle.

Out of the corner of my eye I saw Lailah reach up and untie her cloak. She tossed it outside the circle and stood barefoot in an almost transparent white gown. Her honey-streaked hair hung loose around her shoulders, and I couldn't help but think she looked like an escaped mental patient.

Her disapproving glare landed on me. I shut my eyes tight, determined to focus.

I heard nothing but Lailah's voice after that. "Selene, moon goddess of the night, hear me now, High Priestess of the Coven." Her voice was clear and somehow blocked the dull background noise from the people walking Bourbon Street, just feet away. "Bless these women, your three daughters, with your presence. We call seeking wisdom, strength and, above all, the power to protect our sister from all who seek to harm."

Mist tickled my arms. I opened my eyes to a thick blanket of fog. I could see nothing but the dim glow of the candles flickering low on the ground.

"Moon goddess, we ask you read our sisters' intentions. We give our will to you freely and take nothing but yours in return. We want only to help our sister to be free of the bonds that bind her. Free of the spirit that haunts her. From one to three, and three to one, please let your will be done."

Silence loomed. The foggy mist turned dense, soaking my shirt until it clung to my body. The candles, barely visible, flickered like a faulty light bulb. I held my breath and waited.

And waited.

Then, in a flash, the mist dissipated and the candles stopped flickering. The three of us looked at each other then at Lailah, standing as still as a statue, her eyes closed, head tilted up. I sent Pyper a questioning glance. She lifted one shoulder in a sad deflated shrug.

I let out a barely audible sigh and opened my mouth to speak but was shocked into silence as the blue candles lit and shot a wall of fire straight in the air, blocking us from Lailah and the rest of the courtyard. Kat jerked, trying to get free, but instinctively I held tighter, keeping the circle whole. The flames turned a brilliant sapphire blue before fading to a transparent white.

Through the wall Lailah gestured to me. "Now!"

I yanked Pyper and Kat through the wall without any warning. Instead of heat, sharp stabs of icy cold prickled my skin. The three of us toppled to the ground, and the flames turned brilliant blue once more. The radiant heat warmed the chill instantly.

I stayed still with my face pressed to the ground, breathing deeply. "Did it work?"

"I have no idea," Kat mumbled beside me.

"Pyper?"

Her motionless body faced away from me, and she didn't answer.

Too tired to move, my eyes flickered to Lailah. She stood like a statue, her face blank.

Crawling up on my knees, I tried to get my feet under me but froze when Lailah's face glowed silver and her features changed, revealing long, white-blond hair and clear, pale blue eyes. Her full red lips moved into a grim line, and the voice that spoke was deep and husky.

"I have fulfilled your intentions. What comes next I cannot control. The events that unfold are up to you, my child." She pointed at me. "Reach deep inside yourself to alter the course now set in motion." The silver glow started to fade.

"Wait! Why me?" I asked in desperation.

"You are my daughter." The image faded back to Lailah, now as pale as a ghost.

The blue wall of flames faded back to translucent white. Lailah turned to focus on the circle and yelped. "He isn't Pyper's black shadow!"

My head snapped to the circle. There stood Bobby, radiating frustration. I was more than a little surprised I could read his emotions.

"Yes it is. He's the one who's been tormenting her."

"No! I know him. His energy is bright white, not black." Lailah dropped to her knees, checking on Pyper still curled up at her feet. "Pyper. Wake up!"

I crawled to her side and cradled Pyper's head in my lap. "Pyper?"

"Her black cloud is gone, but so is her energy." Lailah's voice rose in panic. "Oh my God! What have I done?" She slumped down next to Pyper.

I opened my mind and tried to get a read on Pyper's energy. Nothing. "She's just passed out. Do you have smelling salts in that bag of tricks?"

Lailah fished around and handed me a small jar. I quickly checked Pyper's pulse and breathing. Both were a bit weak, but I let out the breath I'd been holding and put the smelling salts under her nose.

Nothing.

"Come on!"

"What happened?" A male voice, Kane's voice, called in panic.

"She's passed out." I tried to sound calm.

"No. She isn't in there. I can't feel her." Lailah crumpled into tears.

Kane's eyes stared into mine for a brief agonizing moment.

Then I heard Kat say, "Yes! My friend has lost consciousness. Send an ambulance."

Chapter 18

Time seemed to stand still as Pyper lay crumpled in my arms. If Bobby hadn't been attached to Pyper, then what was? And where had it come from? A cold chill snaked its way through my body. She hadn't been affected until after I'd moved in. Had Ian's ghost hunting triggered it somehow?

And what about Bobby? How come Lailah hadn't seen him attached to me? Even if he didn't follow me everywhere, she'd been in my apartment earlier that evening. Surely she would have seen him then. Maybe she had been too caught up in Kane. I scowled and forced the petty thought out of my head.

The roar of the siren snapped my mind back to reality. I tore my tear-filled eyes from Pyper's face and peered up at the gate, trying to mentally urge the paramedics to move faster.

"What are you doing?" Kat asked.

I turned to answer her, but she was staring at Lailah. The wall of flame had disappeared, and Bobby was gone from the circle.

"Closing the spell," Lailah said in a barely audible whisper.

I cleared my throat. "Where did he go?"

"Bobby? I let him out. There was no reason to keep him." Lailah gathered up her supplies and stuffed them in her paper bag.

I said nothing but wondered if that was true. I'd thought Bobby had been interfering with Kane and me every time we got close. But was it really Pyper's black spirit, or something else entirely? Anything seemed possible now.

"Excuse me. You're going to have to let her go," a paramedic said, gently pushing me to the side.

Kat pulled me to my feet as the emergency workers loaded Pyper on the gurney. Kane stayed by her side, and the rest of us followed as the EMTs rushed her to the vehicle. An argument broke out when Kane was told only family was allowed in the ambulance. Lailah stepped forward, laid her hand on the paramedic's arm and said something I couldn't hear. After that, Kane climbed in, sat next to Pyper and took her hand.

We watched as they raced away.

"Lailah, what did you say to him?" I asked.

"Nothing significant. I just bent his will a little bit with my energy." She looked at her feet. "It was the least I could do."

"Come on. I'll drive." Kat pulled out her keys and led us to her car.

The antiseptic smell burned my nose as I made my way to the nurses' station. Kat and Lailah trailed behind me.

"I doubt they know anything yet," Kat said.

"Probably not, but we need to know where she is." Plus, I needed to see Kane. My eyes burned with unshed tears as I thought of the anguish on his face before the ambulance took off.

Kat grabbed my arm. "Have a seat. I'll get the information."

I shook my head. "It's okay. I'll go." I left them in the back of the full emergency room and returned thirty minutes later, after insisting the nurse personally check on Pyper.

"She's here, but there's no change. They're running tests. As far as I can tell, Kane is still with her." The nurse had said a family member was with her. It could only be Kane. I sat next to Kat, with Lailah on her other side.

"Here." Kat handed me a Styrofoam cup. "Coffee."

"Thanks." I held the cup, warming my chilled fingers, even though the night was thick with humid summer air.

"What happened back there?" Kat asked in a low voice.

I turned and saw her peering at Lailah.

"Which part?" Lailah focused on the white wall in front of us.

Kat glanced at me and raised her eyebrows.

I cleared my throat. "Let's start at the beginning. You were trying to trap the black spirit attached to Pyper, but instead you trapped Bobby. How is that possible? I thought they were the same being. Bobby is the only one I ever saw."

"I already told you, Bobby has white energy. He's Bea's brother."

"I know. That's why we were trying to get in touch with her. I didn't know you knew him. You've seen him before, I take it."

She nodded. "A few times with Bea. When we were working on some spells together."

"Okay." What kind of spells? I shook my head trying to focus. "But you said before you could see things. You saw the black spirit, so why didn't you see Bobby's energy?"

"Because of you, I guess. Your aura is purple, but surrounding that is brilliant white energy, like all intuitives have. If he was near you, it would have been hard for me to see him."

"Oh." I sat back staring at the admittance door, wishing Kane would appear.

"So because Jade was focusing on Bobby, he got trapped in the circle and not Pyper's ghost. We *are* talking about two ghosts here, right?" Kat asked.

The people next to us turned and openly stared after hearing her statement. She stared back until they turned away. In spite of myself, I smiled.

"At least two," Lailah said.

"At least!" I sat up straight.

"I don't know!" Lailah finally met my eyes. "I have totally fucked up. I don't know anything anymore."

"Calm down," Kat said in a hushed tone. "No one is blaming you."

I suppressed a grunt of disagreement. Kat must have heard me, judging by the elbow she nudged in my rib.

"We're just trying to figure out what happened. Tell us about the vision we saw," I said.

"The vision?" Lailah furrowed her eyebrows. "What vision?"

"The one where you turned into another person and told me I was the one who would have to fix this mess." I jumped out of my chair and stood in front of the two of them.

Lailah's eyes went wide as her head turned from me to Kat. "She came…"

"Who? Who came?" Kat asked.

"The goddess. It had to be." She sat up straight. The remorse faded, replaced by an excited glow.

Kat and I stared at her in silence. She looked around, as if aware for the first time where we were. Standing, she grabbed a hand from each of us. "We need to talk a little more privately."

I glanced back at the admittance door, while Lailah dragged us outside. Still no Kane.

"Tell me exactly what happened," Lailah demanded when we were safely out of hearing distance from the emergency room door.

"I…" I turned to Kat. Suddenly I was overwhelmed into silence.

She gave me a small smile and replayed the scene for Lailah.

"It's for you to alter the course now…" Lailah trailed off, deep in thought.

"What did she mean, 'I am hers'?" I asked.

"You are her daughter. In a cosmic sense. I'd guess your powers are deeper than you ever thought. A white witch, maybe. A natural-born witch." She shrugged. "Hard to say until you explore your powers."

"So the goddess Selene, whoever that is, thinks I have some extra powers?"

"Pretty much." Lailah paced in a circle. "Damn it. I wish Bea was here."

I gritted my teeth and walked back to the entrance, scanning for Kane. I didn't want to hear about extra powers. All I cared about was Pyper's condition. I turned back to them. "I'm going back in."

"Wait." Kat held up her hand. "Just one more thing. What the hell is a low-level angel?"

Lailah stopped pacing. "It means I'm a mortal angel. A messenger from God, but in mortal form. It's why I can do some Wiccan magic, but it all comes naturally for me. I don't have to practice or do special rituals. I can just make it happen. I do have to take precautions to keep evil out, which is what the herbs, candles and circle was about. Though I could have made that all happen without it. Unfortunately, I failed."

"A messenger from God?" Kat asked with a heavy dose of skepticism.

"We come in all forms." Lailah closed her eyes, as if her burden was too heavy to bear. "I still do not know my purpose. I try to do good, but as you can see I'm not always successful."

Too overwhelmed by the night's events, I said nothing and returned to the waiting room.

Soon Kat joined me. "She went home."

I nodded, and we sat in silence until finally Kane emerged.

My heart swelled simultaneously with joy and pain at the sight of him. He held his face taut with his lips in a grim line. Our eyes met as I stood, and his pain ripped through me, almost making my knees buckle. I grabbed him and held on with my face buried in his shoulder.

"She's still the same," he whispered in my ear. "Coma."

"No." I felt him nod and I looked up. "I'm so sorry." Silent tears streamed down my face.

He hugged me tighter and brought one hand up to wipe my tears. "I don't know what happened, but I know whatever it was, it isn't your fault."

His tenderness brought on a fresh bout of emotion, but I steadied myself and willed the tears back. He guided me toward the doors.

"You should go get some sleep," he said.

"And you. You'll stay here?"

"I have to. Let Kat take you home. I'll call if I hear anything."

The last thing I wanted to do was leave him, but I could see by the stubborn tilt of his chin he wasn't taking no for an answer. "Promise to call with any news, at any time."

"I promise." He steered me out the double doors.

I turned to him, my heart aching as I looked into his tired eyes. "We'll get her through this. I promise." I didn't know how, but I knew in my heart, I'd do whatever it took to save her.

He nodded absently and gave me a gentle push toward Kat. But I stepped closer, took his face in my hands and kissed him. All of my anguish and suppressed emotions poured out of me into that one kiss, desperate to show him how much he meant to me, even if I couldn't say it.

Grief, longing, and fear surrounded me as he kissed me back in a slow, bittersweet manner. When our lips parted, he hugged me tight. "Get some rest." And then he was gone, back through the double doors of the hospital.

"Let's go, sweetie." Kat said, pulling me to the car. "You'll see him tomorrow."

I didn't say anything until we were safely in her Mini. "Do you think Lailah is crazy?"

"Definitely."

The bed shifted as Kat lay down next to me. She didn't want to go home, so I offered her the other side of my bed.

"He talks about you all the time, you know."

"Who? Ian?" Jolted out of my thoughts about what just transpired with Kane, I rolled over to face her.

"No. Dan."

"What? You're kidding. Why?"

"I'm starting to think he's obsessed with you." Kat laid back and stared at the ceiling.

"That's crazy," I said, realizing the night's events had hit her harder than I'd thought.

"No it isn't. He's the one who told me about the job opening at the glass school. Told me I should call you. Said it would be good for me to have you here."

I stared as I digested her statement.

"He kept hounding me about when you were coming, and talking about double-dating. I'm so stupid. I should have seen it for what it was."

"What?" I whispered.

"He's still in love with you."

I let out a bark of laughter. "That's insane. He has nothing but hatred for me."

Kat propped herself up on her elbows and turned toward me. "I think maybe it's a love-hate thing. He still loves you, but you clearly can't stand him. So his frustration manifests into schoolyard bullying."

"Are you saying this is my fault?" I narrowed my eyes, feeling the pain coursing through her heart.

"Of course not." She lay back down and turned her back to me.

Irritated, I flopped down on my side of the bed. My eyes felt like sandpaper, but I knew I'd never sleep until I asked the question I'd been holding in for weeks. "Kat?"

"Hmm?"

"Why did you do it? Date Dan, I mean."

She sighed. "I don't know. He just showed up out of nowhere. He didn't even tell me he was moving here, and one thing led to another..."

Her voice sounded so small and dejected, I couldn't help but feel bad for her. "It's okay." I reached for her hand and squeezed.

"No it isn't, but thanks for saying so." She squeezed back.

She was right. It really wasn't okay. She'd known how much Dan had hurt me and yet, she still chose to not only date him, but to move in with him. I'd been lying to myself, saying it was fine, it didn't bother me. But it did. And we both knew it.

"I'm kicking him out tomorrow," she said.

"Are you sure? He clearly needs help. Maybe you can help him get it."

"After he assaulted me? I don't think so. Besides, he's not over you. I deserve better in a relationship. If he wants help, I'll be there, but not as his girlfriend."

I reached over and hugged her. "I love you, you know that, right?"

"Yes. I love you too."

Chapter 19

A dull headache threatened as the florescent lighting glared off the stark-white walls of the hospital. The fact that I hadn't slept more than six hours in the two days since Pyper had been admitted didn't help. I popped two aspirin and washed them down with a large gulp of lukewarm coffee. Food and sleep would have been a better prescription, but I'd take what I could get.

The receptionist waved, and I nodded as I made my way down the corridor. The staff had suspected everything from a drug overdose to a brain aneurism. But after an endless series of clean MRI's, CAT scans and blood tests, the official diagnosis was an unexplained coma.

Entering Pyper's room, I was relieved to see she was alone. Kane had been holding a vigil by her side, and I hoped he'd finally gone home for some much-needed sleep.

I sat down next to her and took her hand.

Closing my eyes, I let my barriers down and sent my awareness toward her. It was tough to sift through the raw energy of the other hospital patients, but with strained effort I managed to keep their signatures in the background. I'd been trying each time I visited her, searching for her distinct energy, but each time I had the same result. Nothing. Frustrated, I sent my energy out with more force. Her emotional energy was still vacant, but with her hand still clasped in mine I felt her body twitch.

My eyes popped open. She was lying there just as she'd been before.

"Pyper? Pyper, honey, wake up. I know you felt me. I felt you flinch from my mental probe. Come on now, we all miss you. Wake up."

"Mental probe?"

I jumped, and dropped her hand. Kane, with damp hair and wearing a clean T-shirt and jeans, stood at the door.

"I was trying to reach her, and she flinched."

"Reach her? How?" Kane tilted his head in thought and then focused on me with wide eyes. "Wait, she flinched?"

"I think it was more like a reflex," I said ignoring his first questions. I got up and wandered to the window, as Kane moved to sit next to her.

Kane spoke in a low voice, trying to coax Pyper awake. When nothing happened, I moved to stand next to him.

"What did you say to get her to move?" he asked.

"Uh…" I sat down on the edge of the bed, faced him and took a deep breath. "Nothing, I just held her hand and tried to get a sense of her energy." How could I tell him about my ability now? But how could I not, especially if I could help Pyper?

"Oh. I see. Did you get anything?" Kane put Pyper's hand in mine.

"Huh?" That wasn't the response I'd been expecting.

"Did you get any reading on her emotional energy?"

Wait. He knew? "You know about my ability?" Had Pyper told him? I'd never told her it was a secret, though I'd thought that was obvious. I should've realized she'd tell him. They were best friends, after all.

His eyes held steady on mine. "Yes. I know about that. I tried to tell you once before, but you didn't want to talk about it, so I let it drop."

"But—"

"Jade," he stroked my arm. "Can we do this later? I'd like it if you tried to reach Pyper again."

I bit down hard on my lip. He knew. He'd known for a while, apparently, and he hadn't run. In fact, I'd pushed him away. *Idiot.* I took a deep breath. "All right."

"Thank you."

"I can't promise anything."

He nodded.

"Okay." I shut my eyes and tried to center myself. After a few deep breaths I relaxed and focused first on Kane. His anxiousness came through loud and clear, with also a bit of relief. That surprised me. *I* was relieved he knew my secret, but why was *he* relieved? I put the question aside and mentally shoved Kane's emotions to the back of my awareness, ready to focus on Pyper.

As before, I couldn't find one thread of her energy. I gathered as much force as I could muster and sent my probe deep into her psyche. My head started to spin as my vision narrowed to only Pyper's face, and suddenly my body spasmed. Pain slashed my flesh.

I jerked, trying to break the connection, but the pain was too much to bear. Everything faded to black.

"Jade?"

"Wha…?"

"Here, lie back." Kane's face came into focus.

"What happened? Did I pass out?"

"Yes, right after Pyper opened her eyes."

"She opened her eyes?" I sat up, and the world spun again. Kane's arms came around my shoulders, steadying me, and my head cleared.

"Whoa. Take it easy. They just fluttered open and then closed again. No words, no other movement. What did you feel?" He pressed the buzzer, calling for a nurse.

I clasped Pyper's limp hand and whispered, "Pain. I felt pain."

Kane's face hardened into granite. "Pyper's in pain?"

I nodded as a nurse bustled in and immediately went to inspect a printout from one of the beeping machines. "Looks like a bit of activity here. Did you see any movement?"

"She opened her eyes but closed them immediately," Kane said.

"That could be a good sign. Let me take a look." The nurse checked her eyes with a light, took her blood pressure and checked a few more readouts. "It could have been a reflex, but I'll let the doctor know. It happens sometimes. We just have to wait and see." She gave us an apologetic smile and left.

Kane turned to me. "Pain, you said?"

"Yes." My voice trembled slightly. I took a shaky breath. "I felt it. That's what made me pass out. We have to help her."

"What do you think I've been doing these last few days?" He stood up and paced. "Hell, the last year of my life? I've done nothing but try to help her. I don't know what to do anymore."

I reached for his hand and pulled him to sit beside me. His words held an edge of anger that could be interpreted as resentment, but his emotions portrayed nothing but general frustration. He was at his wit's end.

"She's the only family I have left, since my grandmother died a few years ago." He turned to me. "Don't you think I would do anything to help her?"

"Of course. I know you would. We just need to figure out our next move." I traced his palm with my fingers. "Your only family? What about your parents?"

He hunched and waved a hand, signaling the subject wasn't important. "They're off exploring the world. I never know how to reach them or even where they are in a given month. Last I heard, they were living in the Cook Islands. They're kind of flaky." He gave me a small smile. "I grew up with Gram. She was my family."

My heart squeezed at his words. "I can relate. I lost my mom when I was fifteen. I have no idea where my dad is. I haven't seen him for ten years. Besides my Aunt Gwen, Kat is my only family."

"I'm sorry. That's a terrible age to lose a mother. How did she die?"

I swallowed. "I don't know. She just…disappeared."

"Abducted?" Kane grabbed my hand and squeezed. "No trace or anything?"

"No traces." I pursed my lips together. I really didn't want to talk about this. "It's been a long time. Like I said, Kat is my family now."

"That's why you moved here?"

"Mostly."

He raised his hand to my face and leaned in brushing my lips with his. "I'm really glad you're here."

I gave him a sad smile and looked back at Pyper. "I've been wondering about something."

He raised an eyebrow and waited.

"Have you tried dreamwalking her?" I asked softly.

Kane's face softened as he took in what I said. "I hadn't thought of that. Do you think it would work for a coma patient?"

"No idea, but I'm not so sure she's in a coma. At least, the way the doctors define one. This is something different. I don't know what, though."

"I haven't really slept much since this happened. But I suppose it's worth a try." He turned back to Pyper, clasped both hands around her right one and rested his chin on top of his knuckles. "I'll see you soon, love," he said to her.

I suddenly felt like an intruder and quietly let myself out of the room. On the way to the nurses' station I ran into Holly. "Hey."

Holly's eyes sagged with lack of sleep, and their redness indicated she'd been crying again. "Any change?" She sniffed.

"No, not really. Kane's with her now. Do you want to join me for coffee?"

"I don't think I could drink one more cup." She held her hands up. "See how jittery they are? Way too much caffeine."

"I think tomorrow after the first pot we should switch you to decaf." I guided her toward the vending machine and bought her a package of crackers. "Maybe these will soak it up a little."

We sat on the hard plastic chairs in the sterile waiting room.

"Thank you." Holly stared at the package.

"It's really not a big deal. Don't worry about it."

She looked up at me. "Not the crackers. I meant for all you're doing to help Pyper with the café and the club. She doesn't have a lot of people to count on, you know."

Her statement startled me into momentary silence. I'd been rotating duties with Holly and Charlie at both The Grind and Wicked, to cover for Pyper and Kane. I blinked and said. "You're welcome, but she does have people. You, Charlie and Kane come to mind pretty quickly. That's more than a lot of people I know."

She fiddled with the plastic wrapper on her crackers before answering. "I haven't been very friendly toward you."

I continued to watch her. The statement was true. I didn't know what to say.

"I just wanted to say I'm sorry." With her face set in determination, she met my gaze. "I was jealous. I have no excuse."

"Oh. I sort of thought it had to do with Kane. It's okay, I understand."

"Kane?" She laughed. "Oh no, not because of him." Her laugh turned into a schoolgirl giggle. "Because of the time you were spending with Pyper."

"Pyper? Why?" Did Holly have a crush on Pyper? That made no sense. She was giddy when she'd mistaken us for a couple.

She shrugged one shoulder. "Pyper's my closest friend. The closest one I've ever had actually, and when you two started spending so much time together I just assumed you were becoming a couple. She doesn't get close to people easily. But when…"

"When you realized Pyper and I were just friends, you were afraid I'd take her away from you?" I finished for her.

"Yes," she said. "It's stupid I know. I don't have a lot of experience with female friendships."

Apparently today was the day for confessions. I put on what I hoped was a reassuring smile and peered into her eyes. "We all have insecurities. I understand, but I think you should give Pyper more credit than that. She has room in her heart for more than just one person."

She smiled back at me. "I know. And I see what a great friend you've been to her. I hope one day you and I can be good friends too."

Movement in the corridor caught my attention. I stood. "I think we're already on our way. Here comes Kane. Why don't you go see Pyper now?"

Kane reached my side just as Holly waved and took off down the corridor.

"What were you two chatting about?" he asked.

"Just clearing up a few things. Ready?"

He nodded and took my hand as we left the building.

I propped my feet on the coffee table in Pyper's apartment. We'd decided it would be better to be in her space when Kane tried to connect with her.

"We could order some takeout." I said, closing my eyes and relaxing into the overstuffed cushions. Kane hadn't eaten anything but cafeteria food in days, and I certainly didn't have the energy to cook.

"That's a good plan." A moment later I heard him order a pizza. Worked for me. "It'll be here in thirty minutes," he said.

"Thanks." I opened my eyes and smiled when I saw him sitting exactly as I was in the chair beside me. "Mind if I borrow your shower?"

He opened one eye and his lips quirked up in a half smile. "Want some company?"

My smile blossomed into a grin. "Someone needs to wait for the pizza."

"Damn."

I left him with a mournful expression on his face and took my time in the water, letting the hot stream soothe my aching muscles. When the water turned tepid, I reluctantly turned off the tap and reached for the oversized bath sheet. That's when my phone started to ring. I wrapped my dripping hair in the towel before making my way to the bedroom, where my phone lay on Kane's dresser.

"Yeah?"

"Oh good, I caught you," Kat said. "I just got off the phone with Ian."

"Finally. Where the hell has he been?"

"With his aunt. Apparently they went to consult a paranormal expert and got caught in a ghost hunt. All of the electronic equipment went haywire, including his cell phone. He hasn't been able to reach anyone for five days. He just got our messages. He says he'll be back in town late tonight."

"Okay. I'm not sure what good he'll be to us now. But at least we don't have to worry about him." I wrapped my free arm around my bare body, chilled from the air conditioner.

"He feels terrible and says he might be able to help. Apparently he learned some new tricks." Kat chuckled. "He sounds like a boy at Christmas."

"Boys. All right, then. Kane's going to try to dreamwalk Pyper tonight. We're hoping it might help us understand what's going on."

"That's a great idea. I'll get Ian to come by in the morning."

"Sounds good." A door clicked shut in the other room. "Dinner is here. I better go."

"Later."

I flipped the phone shut and as I started to make my way back into the bathroom, the bedroom door opened.

Kane filled the doorway and froze. His gaze roamed the entire length of my bare body. Twice. Then his eyes met mine. "Sorry. I thought you'd be in the bathroom."

I stood still, like a deer caught in headlights.

He walked into the room, never taking his eyes off mine. "Dinner's ready."

I gulped as his eyes turned from cinnamon-speckled mocha to molten chocolate. "All right," I said, my voice barely audible.

He choked out an oath, his voice as rough as his hands when he grabbed my hips, yanking me to his solid frame. Our lips met in a crush of impatience. Need clutched at my heart as it pumped rapidly, threatening to jump out of my chest. I wanted this. I wanted him like I'd never wanted anyone before.

My impatient hands found their way under his shirt as he pushed me up against the wall. I pressed the length of my body closer, desperately trying to fuse with his.

"I'm at a disadvantage here," I whispered against his lips.

I felt his slow wry smile just before he kissed me again and moved my hand to the fly of his jeans. "Do something about it."

I rose to the challenge, flipping the button open with my thumb and forefinger. He stilled as I undid the zipper. With one stroke of my hand over his silky shaft, he groaned. Heat shot to my center. I placed both hands on his hips and yanked down, stripping him of his jeans.

I consciously did everything I could to keep his emotions from merging with mine. Once that happened I'd be lost at sea, overwhelmed by the tide of his desire. I wanted to feel his strong hands and muscular body, to get lost in all the delicious little details of his exploration. Like right now, the way he gently held my nipple in his teeth while the tip of his tongue teased.

I pressed my back to the wall, arching my hips against his full erection. A deep, satisfied chuckle rumbled in his throat. Humorous, was it? We'd see about that. His lips trailed a line of kisses up my collarbone. I shifted, making space between us, then placed one hand around his neck and the other around the base of his cock. His lips froze mid-kiss. I stroked the length of him until his hips moved in rhythm with me.

It was my turn to chuckle. Not so funny now.

His kisses resumed, more savage than before, and my body lit like crackling fire. A moment later he produced a condom from the nearby dresser.

Thank heaven for the prepared.

His hands moved to my ass, boosting me up, and I wrapped my legs around his hips. The tip of him pressed at my opening. Our eyes met for two long beats. The intensity broke though my defenses and as his unrelenting desire flooded my core, he rocked his hips and entered me.

A cry of pleasure ripped from me as I came almost instantly. I held on, letting myself ride Kane's desire as he pounded into me, over and over, bringing me once again to the edge. Until this time we shuddered together.

"Lord, help me." His lips were pressed against my neck, muffling his voice.

"I think it's too late for that."

He pulled back and grinned. "I'm going to need some for the next round."

I raised an eyebrow. "Greedy."

"Yes." He set me back on my feet and stepped backward, pulling me with him. "I need to lie down."

I stopped, rooted to the floor, and stared over his shoulder.

Slowly he turned toward the direction of my gaze.

"Do you see that?" I asked.

"Yes."

Chapter 20

Kane moved, shielding me from the ghost as I grabbed the discarded towel. I covered up and peered over his shoulder. A red/orange rage illuminated from Bobby, gripping my interior like a vice.

I stumbled forward and held onto Kane's shoulder with one hand, trying to stay conscious. He tensed. Protectiveness flowed from him, easing Bobby's emotional hold on me. Sighing in relief, I moved to Kane's side. He radiated disapproval. I squeezed his arm. "It's all right. Just stay next to me. Your emotions help."

Uncertainty flashed over his face, but he nodded.

The energy around Bobby turned a deeper red as his rage grew out of control. I clutched Kane's arm as a tremor of terror ran up my spine. Determined, I took a small step and stared into Bobby's eyes.

In a quiet voice, I spoke. "Bobby, stop this. I am not your wife. I know I look like her, but I do not belong to you. I belong with Kane."

Kane's pleasure seeped through the fierce protective vibe he had going on, strengthening my resolve.

The rage stronghold had begun to fade, but as Bobby turned to Kane, a fresh wave of angry possessiveness lashed out, making my knees buckle.

"Stop it!" I yelled. "Even if I was who you think I am, is this how you'd treat your wife? Is this how you treat someone you love?" I hugged my arms to myself, trying to see past the pain searing though my chest. "Please, just let me have my life."

Kane's arms wrapped around me, and a fresh wave of his affection circled me in a gentle caress. Bobby's hold on me vanished. I reached around Kane's torso and stared at him with wide eyes. "How did you do that?"

"What?"

"Your energy replaced his. He isn't affecting me right now."

His eyes searched mine. "It must be because you belong with me." He tilted his head, tightened his hold and gave me a slow lingering kiss that made my toes curl in pleasure. I leaned into him, cherishing the tenderness of the moment. When we broke apart I let out a soft sigh and leaned my head on his chest.

Kane stroked my hair and whispered, "He's gone."

"I know."

"Come on. You need to eat." Kane took a few steps back, deeper into the bedroom.

"But the pizza is out there." I pointed toward the door.

"Yes, but I really need a shower first, and I'm not letting you out of my sight."

I laughed. "I knew you'd find a way to get me in the shower."

He grinned and pulled me along after him.

After a second round of lovemaking, we finally emerged flushed and smelling of the rainforest.

"I'm starving," I said as I placed a full plate of pizza in the microwave.

Kane picked up a cold piece and ate half of it while pulling two beers from the refrigerator.

"Yuck. I love pizza, but cold pizza is just not right."

"What? You can't be serious. Besides, I can't wait. Someone used up all my reserves."

I chuckled when he leaned in to nuzzle my neck. "Stop. Go into the living room. I'll meet you there with warm pizza in hand."

The microwave dinged, and I switched the plates.

"You go. I'll be right behind you." Kane handed me the beer bottle and gave me a tiny shove.

With the pizza in one hand and a Guinness in the other, I curled my feet under me and sank into the couch. I'd finished two pieces by the time Kane appeared. He lifted an eyebrow. "Must have had a good workout."

"Something like that," I said between bites.

We ate in companionable silence. When the last slice of pizza was gone, I grabbed both plates and took them to the kitchen. It didn't take long to load the dishwasher and clean the counters, but desperate to avoid the upcoming conversation I moved on to scrubbing the sink. By the time Kane came to find me, I'd cleaned the stovetop, wiped down the appliances and had moved on to sweeping the floor.

"What are you doing?" he asked.

"Just a little cleanup."

"A little?" His eyebrows rose as he looked around at the sparkling kitchen. "Are you cleaning out the refrigerator next?"

"Uh…no." I put the broom back in the closet.

Kane smiled and took my hand. "Thank you, but that wasn't necessary."

I shrugged and let him lead me to the living room.

"All right, what is it you don't want to talk about?" he asked after pulling me down on the sofa next to him.

I shook my head. "I can't keep any secrets from you." How did he do that? It must be some kind of special gift. Only, not a weird psychic or dreamwalker gift. Just a natural gift of perception.

"It's hard to hide from the people who love you." He wrapped his arm around me and pulled my head to his shoulder.

Love. There it was. I knew he loved me. I could feel it just as I felt the love growing in my heart for him. A lump clogged my throat and I took a shaky breath. "I'm sorry I hid my ability from you."

"It's all right. I understand."

I sat up, unwrapping myself from his embrace. "It's really not okay. I wasn't honest with you, and considering how hard I was on you after you told me about the dreamwalking, I can't understand why you aren't more upset."

"Maybe it's because I knew about your ability. You didn't tell me, but I felt it and knew what I was getting into. Plus, you weren't influencing the way I felt about you."

"But you weren't upset when I wasn't honest with you. Why?"

"Is it so hard for you to understand?" He tilted my head to look in my eyes. "I know what it feels like to have people run from me due to my ability. I already knew why you didn't tell me."

My heart squeezed. He'd known his share of rejection, just as I had, due to something neither of us could control. And what did I do right after he told me about his gift? I ran. "I'm so sorry." I tore my gaze away and focused on our clasped hands. "I hurt you."

"I deserved it." I could hear the smile in his voice. "But you should know I really didn't dreamwalk you on purpose. My subconscious took me there and was in charge in my dreams… at least at first. So everything that happened, well, I didn't control it. It's just what I secretly wanted." He paused and his voice hitched. "And my emotions…those were real."

I lifted my gaze to really study him. "You were never trying to manipulate me." It wasn't a question, but he answered with a shake of his head.

"I love you, Jade." His hand tightened on mine. "I want you as my partner, my friend, my lover. But I only want you if you want me the same way. I wouldn't try to trick you into anything, or expect you to be anything other than who and what you are. That isn't who I am."

"I know," I said with intensity. "I know that isn't who you are."

He pulled me into his lap and held me close. "So what do you say?"

Joy spread and filled all the empty corners of my being. "I love you, too."

Kane's arms tightened around me, while his lips brushed mine. I leaned into him, hugging tight and sank into the kiss. When I pulled back, the softness of his eyes matched the tenderness escaping from his being.

I snuggled back into his chest and rested my head on his shoulder. "We need to talk about Pyper."

"All right."

"I feel guilty being happy about us when she needs help." I buried my head deeper, as if to hide from myself.

"Don't. I know Pyper and she'll be thrilled for us, no matter how or when this came about." He stroked my back.

"I know. It's not that. It's because I don't know how to help her. At the calling Lailah did," I cringed at the use of her name, "the vision of the so-called 'goddess' said I needed to change things. That I held the power to alter the course now set. I don't know what that means. I don't know what I can do, other than try to reach her emotional energy. And that isn't working."

Kane sat silent for so long, I finally glanced up to catch his eye. "What?" I asked.

"I don't know. I really don't. And as far as Lailah is concerned, I'd just as soon not have you involved in any more of her brand of magic."

I sat up. "I'm not too keen on it either, but I feel like I have to do something."

"Okay, we'll try to figure it out, but not right now. Both of us need sleep. Will you stay with me while I try to dreamwalk Pyper?"

I nodded, got to my feet and held out my hand. "Come on. Let's go." I couldn't help my lips from curling into a small smile.

Ten minutes later we climbed into Kane's bed. I stared at his chest, my eyes lingering. I reached out and ran a hand the length of his torso. "I wanted to do that since the first time I woke up next to you."

Kane caught my hand and kissed it. "If I hadn't thought you had a concussion, I don't think I could have kept my hands off you."

I scooted closer and snuggled up next to him. "There wouldn't have been much of a fight."

He groaned. "Now you tell me."

"I think you'll live." I lifted my head. "Will you take me with you in the dream?"

"I already planned on it."

Pressing my head to his chest, I relaxed. "Thanks. I want to try to reach her mentally before we go."

"You can do that from here?"

"Maybe. The closer I am emotionally to someone, the easier it is. And the fact we're in her apartment helps. Plus, you're her best friend. If we're connected I might reach her."

"It's worth a try." Kane reached over and flipped off the light.

"Okay, I'm going to read you first. I need to lock in your emotions so I can differentiate and concentrate on Pyper," I said.

"All right."

Because Kane and I were now connected emotionally and physically, reading him became as effortless as breathing. His energy flowed through me as if it were my own. I didn't think I could block him now even if I tried. His pleasure warmed my skin, and I lightly trailed my fingers over his as I paused to enjoy the moment. But soon the weariness and worry for Pyper intruded.

In my mind I conjured up Pyper's distinct energy. It wasn't long before I entered the void I'd been experiencing at the hospital the last few days. I was close. As I had earlier, I forced my essence deeper. Instantly, pain rippled down both my arms and legs. Through the haze I barely heard Kane gasp in alarm. Instinctively, I stiffened, trying to hold as still as possible and the stabbing jabs eased to a dull ache.

"Pyper," I whispered. "We're here. I can feel you. Please, tell us where you are."

Anger and despair filled the void, masking hopelessness.

"It's not hopeless. Kane and I are coming for you. Tell us where to look."

Pyper, I'm here. We both are. Don't give up. We're coming for you. Kane's voice rang in my head.

I jerked, momentarily startled. How did he do that? My focus waned, and I felt Pyper slipping. "No," I said in a raised voice and concentrated. "Where are you?"

Pain pierced my hands, and I bit down on my lip to keep from crying out. Kane's arms tightened around me with fierce protectiveness.

Roy. Kane, Roy has me. Help. Pyper's faint voice barely registered in my mind. A white-hot bolt of terror punched me in the stomach, and the connection was lost.

Kane shot straight up as I rolled away and vomited right there on the bed.

"Oh, God. Oh, God. Oh, God," I said over and over. "I'm sorry."

Kane grabbed the quilt and carried it out of the room. In no time he was back. "Are you all right?"

Barely holding back my gag reflex, I shook my head and wobbled my way into the bathroom. When I was sure I could hold down the rest of my dinner, I reemerged and found Kane hovering by the door.

"Jade." He rubbed my back as I padded back to the bed. "Are you okay?"

I nodded and sat with my back against the headboard. "All of that pain was Pyper's"

"What pain?"

"Oh, you didn't feel it?" When he shook his head, I continued. "Her hands are in awful pain, like she's been stabbed or something. I got sick because I experienced a sucker-punch of some sort. Only it wasn't me, it was her."

Kane's eyes darkened to almost black, a shade I had never seen in my vast experience of analyzing his eye color. Fury and hatred engulfed me.

"I know. I feel the same way." I ran my hand up his arm. "Why did you gasp? What did you feel?"

"Your energy changed. It went from a light airy feel to heavy and somehow foreboding. I knew something wasn't right."

"That's when I felt all the pain." I rubbed my palm. "Who is Roy?"

"I only know one Roy. He was the previous owner of the club." Kane paused. "He died six months ago."

"A ghost," I whispered.

Chapter 21

The turbulence coursing through Kane was like nothing I'd experienced before. Hatred, compounded with a fierce possessiveness, overwhelmed his other protective instincts. I imagined a wolf protecting his den while he simultaneously stalked his prey.

"Kane?"

He turned, and his emotions surged through me, zapping my remaining energy.

"I know you're upset. You have every right to be, but I need you to calm down. Please."

He took a deep breath and let it out slowly. "Sorry."

I pulled him down in the covers and cuddled up close. "Just focus on me for a while, okay?"

He kissed the top of my head. "I'll try." The intensity of his emotions faded, but the anger didn't disappear.

"I'm going to try to relax and sleep. I'll be waiting for you when you're ready."

"I'll see you soon," he said.

I closed my eyes and stretched my aching limbs. Kane felt good, too good in my arms, and it didn't take long for me to drift off. Immediately Bobby appeared at the foot of the bed, shining in his bright light. All the red anger he'd displayed earlier in the night was gone, replaced by a peaceful acceptance. I dozed in his presence until finally, after what seemed like hours, Kane joined me.

Bobby came and stood next to the bed, his light washing over both of us. I looked from him to Kane and back again. Bobby nodded, turned his lips up in a sad smile and faded into the night, his light going with him.

That was weird. I stared at the spot Bobby had vanished from.

Focus, Jade. I need to take you to Pyper. Kane's voice rang clear in my head.

My eyes found him. His determination and sense of urgency snapped me back into the moment. With our hands clasped, our bodies rose together in a transparent image of ourselves. We floated through the walls and floors, ending up next to the stage in the middle of Wicked.

The club pulsed with activity. One of the strippers crawled across the stage toward an eager front-row participant. I spotted Charlie, busy at the bar handling a line of bachelor party shots. The room was half-full with tourists, party goers and, of course, the regular at the table in the corner, sitting the same as always, with a cigarette and a bottle of beer on the table. He stared across the room at something. I followed his gaze.

A platform in the back of the club levitated above the velvet couches lining the wall. I pointed and floated off toward it. As I got nearer, someone's anger engulfed me, muffling my senses. The emotional imprint seemed vaguely familiar, but I couldn't put my finger on it. I spotted Kane just behind me, horror etched on his face. A twinge of desperation and panic I recognized as Kane's pushed its way through the anger surrounding me. I sent my energy out to him, trying to link us together, but his emotions were far away and barely reachable. Disoriented, I turned back to the platform and floated up above it.

A piercing cry rang from my lips, and my own terror pushed out all other emotions.

On the platform, Pyper lay encased in a silver-outlined, clear box. Stripped naked, she'd been pinned down, spread-eagle with nails through her palms and feet. Barbed wire wrapped around her limbs, causing her to lie still or suffer more puncture wounds. Her eyes, pleading, moved from me to Kane and back again. Her lips moved, but no sound was audible.

The foreign, angry energy mixed with my own desperation, and I raised my arms over my head, ready to strike. Using all of my force I slammed my hands down, intending to shatter the silver-lined box. I barely felt anything as my hands bounced off the structure, propelling me backwards. Reminding myself my body was back in Kane's bed and this was just my dream self, I changed tactics. Turning in a circle, I sent my energy out searching for the unwelcome visitor still crowding my awareness.

Kane hovered above Pyper trying to communicate with her, his mouth working and hands waving. Charlie was oblivious to the action, as was everyone else in the club, except for one man; the quiet, creepy regular with the beer bottle and unlit cigarette whom I'd seen every night I'd ever been in the bar. He sat in his regular corner staring right at me, hatred ripping holes in my senses as it radiated off him.

Our eyes locked, and in that moment I knew he wasn't alive. A ghost. This had to be Roy. How had I missed it? Digging deep, I sent all of my awareness toward him and was engulfed into blackness so dark it was as if I'd gone blind. I floated back to Kane, reining in my energy.

"There he is. It's Roy, isn't it?" I pointed to the ghost across the room.

Kane turned, following my direction. "Son of a bitch!" He flew across the room, fists raised in challenge. Just as Kane came to a stop in front of the man, Roy's hatred heightened, slashing at my very essence, and then disappeared as the ghost vanished. Kane whipped around, back and forth, and then glided back to me.

I sent my awareness back out in search of him and felt a small tug. Then my energy was grabbed with such force, I felt as if it would be ripped from my being. Frantically, I tried to merge with Kane as I had earlier in the evening when Bobby had invaded my senses. But I couldn't reach him. A thread of Pyper's desperation reached me and I opened to it, merging with her instead.

All at once, Pyper's pain vanished, along with her restraints. I hovered near the case and melded my energy closer to hers. Pyper rose from the case and floated next to me. Seconds ticked by, and then I faded into nothing.

I woke with slashes of pain radiating throughout my limbs. My eyes blurred with unshed tears and when I tried to move my arm, a ragged cry burst from my throat as sharp barbs pricked my flesh. The tears ran down the side of my face, and Kane's face came into focus.

I could see his mouth forming the word "Jade" over and over again, but I could hear nothing. Worse, I could no longer feel his energy. I was trapped in a void.

You freed her—I needed someone to take her place, a sinister voice said in my head.

"Why?" I asked in desperation.

To punish you, of course. To punish them.

I focused on the glare above me. I was now trapped in the case with my limbs wrapped tight in the barbed wire. Pain pulsed from my hands and feet, and I knew nails held them down. There wasn't anything I could do to get free. I stared at Kane, looking as helpless as I felt, and cried out in anguish as he disappeared from my sight.

He's left to be with her, you know.

"No!" I cried. "He'll be back for me."

He's always loved her best. There will never be room for you in his life.

"Lies. You're an evil, lying bastard."

Roy chuckled, and his laughter rang in my mind. *Call me whatever you like. You're mine now.*

"I'll never be yours." My voice was flat to my own ears. Where had Kane gone? I couldn't believe he'd left me here like this.

That's right, Jade. He left you. Really, what did you think he would do?"

"Stop it! Just stop it!" In my rational mind I knew Roy was playing off my fears, but I was powerless to stop him.

Roy continued to spew his brand of hate at me for what seemed like hours. Tired and worn down, I turned inward, pulling my guards up. Suddenly I couldn't hear him anymore. The pain in my limbs dissipated to a dull ache. Why hadn't I tried that before?

This isn't real, I told myself. Of course it wasn't. Pyper had been in a coma in the hospital with no visible marks at all. Roy had stolen just her conscious self. Now, I'd traded places with her. All the pain was an illusion in my mind.

I tried to lift my arms, but all I felt was weight holding me down. There wasn't the sharp stabbing pain as before, but I couldn't lift my arms or legs. Still trapped. Damn it!

With nothing else at my disposal, I decided to try merging with his emotional energy again. It was the only thing I could think of to do. After taking a few deep breaths, I let my guards down. My arms throbbed in pain from where I'd tried to lift them against the barb wire. I pressed my arms down on the platform, trying to get as far away from the prickling metal as possible.

That won't help you, Roy said.

"Shut up, you bastard." I glared up into his twisted face.

He gave the mechanical laugh of someone destined for a padded cell. His image floated above me, and I sent my energy toward him.

Stop trying to invade my soul, you witch! I'll kill you if you keep it up.

His venomous thoughts spurred my determination. I pressed harder, seeking to merge my energy with his. The hatred crawled up my spine, making me squirm and cry in pain as wire stabbed my limbs. I stilled and fought to keep a hold on his emotions. As I pressed deeper I sensed a twinge of his panic, but his toxic, determined energy took over as he loomed over me, staring into my eyes.

I stared back, determined to break his hold on me. Sweat broke out on my face. I struggled to keep connected with him. His hateful emotions wore me down faster than I anticipated and before I could build up my walls, he lashed out with his mind. Wielding an imaginary whip, he slashed at my torso, leaving raised welts. My cries of terror mixed with hot tears as I struggled to shut him out, but the pain and fear took over.

After half a dozen strokes, he stopped to peer at me in the box. *Are you going to behave, or do you need to be punished some more?*

I turned my head so I wouldn't have to look at him, using the moment to build my guards. I vaguely felt the imaginary whip come down a few more times, but when I didn't flinch or respond, Roy retreated.

That plan didn't go well. My earlier panic had faded, and I was left feeling only despair. Where was Kane? I couldn't believe he'd left me alone. He had to be coming back. Somehow I knew if he was here, we could fight this together. I hoped Pyper had woken, and he'd gone to see her.

Time became nonexistent as Roy hovered, waiting for my resistance to fail and doing his best to taunt me and break me down. But no matter how tired I got, I wouldn't give him the satisfaction.

Eventually I started to fade into an unconscious sleep state. Something familiar reached out to me. Something comforting and pleasant. I reached for it with my mind, and then Kane spoke. *Jade, there you are.*

Kane, where are you?

I'm with you, next to the case you're trapped in. I have been for hours. But your guards are up, and I couldn't reach you.

Is this a dream? Confused I tried to look around, but saw only darkness.

I'm speaking to you in your dream state. It's the only way I could reach you.

I don't understand. Nothing made sense to me. I hadn't seen Kane or felt him since I'd freed Pyper and became trapped in the box.

Your guards are up. I assume it's helping you keep Roy away, but it's also shutting me out.

Oh. Is Pyper safe?

A rush of gratitude and love streamed from him. *Yes, love. She's fine. You, however, have now taken her place at the hospital.*

Great. I mentally groaned. *Kane…I don't know how to get out of this.*

That's why I'm here. We're coming for you. Me, Bea, Ian, Lailah, Kat, Holly and Charlie. All of us. Be prepared to let your guards down. It's the only way we can help you.

How?

I don't have all the details. Just be ready. Bea says you'll know.

Okay. I'm ready now.

Kane gave a sad chuckle. *Me, too, love.*

His energy started to fade. I mentally reached out to hold on to it. *Don't go!*

I'll stay as long as you need me.

Forever. I need you forever. But for now, just until I feel strong again. I don't know why, but Kane's energy fed me. Already the weariness of holding Roy off waned.

I'm here. I'll stay, he said.

Just until I'm strong again. Then come back and kick that bastard's ass.

My pleasure.

Chapter 22

Kane faded from my consciousness and as I lay there, staring through the top of my prison, boredom set in. My barriers were firmly in place and all the pain had subsided. I had nothing to do but wait.

Roy kept his distance, and I suspected he knew I was stronger. I contemplated letting my guards down to see if I could best him in another energy match. But I didn't want to risk wearing myself down for when the group showed up. Whenever that was.

Some time later, Roy edged closer to my case, as if to test the safety of coming nearer. I wanted to laugh. What exactly could I do in my position? Clearly, he still had the upper hand, considering I was trapped, even if he couldn't cause me physical pain.

Roy floated above me, back and forth from the box to his corner. The cigarette hung unlit from his lips. Was he doomed to roam forever in his ghost state, always wanting to light that cigarette? A small twinge of satisfaction rolled through me at the thought of him in permanent nicotine withdrawal.

"Serves you right," I said.

Roy appeared above me, peering in.

I lifted my eyebrows and watched him. It was nice not having to feel his foulness. Maybe after my friends freed me from this hellish box, my new connection with Kane would help me keep other people's emotions out of my awareness.

Roy's face contorted into a scowl as his mouth worked overtime. He was yelling at me, but I couldn't hear him.

My indifference seemed to fuel his hostility. Fascinated, I studied the increasing animation of his face as he ranted. His scowl deepened, and his eyes bugged as he did an excellent impression of a demon possession. Suddenly, he launched himself and ended up lying flat, facedown on top of my box.

I narrowed my eyes. "You have nothing on me, you sick, demented bastard."

His face turned beet red, and he roared. The case shook, but I still couldn't hear it. It was weird how a ghost's skin tone could change with anger. Although, this was an alternate reality, so I guess anything was possible.

I don't know how much time went by as Roy continued his temper tantrum. Periodically I'd say some snide, colorful remark just to satisfy my own perverse need to get under his skin. It probably wasn't wise, but I had nothing else to do to entertain myself.

Eventually Roy moved from my sight. Bored out of my mind, I closed my eyes and faded in and out of a semi-conscious state for what seemed like eternity. In my weakened state, my barriers started to collapse as someone pushed at my walls. I imagined armor forming around me, determined to not let Roy push his way into my emotional field.

No! A chorus of voices rang in my mind.

My eyes popped open wide, and I turned my head back and forth, searching for my friends. A faint outline hovered above me, and I smiled in relief at the sight of Kane. I let the armor fall but still kept my emotional barriers in place.

There you are, I said, again with my mind.

And I'm not leaving without you. Kane turned his head toward the center of the club where Bea sat in an old tattered chair, surrounded by Ian, Holly, Charlie, Lailah and Kat.

Where's Pyper? I asked.

Sitting at the hospital with you. She wanted to come help, but I refused.

I nodded. *Good call. Roy's fixation on her is too dangerous.*

Exactly.

I turned my attention to the others. Although I still couldn't hear, they appeared to be chanting. As they did, Roy got even more agitated (if that were possible) and flew around the room. His image moved so fast I had trouble following him.

Kane hovered closer. *Be ready, Jade.*

For what? I couldn't get over the weirdness of communicating in our heads. Though I suppose it wasn't any weirder than being held prisoner in another dimension by a ghost.

To leave that case. It's almost time.

I waited with growing impatience. Testing my restraints, I tried to lift my arms. Pain jabbed at my wrists.

Not yet. I'll tell you.

Okay, so Roy couldn't get in my mind, but the barbs still stung. And I wasn't asleep, at least not in this reality, and Kane was talking to me in my head. Color me confused.

I shook my head to clear the thoughts and tried to focus. All of the people who normally worked at Wicked were absent. Either it was daytime, or Kane had closed the place down for this event. To me, it didn't matter much. They couldn't see this anyway. Too bad. It would have been a show-stopper.

As Bea chanted, the bright white light surrounding her started to dissipate, fading into a foggy mist. She stood out, vibrant and full of life. For the first time, I realized the other five people appeared to be slightly translucent, and so did Kane. They had to be in their dream states. But what about Bea? Was this a witch thing?

Kane, did you dreamwalk all of them here?

Everyone but Bea. She came on her own.

Is she dreamwalking me?

No. She's awake.

Impressive. In all of my dreams when Kane dreamwalked me, had we been translucent? I couldn't remember, but I supposed I'd been too preoccupied to care.

He floated over my case, smiling down at me. *You haven't seen anything yet.*

Since I couldn't do anything else, I laid there staring up at my boyfriend. Yep, that's right. My boyfriend. My smile widened as I explored every inch of his body with my eyes. What I wouldn't give to have another night wrapped in his arms, leisurely kissing every inch of his tender flesh. My mind wandered to the events that took place in his shower, just before I'd replaced Pyper in the box. In spite of my current situation, my body started to tingle.

Jade!

Huh?

Stop it. You're distracting me.

Oops. I guess in this state you're a mind reader.

Kane put his hand up, signaling for me to be quiet, while he watched our group of friends. I couldn't really tell what was happening. After a moment he turned back to me. *I can't read your mind unless you direct your thoughts to me. What I can do is sense your emotions. I can't believe you're getting turned on right now.*

I was staring at you, I replied in defense.

A hint of humor mixed with satisfaction escaped from him into my awareness, and I chuckled.

Get a hold of yourself. Bea is chanting now. In a moment it will be time for you to join me, Kane said.

Okay. I waited, suddenly tense and feeling totally unprepared. They obviously had a plan. Unfortunately, I had no idea what it was.

Out of nowhere, Roy appeared right above me, his eyes bloodshot and a crazed expression on his face. We stared each other down, neither one of us willing to look away.

"You can't keep me, you bastard," I said with venom.

He raised a fist and opened his mouth but before he could speak, some invisible force flung him backward.

Now, Kane said with a fierce nod.

With my heart racing and fear curling in my belly, I stared into Kane's eyes and gathered as much courage as I could. *Come on Jade,* I told myself. *Get on with it.*

It's all right. I'm here, Kane said.

At the sound of his voice, I lowered my guards. Roy's fury reached me like a flash of lightning, and I struggled to keep my defenses down.

"Stay with me." This time, Kane wasn't speaking in my head. The sound jolted me. I lurched forward. My hands and feet came free, and my body rose to float next to Kane.

"Thank God it worked." Kane pulled me to him, his solid arms wrapping around me.

"This is just weird," I whispered into his ear.

Kane pulled away, holding me at arm's length. "You're just now coming to that conclusion?"

I shook my head. "No. Not this." I waved toward our friends standing in a circle in the middle of the club. "This—" I pointed at him, and then back to me, "—you and me, hugging in shadow form."

Kane shook his head, looking exasperated. What can I say? I'd gone so far past my fear threshold, I'd completely given up on being afraid.

"What now?" I asked.

He started to answer but was drowned out by a sudden howling wind. Hot air swirled through the club, scattering advertisements and a few chairs. I pushed the hair out of my face. Lailah stood outside of the circle, arms raised. She appeared to be chanting, but I couldn't hear over the roar.

Roy twisted as if in agony, suspended directly above Bea. She sat still as a statue, staring up at him, her eyes never wavering. The other four, Kat, Charlie, Ian and Holly, stood circled around Bea, their hands clasped.

I couldn't help but be worried for Lailah. She wasn't part of the circle anymore. Who was protecting her? If anything went wrong with whatever piece of magic she was wielding, there could be serious consequences. It dawned on me Kane and I were outside of the circle as well, but for some reason I had no fear for my safety anymore. I had to help.

I forced my way through the roaring wind down toward Lailah and pressed my senses toward her. Determination, mixed with a thread of frustration, met my inquiry. Frustration. Maybe the spell wasn't working properly. I glanced back at Bea, still rigid in the chair. No help there.

Kane flew to my side and gripped my arm. "Keep your energy with me."

"I can't. I have to do this!" I shouted. We'd never be free of Roy if we didn't finish it now.

"No! You will *not* merge with him again. I won't let you." Kane's fear penetrated my mind.

"Not him. Lailah."

Kane's face relaxed, but I knew it was a conscious effort. Tension radiated from him like a beacon. He held his hands up as if to say *wait*. "Can you take me with you?"

Could I? I had no idea. Usually I focus on one person and can tune everyone else out. I didn't know if it would work with two. "I'll try."

Standing together, next to the struggling Lailah, I took turns focusing on each person in the room and systematically shutting them out. Everyone except Roy. Then I turned to Kane. Connecting with him took no effort. I sensed his relief at being merged with me. I sent him a small smile and turned my focus toward Lailah.

She frantically strained to complete something. I didn't know what she was doing exactly, but it was clear she was struggling. I gathered Kane's spirit to me and sent everything we had in her direction. She straightened and stood taller. With a renewed air of confidence she tilted her head back, chanting words I didn't understand.

Kane and I stood next to her, our arms around each other, and waited. Everything turned pitch-black. My fingers tightened in his until triumph flowed from Lailah. Then a circle of light formed in front of us, radiating orange and red, and the wind stopped. The room took on an eerie glow.

Curiosity lured me toward the light.

Kane's arms tightened around me. "No, Jade. It's a portal."

"A what?"

"It's where we're sending him." Kane pointed toward Roy.

My eyes went wide as I watched Bea stand. The other four broke away, giving her room to move. Even though they weren't touching anymore, they stayed in a circle formation.

Roy still floated above Bea, contorting as if in pain. She moved slowly, carefully, never taking her eyes off him. We stood transfixed, all of us, watching.

The closer Bea and Roy got to the portal and to me, the harder it was to block Roy from my awareness. I took a few steps back and felt Lailah cling to our connection.

"No, Jade. I need you close. You're the one making me strong enough to hold the portal open," Lailah said.

I took a deep breath and moved closer to her, bringing Kane with me. We formed a barrier on the edge of the portal and waited for Bea to reach the other side.

Even with Kane's and Lailah's strength, Roy slowly worked his vitriol into my being. Hatred and despair wedged its way into my soul, sending small stabs of pain through my body. I clenched my hands tighter around Kane's and Lailah's, trying to block it out. A trickle of her airy essence pressed on my skin, but Roy overpowered it. Then, in a gut-wrenching slash, Roy's energy severed my connection to Kane. Struggling, I sent my own energy out in a panic, desperately trying to hold on to Kane's strength, but nothing worked. Eventually the pain became sharp daggers.

Roy started to seize me.

My eyes blurred as I fought for control. If we could just get him in the portal. I looked up, barely making out the images of Bea, now at the far edge of the portal, and Roy, centered above it.

"Do it now! I can't take it anymore," I screamed through the spasms of pain.

"No!" Lailah yelled. "He'll take her with him."

Kane wrapped his arms around me, as if to shield me from harm. "I've got you. I won't let anyone take you."

I shook my head, with silent tears rolling down my cheeks. "He'll never let me go."

"Yes, he will," a translucent Pyper said from Bea's side.

"Pyper? How did you get here?" Kane's voice rose with panic.

"Not now," she said and turned toward Roy. "Let her go, you sick fuck. It's me you want."

"No!" I yelled and wrenched out of Kane's arms before running around the portal to Pyper's side.

Roy's energy vanished from my awareness just as Pyper's eyes rolled up in the back of her head. I lunged and caught her just before she fell forward into the red light.

"I won't let you have her!" I yelled at Roy.

He still floated above the light, trapped by Bea, but his sick satisfaction flowed straight to Pyper. It crawled over my arms, making me want to release her. I clutched her tighter, painfully aware she'd slipped back into the coma. If we sent him through, she'd be lost.

"Damn it!" I reached a hand out to Kane, who now stood beside us. "Help me."

He took Pyper from my arms and held her propped up against his side.

I focused on Lailah and with her energy mixed with mine, I sent it all into Pyper, determined to either free her or take her place. She didn't have any defenses against him. I did.

Pyper's energy was not void, like it had been in the hospital. It was just hidden. I now understood what Lailah meant when she said she could see things other people couldn't. Her ability helped me focus on the parts that were Pyper and the parts that weren't. Specifically, the areas Roy was infecting.

Her energy was thick, like mental sludge. No, not her energy. Roy's. The realization hit me and I focused harder, mentally battling the sludge. I forced it all together. Roy fought back, but with Lailah's strength merging with mine he didn't have a chance.

Together, Lailah and I mentally grabbed hold of Roy and ripped him from Pyper. He screamed in anger and lashed out, trying to invade me.

"Now!" Lailah yelled.

Roy spiraled toward the portal. Then something changed. My emotional radar was cut off, and I drifted into a hazy fog.

Chapter 23

A steady stream of *beep, beep, beep* entered my consciousness. It took me a moment to realize the sound wasn't an alarm clock. It was the monitors in the hospital. All at once the scene at Wicked flashed through my mind. I jerked up but was stopped by something gripping my hand. Through blurry eyes I traced the source of my entrapment. Pyper sat next to me, both of her hands clasped over my right one.

"Hey," I said, my voice cracking from lack of use.

"Hey yourself," she said with a huge grin. "How are you doing?"

"Water?"

She held out a paper cup.

I sipped the liquid through the straw and cleared my throat. "It's over?"

Pyper nodded.

"It was all real, right?"

"Yes." Tears filled her eyes and she gripped my hand harder. "Thank you," she whispered.

My eyes filled, and I reached out to her. We held each other for a long moment.

"Where is everyone?" I asked. Then panic flared. "They're all okay, right?"

"Everyone is fine. They're at my apartment. That's where they were meeting to sleep, so Kane could bring them to you. Except Bea. She was physically in the club."

Relief flooded through me. "I figured that last part out. Was that Roy's chair?"

"Yes." Her fingers twitched, and a small spark of her surprise tickled my hand. "How did you know?"

"I sat in it once while I was in the storage room. Some of his residual energy clung to it. It's awful. I made the connection when I saw her in it. I assume that's how she tapped into his energy."

"You're good." Pyper said, her eyes wide and eyebrows raised.

I smiled and tried to sit up. "Oh, God. How long have I been here?"

"A week."

"What?" No wonder I could barely move. "It didn't seem that long."

"I know," Pyper said quietly. "I suppose that's a good thing, considering all the pain he put us through."

"Oh, Pyper. I'm so sorry we didn't think of a way to get to you sooner."

"Huh? You got to me after two days. We took a week to get you out." She frowned, and shame seeped from her straight into my heart. "I'm the one who's sorry. I wanted to come. I wanted to go right back, but Kane wouldn't take me."

"Good!" I sat up straight and waited for my spinning head to clear. "I wasn't in pain. I have the ability to block him out. Didn't Kane tell you that?"

She shrugged. "I don't know. He might have tried, but I got angry and stopped speaking to him for a few days."

"Pyper…" I wanted so badly to take away her guilt and shame, but I knew I wasn't strong enough. Instead, I gathered all my appreciation and pushed it toward her.

The tension in her face eased. "I know that didn't help, but I was the only one who knew how bad it really was. It drove me insane, knowing Roy had you." Her eyes clouded. "I wanted to rip his eyes out."

I smiled at that. "Thank you. But I think sending him to hell was a better choice."

"Is that where Lailah sent him?"

"I think so. If not, it was close to it. That portal had some seriously bad juju vibes coming from it." I shivered. "Plus, she told me and Kat that she's some sort of angel."

Pyper jerked back. "Angel? That seems sort of crazy, don't you think?"

"That's what I said. But who knows? Look at what we just went through. It could be true."

"I guess you're right."

I shifted my body, trying to swing my legs out of the bed, and caused an alarm to go off.

Pyper laughed.

"Crap."

The door opened, and a nurse bustled in. "You're awake!" She clapped her hands. "How are you feeling?"

"Fine. I need to get up and move. My body aches."

"In due time. First the doctor needs to check on you." She pushed me back down, and checked my temperature and blood pressure. After asking my name and other identifying questions she seemed satisfied and said, "Looking good. I'll send the doctor right in."

The nurse left, and I returned my attention to Pyper. She held her phone out to me. "You have a message."

I read the text. *Tell Jade I love her and not to move an inch. I'll be right there. Kane.*

I laid back and closed my eyes, imagining the feel of his arms around me, and then sat straight up. I'd been lying here a week. "Give me a mirror!"

"I told him you'd be fine when you woke up." She held out a brush and mirror for me. "I was the same way. As if I'd only been asleep for an extended amount of time."

I went to work, trying to tame my hair. Someone had braided it in one long plait to the side. I undid it, gently combed it out, and fixed it up into a relaxed bun.

"You look pretty like that," Pyper said.

"Ugh, if I wasn't so pasty white."

She handed me a compact and some lip gloss. "This will help."

A few minutes later I surveyed myself in the mirror. Better. At least I didn't look like death. "Thank you." I handed everything back to Pyper and patted the bed for her to sit down and wait with me.

"So, have you been sleeping okay this week?" I asked.

"Not really." She caught my panicked expression and continued. "Just because I was worried about you, not because I was being tortured. That's over. But I did see someone else in my dreams. A fair-haired man and a golden retriever. Anyone you know?"

"Did they have white light shining around them?"

"Yes." She smiled.

"Crap. Why are they bugging you?"

"They aren't. They appeared the first time I slept after I woke from the coma. The man waved and walked off. I think he said goodbye."

"Weird."

"A little, but it doesn't bother me. They seemed harmless."

"To you, maybe," I mumbled. Then, to change the subject, I asked, "Do you know why Roy was after you?"

"Yeah. He thought it was my fault he died." She frowned.

"What? Why?"

"You know he got all that money from selling Kane the club." I nodded.

"Well, he took it all to the casinos and started hanging with the wrong crowd. Seems he gambled most of it away and ended up crashing at some dope dealer's house. There was an altercation, and he got caught in the crossfire. That's how he died."

"And this is your fault why?" I didn't see the connection.

"Because we forced him to sell out. If we hadn't, he'd still be here, running the club."

"That's ridiculous."

"I know. But he'd hated me for a long time now. Ever since I rejected him."

"Ick." A shudder ran through my body at the thought of Roy asking her out.

"Yeah." Her shudder mimicked mine, and we both laughed.

"What's so funny?" Kane stood just inside the door.

My eyes found his. My heart swelled at the emotion I saw there.

Pyper cleared her throat. "Nothing. It's about time you got here. What took you so long?"

"It only took me ten minutes." He shook his head and rounded on her. "What the hell do you think you were doing, showing up in my dream?"

Pyper stiffened. "Stop it. You didn't see her." She nodded to me. "Her body started flinching, and I felt what she was feeling."

"You did?" I asked, more than a little shocked.

Pyper turned to me. "Yes. I felt him mentally attacking you. I couldn't let it happen. So I curled up next to you and willed myself to Kane's dream. It wasn't hard. I'd been there before."

I clutched her hand and mulled over what she said. "Can you sense anything about me now?"

She chuckled. "Just that you want some time with Kane." She squeezed my hand and let go. "And no, it isn't a psychic thing. It's just obvious. I'll see you two later."

She disappeared and Kane sat next to me. "Are you all right?"

I nodded and pulled him closer.

He planted a kiss on my forehead and hugged me tight. "I thought I might have lost you."

I shook my head, too afraid to speak.

He shifted and looked into my eyes. I didn't need to explore his energy to feel the love flowing from him.

"Just hold me a while," I choked out.

"I'll hold you forever." He lay down next to me and wrapped me in his arms. I snuggled in and rested my head on his shoulder. After a moment he undid my bun and spent a long time running his fingers though my hair.

Later that day, the doctor had just left when Charlie and Holly came to visit. They brought flowers and sat with me for a while. I asked about the café and the club, and they filled me in on the craziness of being short-handed. Charlie talked about a new girl she had her eye on, and Holly told me she signed up for my glass beadmaking class.

"You did?" I asked, surprised.

"Yes. I just knew they'd find a way to bring you back. I figured planning a future with you in it could only help. You know, positive cosmic energy and all that." She tilted her head, hiding her face with a sheet of long, blond hair.

"Yes, that does help. Thank you." I tapped her arm. "But did you really want to learn?"

She looked up with a huge grin. "Absolutely. I've wanted to since I met you. It just looks so cool."

We chatted for a few minutes more until Kat showed up.

"We've got to go. See you soon," Charlie said and grabbed Holly's arm to escort her out.

"Bye." Holly waved.

I watched them go and turned to Kat. "What took you so long?"

She sat down next to me. "I had to call Gwen back. She's been frantic ever since she felt you disappear."

"Oh my God, Gwen!" I reached over and picked up the phone. After leaving a short message, I turned back to Kat. "What did she say? Is she all right?" Damn it. That must have been hell for her.

"She's fine. She felt you come back to the land of the living. But I think she's planning a visit soon, so prepare yourself."

My heart swelled. "I'd love to see her. But—" I stared at the door as if she would walk in any minute, "—crap, I won't have any secrets after she gets here."

Kat laughed. "True. That woman can't keep anything behind those bright red lips of hers."

I groaned, but was still smiling. "Have you seen Bea? I want to thank her."

Kat's smile faded. "Yeah. I just came from her house. She nearly collapsed with exhaustion after holding Roy in a binding spell for so long."

"Oh, no. Is she okay?" I inched up on the pillows.

"I think she will be. Ian's going to stay with her until she feels better."

"Ian's staying with her? I didn't know they even knew each other." Then something hit me. "Bea is Ian's aunt, isn't she?"

Kat nodded. "Yes. I didn't know either until this week. They were together at some ghost hunt. That's why we couldn't reach either of them."

"Ian could have told us he was leaving," I said, slightly annoyed.

"They'd only planned to be gone one day, but things got a little wild, and they got stuck. Anyway, I'll let him tell you all about it later."

"Is he coming by?"

"No. He said to tell you he'd call. He doesn't want to leave Bea alone."

"That's good." My heart filled with gratitude at what everyone had done to help me. I reached out to Kat and grabbed her arm. "Thank you."

"No need to thank me. I'm not letting you go that easily." Her tone was light, but relief mixed with residual fear pressed at my consciousness.

"Help me up," I swung my legs off the side of the bed. "I need to get out of this bed and into a shower." I'd been up a couple of times already. Once to use the bathroom and once to take a short walk. After lying down for a week, it wasn't easy.

Kat helped me shower and to my delight had a bag full of fresh clothes and toiletries waiting for me. "You're an angel," I said.

She laughed. "That's Lailah's thing. I'm just a good friend."

"The best," I agreed.

The doctors kept me one more night for observation and by the next morning I was ready to leave. I'd taken to pacing the halls just to get out of bed and move my muscles. When they couldn't find anything after poking and prodding me, they released me into Kane's care with strict instructions to take it easy.

I eyed Kane and chuckled.

"Stop that," he said.

"What?" I asked innocently as I imagined getting him naked.

"Never mind. Behave."

I muffled another laugh as he pushed my wheelchair down the hall.

Kane drove me home in Pyper's Mini Cooper.

"You don't have a car?" I asked.

"Nope," he said. "I used to have a jeep, but a few months back a buddy of mine totaled it. I haven't replaced it yet. I walk almost everywhere I go and when I need a car, I just borrow Pyper's."

"That makes two of us without wheels."

"I know." Kane pulled up in front of the club. I spotted the sign I'd read the first night I'd moved in. *Hundreds of Beautiful Women, and Three Ugly ones.*

"Kane, what's with the sign?"

He glanced at it then back to me. "What?"

"The sign, what's the story behind it?"

He laughed. "You're kidding, right?"

I shook my head. "No."

"I can't believe after all of this, you didn't know." He moved his hands around indicating us, the club, and all that had happened.

"Come on, who are the three ugly women?"

"You're gonna love this." He smiled. "They're ghosts, of course."

"Ghosts!" I shouted. "What? Who? Why didn't anyone tell me?"

"You never asked. Besides, it's common knowledge. Most likely everyone thought you knew." He shrugged.

"Why haven't I seen them?" I wondered aloud.

"You will," he replied.

"How do you know?"

"You'll see."

He got out of the car and came around to my side to help me out.

"Kane–"

He put a finger to my lips. "Shhh. Right now I have other things on my mind." He walked me to the side door of the building, pulled me inside and pressed me up against the wall. His eyes darkened to deep pools of melted chocolate and seconds after his lips and body touched mine, all other thoughts and questions vanished.

When he finally pulled away my heart hammered, and my legs had turned to jelly.

"C'mon," he said, pulling me up my stairwell behind him. When we reached the top, I was panting.

"Are you okay?" he asked.

"Yes. Just out of shape after my week-long hiatus." I smiled and opened my door. "Now, what was it that was on your mind?"

His eyes clouded over and his desire mixed with concern reached me.

"Stop worrying. I'm perfectly fine." I maneuvered closer to him.

He put his arms around me and turned his head toward the bed. "I've been imagining getting you into that thing ever since I brought it up here."

"That's odd. I've been imagining it ever since I saw the headboard in storage."

He pulled me closer. "My grandmother would be so pleased to know that bed is now in the possession of the woman I love."

"It's your grandmother's? You said you were going to give it to a restoration place." I jabbed him in the shoulder.

He shrugged. "I wanted you to have it. I knew you'd take care of it. And I knew you'd never take it otherwise. It's my curse to love headstrong women. Grandmother would be proud."

I shook my head and tried not to laugh at the triumphant look on his face.

"Forget my grandmother." He pulled me down onto the bed, and for the next two hours I focused on all things Kane and the pleasure we gave each other.

When we finally drifted off to sleep, Bobby appeared, highlighted in a warm, pale glow. I watched as he smiled down at me. After a moment he waved, and the light faded into darkness. Still dreaming, Kane appeared and wrapped me in his arms. Bobby was gone, and finally it was just the two of us.

About the Author

Deanna is a native Californian, transplanted to the slower paced lifestyle of southeastern Louisiana. When she isn't writing, she is often goofing off with her husband in New Orleans, playing with her two shih tzu dogs, making glass beads, or out hocking her wares at various bead shows across the country. For more information and updates on newest releases visit her blog at www.deannachase.com.

Printed in the USA
CPSIA information can be obtained
at www.ICGtesting.com
LVHW022253111123
763692LV00015B/1046